ATTEMPTS

a novel

Issa

ISBN-Ebook:979-8-9880675-0-4

ISBN-Paperback: 979-8-9880675-1-1

ISBN Hardcover: 979-8-9880675-4-2

Book Cover Design by 100 Covers.

Part I – An Attempt

A SANT STARED AT HIS friend's hand, and what was in it.

"Take it," the friend exhorted.

They stood by the back of a hut; its mud wall dark yellow, shaded and hidden below a giant magnolia canopy. Both wore jeans, yet different in that Asant's were clean and cheap dark blue, his friend's expensive, stylish, and marked with numerous drawings from a black pen.

Asant continued to stare, then, "No. I can't. I hate these things."

"What? We're robbing a bank man!" said his friend. The friend looked at Asant for a moment and remained quiet, as if trying to read Asant's mind before making a decision. "Fine," he said finally. "It's not a big deal. You won't use it. Don't even take it out. Just show this part," as he pointed to the handle. "Move your shirt like this, all right?" he added, pulling his own brown shirt to cover the better part of his hand and what was in it.

"No. No way. I want nothing to do with it."

"You're the one who complained to me about being hungry all the time and not having money. So, do you want it or not, Asant?"

Asant looked away and covered his face behind his hands, as if to hide from everything, including the magnolia's waves. "I do, I do. I just don't see why we need it, why we need this."

"It's a tool. To help us convince them. It's just a tool, that's all."

"No. I won't carry one."

"Fine, fine. I'll carry it." The friend, exasperated, rolled his eyes, moved his free hand in the air above his head and forced an exhale. "It's too small a change to make a difference. We'll write a note. You'll go to the window, and I will stand next in line behind you. You won't even say anything. The note will do the talking."

It was minutes before closing. The security guard stood by the door, his back slumped, eyes focused on nowhere in particular. This was his same demeanor every time they walked in at exactly 4:56 p.m. - minutes before the end of the afternoon. Today, the only evident difference was in their appearance.

They wore baseball caps, fake eyeglasses, and fake facial hair.

In school, the friend often bought whatever food he wished for, at least once showing off a stack of cash. Asant would gape; his hands usually holding a metal cup with the same daily white rice.

ATTEMPTS

It was some time before they were acquainted...when one day Asant decided to ask about the money.

In the bank, Asant's heart pumped harder and faster with each second.

"Hey, relax," his friend said. "This is child's play. Like I told you, I've done it before, and others have done it many times...and it's only right. It is our money they take anyway. Our sweat. We are just barely twenty years old, and we already work like dogs but get paid beggars' money. This is the right thing to do. It is our right."

Asant's heart pumped harder with each passing minute, reverberating through his body.

The friend sensed Asant's tension and anxiety. He continued to look at Asant, while Asant stared at the security guard and caught his eye. The security guard nodded, then looked away.

Asant and his friend walked through the guiding ropes and stood behind two customers. Asant gazed at his shoes, wanting time to pass; then, he felt a punch at the middle of his back. He raised his head and turned to look at his friend, who was gesturing for Asant to move up the line.

Asant took a step forward. Then, as if a sign from somewhere, he noticed the guard nearby. The guard had moved toward the glass counters and, now, barely yards away, was leaning with his right elbow on the glass and his hand holding up his chin, eyes peering into Asant's.

"I'm imagining it. I'm imagining it," he whispered to himself, then looked behind him at his friend.

The friend admired and considered anything his eyes could find, in an effort to ignore Asant.

Asant adjusted his glasses, turned back to the teller counter and looked at the person behind the glass wall. They stared at each other. Asant's face felt unusually warm, red and sweaty; the other's was tired with drooping and uninterested eyes. One frozen in time; while the other waited.

"Can I help you?" the person on the other side asked after a few seconds.

Asant heard the sounds but did not register the words. By then, he was unaware of anyone except himself. His heart persisted in pushing against his chest.

"Sir. How can I help you?"

Asant's eyes focused on the air, staring at nothing in particular.

"Sir?" the man behind the glass wall said with a louder voice.

It woke Asant from his frozen state. He cleared his throat. "Umm. Sorry. Sorry. I have this. This thing. One second."

His hand in his right pocket, he leaned right and halfway around, wanting to look at his friend, but then changed his mind, turning back to face the glass wall and raising his right arm to the level of the counter.

Note in hand, he looked at the yellow edges showing through his closed fingers.

"Umm. Please. Please take this. There are instructions..."

Asant could not do it. His mind lost control and shut down; his body now acting on its own. He turned left and walked to the door as fast as he could. He pushed it open with both hands. The yellow paper fell out and rested on the frame just as the door closed behind him, the paper laying there in its new home.

Asant did not go to his mentor, spiritual teacher and caretaker's abode—his favorite space and usual destination. Instead, that evening, he asked to stay at a friend's house in an adjacent town. With only his imaginative mind as company, alternating between thoughts and images of being imprisoned and tortured, the night proved to be torturous.

By morning, school was not even a consideration. Months before, he had developed enough aspiration and ambition to pursue engineering in a public school, of course with the ardent support of his mentor. On this morning, however, engineering was not even an afterthought. Instead, he walked aimlessly in the town's center and by its shops, going around the circle several times and through one of its intersecting streets.

In a cafe, his ear caught words screaming out of a television about an attempted robbery nearby. The town's daily paper had a picture of the yellow paper. His yellow paper. Thoughts of jail began to consume him again – blood rushed to his face and trapped his breath. The world was closing in on him.

Thoughts of imprisonment, of losing freedom, of being entrenched in shame, overcame Asant. Then came the panic of intelligence officers and their inclination to torture prisoners; then, even worse, was that of prisoners taking advantage of each other and of him. He thought of his father; how he had died while in prison.

It was not right. Nothing was right.

In the cafe, he sat in a corner with hands holding his head and his eyes glued to the table's surface. He dared to look up only for glimpses of others to see if anyone was pointing at him, or in fear that a picture of his face would appear on the flat television screen in the opposite corner. During one of those glances at the television, pictures of fighter jets, city ruble, fire, and bloodied children standing alone, appeared as the reporter on the screen spoke of a war in a distant country. The picture switched to that of a man in military garb, his right arm raised as if in a sweeping motion he cemented his power. The word Daas slid below declaring his name. The reporter spoke some more about the war and that country's leader.

Asant looked away with temporary relief that the reporter did not speak of the local robbery, and that the screen did not show his face.

But even sitting became uncomfortable. He left the cafe and tried to hide among crowds, cars, and trees. He he could not manage to stay in any one spot for more than a few minutes. The coffee shop, the bookstore, the newspaper stands, the park, the main street—each became an unbearable world. He found his way away from the town center into the woods. The trees watched him with contempt. He begged to rest by one, for it to allow him to rest if only for a few minutes. He crouched down, and allowed his lower back to lean on its trunk with his head between his hands; he could not hold back his fear any longer and let out repeated erratic wailing cries.

Some hours later, he finally found his way to his teacher and caretaker's abode and into his usual room, but could not face anyone directly, certainly not his teacher. The teacher had organized his own home to care for orphans and lost children and teenagers. It was this person who saw Asant walking the streets crying after his mother's passing, who took him in and provided him with stability and security. The house was home to fifteen orphans and abandoned children, with the caretaker the lone father and spiritual teacher for them.

The following morning, after hours of being still and virtually in a frozen state watching the ceiling, there was a knock on the door.

"Asant, teacher wants to see you."

Asant knew the teacher would see through him, that the teacher either already knew or would know in an instant.

"I shouldn't have come here," he uttered to himself. Minutes passed.

"Asant, teacher wants to see you."

It was a different voice this time. Another person. The teacher knew. Asant felt he had no choice but to make his way out to see his caretaker.

The plain and round room was essentially empty, with only Asant, the teacher, and some unadorned pillows. Asant sat facing his teacher, but attempted to avoid looking directly at him.

Asant's eyes wavered back and forth between two sides, catching glimpses of the other man in between. Eventually, Asant tried to look at his teacher's eyes as he usually did, but now he could neither look nor hold his teacher's gaze. He instead attempted to steal glances, his head moving down, up, down.

Neither made an attempt to speak.

He could not stand the silence. Something inside him—a pressure, shallow breathing—pushed him to the edge. "Teacher, if there is nothing, I must go."

"You are to go nowhere," the teacher said. His response was immediate, as if he had expected Asant to attempt to evade reality.

"Teacher, please."

"You must face your actions, Asant." The teacher's tone was low, but certain.

Asant, surprised in spite of his expectations, saw a subtle quiver in his teacher's face, perhaps pain.

He had long before recognized how much he appreciated the teacher, his caretaker, such that now he could not face a disappointment. He worked to avoid it and decided he did not want to think about it.

While on the bed the night before, he had considered how his teacher would see through him, even without any eye contact. And now, in the round empty room, it was clear to him that his teacher already knew what Asant was feeling even before Asant had walked in. Facing truth is never easy.

In spite of his attempts of avoidance, something became clear. He had a choice to make—to admit his fear of being imprisoned, or to maintain his composure and deal with it all on his own without assistance. Perhaps he would find a way to avoid it all.

His teacher studied Asant's face. "A punishment is, in fact, not a punishment at all, but a response to an action.

Do you agree, Asant?" The teacher asked this with the same low tone, any reluctance borne of his care for the young man opposite him undetectable to the ordinary ear.

"That is not necessarily true, sir," Asant said, attempting to change the direction of the conversation. "What if the person did not do anything wrong?"

The teacher's mouth widened a bit, eyes narrowed, displaying a faint and understanding smile. He did not reply.

Asant still had not yet decided whether or not to face any fact—or, for that matter what he wanted to do. Moments passed. He felt his eyes, his expression, gradually changing. At first, he was strident and held his ground. Then, his blank face gave way to a long sag and dropped eyelids. His body gave way to fear and stress.

"Teacher, I fell into a trap." His words were choppy, uncommitted and shaking with every syllable, failing his desperation for a plea. He wanted to trust his teacher, but still could not control his body or his fears. His eyes found a pillow. "I regret that I allowed myself to succumb..." he started but could not finish the thought.

The teacher inhaled a long breath, raising his chest. "It will be all right, Asant;" he said, voice as soft as before, unchanged. "However, you are aware of the laws of our existence."

How his teacher, another human, managed to maintain composure was beyond Asant. The teacher had tended to him for years, through some of Asant's most difficult times, and Asant knew his teacher's care was without bounds—providing life all the orphans and abandoned children at the school. Yet, his teacher maintained his composure with almost no sign of despair or anger.

"Teacher, I do not understand."

"It is best to be direct, Asant. I will choose to be so, regardless of your challenge or mine. You know I cannot bare seeing you or any of your brothers and sisters at this school, this sanctuary, experience more difficulties than you already have."

"Yes, sir."

"You understand well what I mean," the teacher continued.

"What? No. Teacher, please, there must be another way. There must be. I cannot. I cannot..." Asant shook his head vehemently. Anxiety again overcame him; he began to sweat and wail while still trying to get some words across.

The teacher remained quiet for some time. "I am afraid there is not, my dear Asant. It pains me that you must face this consequence; nevertheless, it is your choice how you confront them, always, regardless of where you are."

"No teacher. Please, there must be another way. Please believe me that I cannot. I truly regret my choice."

"What is it that worries you, Asant?"

"Prison, sir. I will be violated. It is not only about my freedom, sir."

"It is a dark place; still, it is not necessarily true what you say." The teacher was calm, his face without expression. He remained quiet for a moment. "There is also the possibility of not being imprisoned at all."

"No sir," Asant said, his voice shaking. "Please do not allow me to be in such a place. No matter what, they will interrogate and torture me. They will beat me. As they did with my father. Please, sir!"

"It is not me, Asant. I did not make the rules of our universe or the rules of our society."

"Sir, please, I will not survive sir," Asant said as his eyes trembled and lost focus. "I beg you."

The man looked on, feeling his student's pain. "Asant, my dear boy..."

"Sir, there must be something. You have the power. Your mind, sir. Help me with your mind and spirit. I know you can."

"One would wish. But our gifts are not to be used to erase our individual mistakes. It is your mind that must transform and overcome. You must live through this experience to rise above it."

"I know sir, I know. But prison is a cruel response to what I tried to do. Please sir help me repay in another way."

"I agree it is cruel, and its extent unnecessary, but it is where we were sent and born. There is no way around it. We cannot alter the responses to the actions we choose, just as we cannot alter each other's actions." The teacher seemed to sigh.

"That is not true sir. You told me we can. You told me we can go back to our past and revisit our errors. You told me there is always more than one possible reaction. With your help sir..." Asant was now physically shaking. His mind shoved him to the darkest of places and sobs took hold of him. "Sir," he said, trying to sound another word between sobs. "Please sir."

"You must gain control, Asant. Do not allow fear to control you."

Asant was unable to reply. Pictures of dark, windowless, locked spaces spread into eyes and overwhelmed him. Then it was images of his father's beaten and bruised body, violated, bones broken. Minutes passed before he managed to look up.

"Sir?"

The man inhaled, breathed out. "You made your choice, Asant, my boy." His voice was now even lower. "You gave your effort and energy for the possibility of an easier life and pleasure, for a false promise. You must now believe in your ability to handle what comes back to you. What does come, however, is no longer in your hands—or mine."

"No sir. You are being too tough. Please sir...Teacher."

"There is no erasing what was done, Asant. I am saddened, but I also need to be direct. You must leave the house."

"No sir. I will not go. I will stay here. I will stay right here."

"My dear, your spiritual training from your tenure will help you survive." The teacher turned his head an inch to the right, and he spoke in a slightly louder voice. "Umar, Yohan, come help Asant."

The two students entered and helped Asant to stand while Asant looked at his teacher and searched the air for words to say.

The students led him to the entrance of the house. The instant they let him loose, he ran back to his teacher's space, and fell at the teacher's feet. "Please Teacher. You must understand I will not survive in prison. I will leave this country if I must to."

"Control your mind, your emotions, Asant. You know well that the experiences we receive are always for our benefit."

"I know sir, but not prison. It will destroy me. And you told me in the past that there are always alternative ways of accounting for one's actions."

"There are. I also told you that alternatives are always more challenging and come at the higher price requiring more effort and without guarantees. Moreover, leaving the country is running away and not an alternative."

"No sir. I will leave the country. I will leave. It is an alternative. I will do what I must."

"It is your choice. Your challenge."

Asant nodded, hope returned to his mind, to his body. Yet, what he had suggested did not sink into his psyche.

"Asant, you understand avoidance is an illusion. The consequence will chase you and find you no matter where you go."

"I know sir. But not prison. Not here."

The teacher gazed at Asant, into him; then he looked in another direction and into the distance. "Very well. Stay with me here tonight. Stay awake if you are able, and we will pray together. The sun's rise will bring us answers."

Asant's lower lip trembled out of anxiety. He nodded as best as he could, and positioned himself for prayer and meditation. He did his best to allow waves of thoughts race through his mind's eye, to no avail. Moments passed, then hours. He attempted to pray, to meditate, but his mind continued to race. He eventually nodded off out of exhaustion and dropped at his teacher's feet into a nightmarish sleep. His arms smacked the air every now and then.

The teacher watched for a while, recalling the day he found Asant sitting on a dirty curb and wailing. *A bird with two broken wings*, the teacher had thought, before walking over. And with a charitable touch, he helped Asant to his feet and walked him to the school. Along the way, Asant repeatedly begged that she be brought back. *She cannot be gone. I beg you bring her back.* His mother had just moved on, merely months after his father's passing.

An hour before dawn, the teacher caressed Asant's head. "Asant," his teacher whispered.

They ate a simple meal together, and soon enough sat on opposite sides once again.

His teacher spoke first. "To address a wrong act, you can accept the reaction—the consequence—or you can do tremendous good that will allow for consideration as replacement of that consequence. That is the rule."

"Anything teacher. Anything at all. I know I did wrong, and that..." His voice broke. "I know I cannot take it back."

"If it is leaving this country that you choose, there is a city called Kamur, in a country torn by war..."

"War?" wailed Asant in surprise, immediately recognizing the prospect of being in the midst of violent conflict.

"Yes. What I hear is that its people have become fractured and have succumbed to fighting each other, with no end to their despair. They have killed thousands and destroyed their cities and just about all that has tied them together. The images I have seen, of pain and destruction, are heartbreaking. These people need not suffer any longer. You are to help end the war. People in the city of Kamur can give you some guidance. I am confident they will direct you. You cannot escape your truth, but doing such a tremendous good might be of help."

Asant moved his agitated body, his head down in an attempt to escape his surroundings. Then, he tried to adjust and collect himself. "Sir, that is impossible!" his said, his voice shaking. "I am but one person. And it is against our teaching to use weapons or to harm. I cannot carry weapons."

"You will use peaceful means only. Also, your training has shown you nothing is impossible aside from evading your truth. You have met other teachers, brothers and teachers of mine, one teacher who had not eaten in fifty years, another who manifested himself in front of your eyes at will, and yet another who created a palace in the mountains in a whim. You are to help end the war, and while this will not necessarily guarantee you redemption, it is the extent of your effort that will be determinative." The teacher stopped to look through his student.

Asant again wanted to hide his fear, but his wet and quivering eyes and trembling body failed him.

"Asant, my boy, much of our lives are determined by us before our birth. What we are to do; what we are to accomplish. We decide the 'how' after coming into life. Only we have the ability to resolve our past actions; we have that choice in how we receive and face our truth and the type of karma we add. The appropriate response will find you."

"But sir...wouldn't injecting myself into an armed conflict be worse than prison itself? I mean—"

"It is your choice. Regardless, no, not necessarily. It is a bigger risk, yes, but with that, your chance to do good is greater. It is an opportunity to assist a whole people. Nonetheless, as I said, this is your choice."

His teacher repositioned himself. He placed his hands with open palms on his bent knees as if ready to receive from above. He moved his focus away from Asant into the distance and worked to begin his daily practice.

Asant wanted more time, more guidance, but he was realizing there would be none. He watched his teacher, and understood they were done talking and that the teacher readying himself for his next task. Asant cleared his throat, allowing himself a second's thought. "Well. Umm, what country is it?"

"Siljap."

"Sir, that is several borders away from here, and no guarantee!"

No words came from the teacher.

"But sir," Asant stated again. Then he bellowed and fell crying, again overcome by the enormity of the task. It was more than he could handle. For an instant, he resented his teacher. How could he do this? Then, it crossed his mind that the person in front of him was the one person he has come to trust; how it was this teacher who took him in, fed him, and taught him patiently. He recalled how he realized time after time that his teacher knew more than he let on.

More gravely, it occurred to him he would not be able to stay with his teacher after his act. It was his choice. He could walk the streets of a neighboring country aimlessly, or follow his teacher's guidance.

It was a while before he picked his head off the floor.

"Yes sir. I will beg and find help to fly there immediately," he finally said.

"No. Inadvisable. Better to walk. Do not let yourself seek alternatives. Do not attempt to escape difficulties. Instead, help will find you when it is warranted and deserved."

Part II – Journey

THE CONTOURS OF HIS birth country were familiar enough, allowing him to ease into the journey. For the most part, he walked by the shores, letting the water guide him. The sea was kind in its own way. Its smell, its saltiness and its fish became a comforting presence, a confirmation that he was going in the right direction. Within a couple of days, the beginning of the trek became acceptable.

However, in spite of rationing and consuming minuscule amounts, his food ran out by the fifth day. Cooking flames began to taunt him. As he walked, becoming more cognizant of increasing pains in his stomach, he looked at restaurants and shops with wanting. He began to take notice when a particular place appeared to be unattended, his mind sometimes twisted his logic into deciding that the place was abandoned altogether—and, perhaps, its left behind contents available to those in need. As if to awake him from his stupor, however, a person would always enter or exit the place. Then a couple of miles later, there would be another. Another temptation.

The thought would somehow creep back into his mind, that it would be acceptable for him to grab something small since his ultimate goal was noble. At first, he persisted in shaking it off. But then, one day, there was a sort of a stand or a hut on the side of the street some yards ahead. Its door was loose, open, moving back and forth inches with the brief but recurring breeze. The hut had dried bamboo sticks holding up a torn awning, providing some shade to the rust of a few metal sheets that acted as walls. It was an old structure, perhaps yet another "abandoned" shop. It made him wonder just enough, that he decided to enter when he reached it.

A bell rang the second he passed the door's frame. Still, no one appeared. A song about silence was playing. He looked left and noticed a small black radio sitting on a triangular shelf, silver antennae piercing the air. He regarded and inspected the other shelves—the ones with cans and shining bags of food. Everything was cramped close. His eyes eventually came to rest on a menu dangling overhead, directly in front of him. It all brought his attention back to his hunger, his longing for something to eat. His stomach growled on cue. His senses and imagination wished everything on the menu, but then he remembered he could not afford any of it. In fact, he could not afford anything in this little eatery. He looked around again, allowed the smells to taunt him. There was the sweetness from a sparkling dessert, and something else with spices, perhaps rice.

He shook his head. Then another thought came to him. There were a few small prepackaged foods and drinks by the outside walls, by the rusted metal sheets facing the street. He waited another moment for someone to tend to him before deciding to consider the items outside when no one appeared.

Just as he turned his back, a voice said, "Hello. Can I help you?"

The words froze him in his spot, his conscience tearing and battling his hunger and emotions. Adverse feelings surprised him—guilt combined with frustration. There was the possibility of faltering yet again, in contrast to the jeopardy of losing an opportunity at obtaining food.

He wanted to say "no thank you", but then he noticed the person at the counter resembled his teacher, almost an identical image. Each watched the other.

The man asked again, "Can I help you?"

"No," Asant finally replied and turned to leave. He stepped once again through the door's frame, downcast, wanting to weep, and turned right down the street. *It was my choice*, he thought to himself as he continued on the street, head down, eyes watching his footsteps, his torn sandals.

"Excuse me. Hello. Hello," a man's voice called out from behind him.

Asant allowed the calling to flow through him, deciding it could not be for him, and continued on walking, his eyes down at the pavement.

"Excuse me. Young man?" The voice sounded much closer, as though the man were directly behind him but damped with a vehicle passing by along with its loud exhaust.

The man tapped Asant's shoulder. "Young man. By the looks on your face, and your sandals, it appears you have been walking a while, perhaps on a mission." The man smiled.

It was the man from the hut. He was close enough to Asant for him to see the wrinkles around the man's eyes and to better take in his dark complexion...looking less and less like Asant's teacher.

"I did not take anything from your store, I promise," he said. His tone was soft, his words slow. He seemed tired.

"No. No. I wanted to give you a few things, to help you on your journey. It is my duty." The smile was persistent on the man's face. "I noticed your torn sandals. Here, please take these. They are mine but barely used. I have no need for them."

Asant looked down at his sandals and saw the two remaining straps over his right foot, three others torn and dangling to the side.

"Please accept them. I truly have no need for them."

Reluctant, Asant used the moment to consider the offer. He gazed at the man and saw a gentle smile, and then decided there would be no harm in accepting. "Thank you, sir. It is kind of you."

"I also wanted to give you water, milk, and some bread. You will need some water to withstand the heat." The man offered a bag weighed down by its contents. "It is not much, really, but..."

Asant gaped at the bag in disbelief, surprised and amazed by the man's kindness, bewildered by the possibility of having food.

"You do not have to pay me. It is my duty. Please."

After that encounter, Asant dared not enter another restaurant or shop with the thought of taking. His teacher's image and the man's kindness had an effect on him—prodding him to think back to the teachings of his teacher —the same lessons that had been repeated over the years—lessons of not allowing desires for comfort cloud his mind, and that he would be provided for. The same lessons he would not commit to. Now, finally, he consciously decided to worry less.

He found food and shelter in the trees, in prayer centers and from villagers . There was the occasional uncomfortable night on a sidewalk, but over time, as he continued across his country, his thoughts about his needs decreased and without much attention to food, his bag was soon empty except for a bottle of water and a towel.

A discernible change became evident in the signs along his path. Now on a road leading to his country's edge, to the border of its neighbor, he saw the signs for directions and an occasional military hut or vehicle.

A couple of miles before the border, soldiers and machine guns gradually became a common sight. When he arrived at a checkpoint, a group of his countrymen were keeping the first few customs soldiers busy. They stood bunched up in a few circles, rather than lines, each facing one soldier, holding up passports above dusty and worn out clothes. About twenty yards to the right were lines of cars waiting under concrete structures painted yellow.

Asant passed a few of the circles and then after some steps between other travelers, waited for the soldier to direct him. The soldier grabbed Asant's passport and handed it to another directly behind. The second soldier motioned for Asant to approach.

"Where are you going?" the soldier asked, focusing his blank gaze on Asant.

"Siljap," Asant replied.

"What?"

"Siljap."

The response took the soldier by surprise. He raised one eyebrow as his eyes scrutinized Asant. He continued to stare at Asant, searching, almost glaring. "Why?" he asked.

"Because my teacher said I need to." Asant replied with no hesitation. By now, it had been weeks since he last saw his teacher. After a few hundred miles of walking and volunteered rides, his response had become automatic.

The reply did not appear to shake the soldier. Perhaps being from the same country and culture played a part in him accepting Asant's answer.

Asant watched the soldier open the passport and inspect the first page.

After a minute, the soldier looked up, observed Asant, and turned toward an enclosure a few feet away. When he called out, another soldier appeared and approached. He took the passport and went back into the enclosure.

Asant felt his heart react. It beat faster. Sweat rolled down his forehead. As it was, the presence of people with authority usually caused him anxiety, more so those with military gear and camouflage after having seen their kind raid his former village. And, images of the bank, the guard, and the yellow note, all rushed back to him. He turned to avoid the soldier's eyes, wanting to hide his mounting nervousness, anxious the soldier would somehow see through him and become suspicious.

"Comfortable ride. Comfortable ride to the other side," a man was yelling down the line of people holding their passports, some twenty yards away. He stepped up to each person offering a ride but was generally ignored. "Comfortable ride sir. You will not regret it."

"No. Go away," one person yelled. "Go. Go."

As the man neared Asant, one person became physical and pushed the man in Asant's direction.

"Comfortable ride sir," the man said to Asant.

Asant, still feeling his heart beating faster than usual, conscious of his sweating forehead, was pulled from his thoughts. He was barely able to see the man. "What?"

"Comfortable ride sir. You will need my help crossing, sir."

Asant, still conscious that the soldier has not returned the passport to him, shook his head in an effort to retain some control of his mind. "No. Please leave me."

"I will give you a ride sir. I speak the language they speak on the other side sir."

"No. Sorry. I cannot request rides, and I cannot pay."

"It would not be requesting sir, it would be accepting. I will take you there."

"Sorry, really, I do not have money," Asant said, now more focused on the man's persistence.

"Then you take me along. I speak languages, many languages. You can pay me later."

"No, thank you. That would be a debt."

"Sir, take me along. Your payment will be your company and the food we find."

"Take you where?"

"Open your bag," interjected the soldier, disregarding the man, and handed the passport back to Asant.

"Sorry?" Asant asked, surprised, looked at the passport, and for a second was unsure if he was cleared.

The soldier looked into the bag, then motioned to Asant to move along, but did not question the man with the cart. The man walked along Asant's side.

"I'm Ismael, sir."

"I'm not a sir."

"Yes. Yes. We will take turns."

"What? Take turns with what?"

"Pulling the cart, sir."

"What. No."

"You're too proud, sir. It's better to have company than not. You will need help."

"How can you help me?"

"We do not know the future, sir. You need me at least to translate."

"No, I can speak the common language."

"Sir, not everyone speaks the common language. You will have a difficult time communicating. Really, sir, the price of pulling the cart is worth having assistance and also company."

Asant walked ahead without responding.

Ismael continued. "Then it is set. I agree to accompany and assist you, and you will pull the cart, sometimes... only sometimes."

Asant turned to look at Ismael. "You can do whatever you want, and I will do whatever I want. So that means you shouldn't get funny ideas because of course I won't pull the cart. As it is I have too much in my head to carry anything."

"Then I will leave the cart once we cross the border. I will sell it; the money will be helpful to us. We only need it to cross anyway. They let me cross when I have it you see."

"You don't even know where I'm going. It doesn't make sense to just pretend you want to come."

"You're going a long way sir. It is clear."

"Why do you want to come anyways? Don't you have a family and a home?"

"No sir. I have not managed either."

Part III – Crossing

NOW IN A FOREIGN COUNTRY, it was a different world. The common language was helpful to Asant, that was true; nonetheless, it was not consistently accepted, barely on the remote and desolate path he was on, and everything else was just that much of a shift to make it all entirely different from what he was accustomed to.

It was noticeable from that first day on the other side of the border.

After a few hours of walking under a high sun, he thought out loud, "I'm going to stop for water and food."

"Yes, yes, true sir, we need water and food," Ismael said in response.

Asant had forgotten he had company. It occurred to him that he was glad to have someone with him. Inside the next near-abandoned shop on their path, Asant spoke in the common language. "Hello. We are in need of water. Please provide us with some," he said while raising his arm to chest level, wrist turned somewhat with a bottle in hand.

"There are bottles right there," the attendant replied with the local tongue and pointed, in spite of knowing the common language – expressing his intolerance of those from other nations.

Asant followed the man's hand to see a stack of bottles. "Sorry. I just meant if you would fill our bottles," he said.

"You must buy," the attendant replied, again in his country's language.

Asant started to say something; the attendant, however, interjected. "Buy or leave. This is a shop," he said motioning to the door.

"But, wait, please..." Asant spoke with more urgency.

The man, however, came from behind the counter to stand between Asant and Ismael. He placed his hands on their shoulders and worked to turn them around. "Hallae, hallae, hallae. I am not a charity," he shouted while prodding them in the direction of the door. "Work for your water or get it yourself. The sea is fewer than two thousand steps from here."

"My friend, what are you talking about. That's salt water. The rest of the country is mostly desert," Ismael said in disbelief at what the man was suggesting.

"Hallae. Find a way. You can. It is manageable for lads like you. Both of you."

The two stood outside the shop for a few moments. Eventually Asant knelt down and sat on a sandy curb.

Ismael followed and said, "Don't be bewildered sir. It is okay."

"We cannot survive without water."

"You know sir, people tell me that in some countries it is against the law and principles to refuse a person water."

"Good to know, Ismael. It is not helpful to us right now, I'm sure you agree."

The two walked for a while, until their need for water was too overwhelming. They decided to take advantage of what refuge they found under a small tree by the side of their path.

"Ismael, remember when I suggested that you go to your home and family, you said you did not manage either. What happened?"

Ismael sighed. "The war in the north. My village was one of those in between the two sides. It became strategic, you know, as they say. Some died. Some escaped."

Asant waited for a moment. "And your family?"

"My family." Ismael looked at the gravel between his feet. "Killed. Three lives wasted. My father, mother, sister. All three. I was a teenager. That day I was trying to find us a way out of the village. I have been pulling and pushing carts since then. No home, no family, no money and no time to build anything of my own."

"I'm sorry, Ismael." Asant looked into the distance. "You know, it is strange that we met, that you spoke with me. My life so far is not all that different from yours. There was no war, but I, too, lost my father and mother early. I have to say, I was lucky that my teacher took me into his home. I have loved him ever since. And trusted him with everything, even with my life. He sent me to school, educated me, taught me and fed me. I suppose he is my family."

"What happened to them?"

"My mother and father?"

"Yes."

It was Asant's turn to sigh. "Father was caught taking food. They said he was stealing. He was trying to feed me.

They took away his freedom. Beat him. He died inside. From injuries." Asant thought back, trying to remember what his father looked like, what he may think of Asant if he were to see him now. "He worked very hard for me and for my mom—his wife— to find work, to feed us." Asant looked at Ismael, then in front of him, into the air. His eyes burned as he shook his head. "My mother was alone in our county—men not respecting her—she could not, could not continue to live. I found her still and cold one morning. That day I begged for her to come back. I begged the sky. For hours hoping that she could be brought back. I prayed and prayed."

The two decided to say no more. They sat staring at the sand and gravel between their feet.

Wind brushed their hair and moved the sand.

"You smell that?" Ismael asked.

"Smell what?"

"It's cattle and horses, sir."

"I don't see anything, Ismael."

"They're nearby. I think they're moving in our direction."

"Either way, it does not matter to me... to us."

"But it does sir. The ranger or shepherd might have water for us."

"Hmm. True. I suppose no harm in asking. But I still don't see anything." Asant looked in both directions. "Oh. I think you're right, Ismael. I see them. Maybe a carriage too. That's it."

"It's too slow for a carriage, even for a cart. But we can wait. Whatever it is, it will be here soon enough."

Minutes passed. Eventually, in the distance appeared the heads of a person and a few horses, then just behind a few cattle and more people.

The beginning of the caravan came close enough for the herders to see Asant and Ismael.

"Let's go, sir. I will talk since they most likely won't understand you."

Ismael greeted the leader of the caravan, and asked if there was water to spare. The leader looked at Ismael, then at Asant.

"Gentlemen," the man began with the local language. "I am Zeke, leader of this caravan. Kindly tell me who you are."

"I am Ismael, sir. And this is Asant from across the border."

"Ah, across the border!" exclaimed Zeke to Asant, and on que now turning to the common language.

"You know the common language?" Asant asked, relieved that communicating was still possible for him.

"Sure. Everyone in these countries does." The man squeezed his face, perplexed at Asant's question.

"We are in need of water, if you would be so kind," said Asant.

"Of course, of course. Come on aboard the second carriage. There is some water that will hold you for now. We will stop for day break soon."

The water was beyond refreshing. It was revitalizing. It even brought happiness with it. It was as if it transported them from one world to another, from one of desperation and near-death, back to life.

True to his word, Zeke led the caravan to stop and set up camp before the skies grew dark.

Around a fire, Zeke had Asant and Ismael sit near him. "Another night with beautiful skies," Zeke said looking up. "The dotted lights from the stars astonish me. They remind me how small our role is."

"Perhaps small among the stars; I present that our role is always significant among men and women," said Asant.

"Yes, perhaps," replied Zeke with a smile. "Do you look up often, Asant?"

"Often, but likely less often than you."

"Ha," chuckled Zeke. "It's a nice and diplomatic answer. It is a privilege nonetheless to be on the move and to have the stars as your roof," Zeke replied. "Here, put a blanket around you, Asant." He handed a white and green blanket to Asant and another to Ismael. "The temperatures drop fast at this altitude. You may not recognize it. We are near the summit of a mountain range. Our ascent has been gradual but consistent since you joined us today."

The area had few small trees, otherwise was an open space. The wood in front of them spewed a few sparks, releasing its essence, a sharp pungent smell, something of a combination between cedar and sage.

"Some say this wood, this tree, helps us reconnect our spirits with the mind." Zeke smiled. "This world, life... shares much with us."

Asant regarded Zeke, admiring, wondering. "Are you truly constantly on the move, Zeke?" asked Asant.

Zeke took a deep breath. He appeared to take in the smoke from their fire. "Yes. Just about every lit moment." His eyes focused on the fire. "How about you, Asant, Ismael?"

"For me it's been only around the nearby border, transporting travelers and their belongings," said Ismael.

"Ah, and Asant?"

"To be truthful, this is my first."

"And where is your first taking you?" asked Zeke.

"Siljap," whispered Asant.

"Excuse me, Asant?"

"Siljap."

"Siljap?"

"Yes. Yes!"

"Very well. We can accompany one another. Siljap is on my path. It is meant to be."

Asant looked at Zeke again, thankful, while Zeke tended to the fire.

"It will be a good adventure, Asant. The world, Creation, has much to show us and teach us, if only we choose to listen and observe."

Life on a caravan was neither simpler nor harder than any other, but it was different. Even for Ismael, time was necessary, allowing him to become accustomed to constantly moving, tending, and selling. Through hundreds of miles, both Asant and Ismael learned to help, and listened as Zeke expressed admiration for their surroundings—deserts, steppes, woods, hills, among other terrains. Occasionally, a few members of the group went off course to visit a specific site.

Weeks after they had first met, Zeke told Asant and Ismael about one particular site—a cave that he visited during every passing. Once they were nearby, they found a site to camp, and planned for the brief excursion the following morning.

The cave's entrance stood on a rocky new-moon-shaped hill, the entrance hidden behind a curve and hard to discern from its surroundings.

"It is tremendous!" Zeke said to himself while looking up, then turning to Asant and Ismael, he added, "It's a miracle, my friends, everything about it. Its water, the light rays that find a way in, the colors, all of it." Then he motioned for them to continue walking.

Zeke was not exaggerating. Once deep inside the cave, the colors were bright and surprising, appearing luminescent. There were red and purple formations on the cave's floor. Water dripped slowly to intercept light rays coming from mysterious sources. The three of them came across even more colorful formations as they walked farther in.

Soon thereafter they reached an edge, a balcony of sorts, that looked over an open expanse a few yards below. A few small plants looked up with patience, one for each ray of light. A few firefly-like insects hovered in the open air. The peace of the space, among life and the quiet colors, stunned the two new visitors.

"Let's sit," said Zeke.

"It is amazing," Asant exclaimed.

"Yes. I am glad you appreciate it."

Two men walked through a crevice on the other end of the open space; they talked animatedly, arms in the air, repeatedly turning to look at each other. Minutes later after they passed, another person, on a slow walk, reached the same crevice and examined it and the walls surrounding it.

Zeke glanced at Asant and Ismael and asked, "How about we begin our trek back my friends?"

Once at the entrance, the three of them noticed the two men standing still talking, and the third on the opposite end of the hill still alone. The first two men now facing each other grew even more animated in their conversation and hand gestures... their voices grew louder and louder.

"I think they are having an argument," exclaimed Ismael as the two men's voices and body language increased in agitation.

"You're right, Ismael. I should try to help them. I will be right back," Asant said to Zeke.

"No. We should get going." Zeke said as he reached for Asant's shoulder.

"But Zeke, it is our duty," exclaimed Asant.

"No, my friend. Come, please allow me to tell you a story while on our way. I promise it's timely. You see, there was a man who was down to his last three coins, albeit they were three gold coins. But nevertheless he had become distraught and knew not what to do. He walked aimlessly in his city, and eventually made his way to a coffee shop...perhaps to forget his misfortune and misery, even if only for a short hour. He busied his mind with the surroundings, watched patrons and pedestrians. Opposite where he sat was a row of shops. One in particular caught his eye. It had a sign with the name, 'Haden's.' Below that name was another sign with the words, 'One Gold Coin for One Piece of Wisdom and Good Fortune.' The shop attracted our desperate friend. Considering his state, he got himself up and walked to Haden's."

Zeke continued, "The man in the store, bearded and ornamented with necklaces and a bright colored robe, looked up as our friend entered, and said, *Welcome. How can I help?*"

"*Well, the sign says one gold coin for good fortune, and I am in need of good fortune.*"

"*Very well. Are you in possession of a gold coin?* asked the bearded man."

"The man began to reconsider. *A gold coin is a lot for...What, I don't even know. Then again, there isn't much I could do, and I will spend it either way. Maybe one coin is worth the risk.*"

"*Yes, we have a deal, I have a gold coin,* the man declared."

"*Very good. Here is what you need to know. Mind your own business,* said the bearded man."

"Our friend waited for a moment, expecting more. When nothing more came, he exclaimed, *Is that it?!*"

"*Yes. One gold coin for one piece of wisdom.*"

"Disappointed, our friend left the shop and went back to his seat at the coffee shop. He sat in continued despair and watched the people around him, deep in thought that everyone had a better life and better circumstances than he did. Then, he noticed two men having a heated discussion. The two men stood up, moved closer to each other and continued with what now seemed to be an argument. They yelled, gestured, frowned. Our dear friend felt strongly against anger and immediately started toward the two men to help them resolve their issue.

"But then, the bearded man came to his mind along with that piece of wisdom about minding one's own business. Our friend stopped himself and reconsidered his intention, that perhaps the matter between those two men was not his business after all. Just as he thought this, he noticed another person running to the two men, right arm raised yelling, 'Friends, please, stop your fighting. You are brothers.' He approached the two and stood between them in an attempt to bring peace."

"*What are you talking about? We are friends,* one of the two men said. *And who ever said that friends cannot argue or discuss matters?*"

"*Right. And who are you to make these assumptions about us?* The second of the two men asked."

"*Brothers, please, I wanted to help, it was only too clear that you were arguing and that you were about to fight each other.*"

"*What are you talking about? We just told you we are great friends with strong opinions,* said the first of the two men who then pushed the third person."

"*That is right,* said the second of the two men. *Why are you trying to come between us?* he asked, while also nudging the third person. *You are interfering. You interrupted our discussion,* he said, pushing the third person even harder."

"Their reaction caught the third person off-guard. He lost his balance from the repeated pushes and fell.

Gentlemen, you have this wrong. I only wanted to help. I thought you..."

"No, you have this wrong. And you thought wrong, the first of the two said."

"And it went on for a bit longer," continued Zeke. "The third man was physically injured in the end; the first two went off angry."

"But that third person had only good intentions," Asant said.

"Maybe so, Asant. Still he did not have the entire history or picture in his mind. He jumped into a scene in which he did not have a place."

Asant thought for a few moments. "Zeke, I want to ask you," he said sometime later, "I am going to Siljap to alleviate the war now happening. From this story, am I wrong to be going?"

"Ah, what I understand from our conversations is that you received advice. It is different in such a case, in the case of advice, especially when it is from a guide you trust."

"What do you mean?"

"Well, advice such as that can create a role for the person, usually to do good. Also, the incident today is different from your situation, in large part because in the latter, you will learn the history behind the issue. History—knowledge—often helps us reach better decisions."

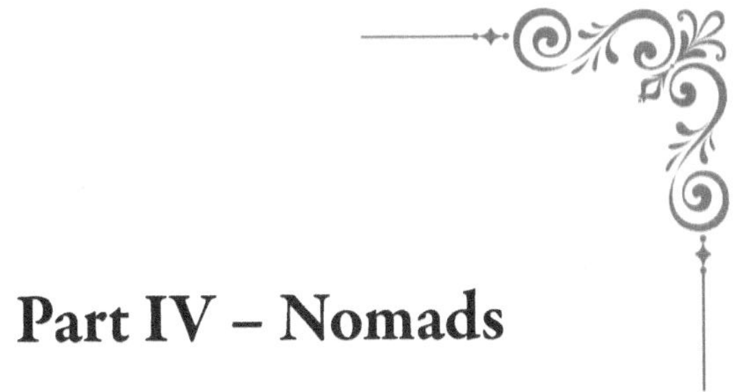

Part IV – Nomads

ASANT AND ISMAEL CONTINUED to accompany Zeke. In return, they contributed to Zeke's trading efforts as the caravan moved west, crossing several man-made as well as natural borders. Like a bee that moves pollen, Zeke moved the likes of spices, teas, and sometimes information, between the different regions he reached. Meanwhile, Asant and Ismael managed to learn parts of the trade and worked to repay Zeke. Along with other members of the caravan, the two also continued to accompany Zeke on excursions. One such excursion was to an ancient prophet's burial site. The most recent of which was to the ruins of a city that once was home to a thriving civilization. This excursion, however, was different, for not too long before they had crossed into Siljap.

Zeke did not announce it, but he did not have to. Asant was aware of where he was on his own. Somehow, he knew that his duty was approaching him. He treaded with anxiety and with the knowledge that he needed to begin the search for how to do his work.

"Zeke, what is this place we are going to?" he asked.

"Ah, it is the ancient City of the Green Desert. The name given to it by an ancient empire for the oasis that it is. It was the city of a great civilization. A civilization so great that one of its queens challenged that same empire, in spite of the empire being multitudes larger. In desperation, the queen declared herself empress of the land, but succumbed to the empire's armies and was taken prisoner." Zeke looked in the direction of the ruins with admiration. "I must say, I adore this place, and hold its ancient inhabitants and what they built in awe. These ancient columns ahead have much to teach us and hold knowledge long forgotten. They humbly reflect the light of the desert with majesty and exude perseverance against time."

Zeke walked in the direction of the ancient city's ruins. They all reached the first of the columns, and along other members of the caravan, Asant and Ismael walked between these tall golden pillars, on a long-ago established street, now abandoned and left to visitors of the new world, and students of the old.

On their way to the end of the street, they approached a sculptured arch, acting as a gate to and from the same street, perhaps a gate to the ancient city itself. Just ahead, on the other side of the arch, stood a woman and by her side a boy of perhaps ten years. A black scarf protected the woman's head and shoulders; a brown cloak covered the boy and a red and white turban protected his head. The two stood close enough to Asant and Zeke to exchange greetings. They stood tall, confident in their stance and in their place, their eyes gentle but unwavering.

"Who is that, Zeke? Do you know their people?" asked Asant in a whisper.

Ismael moved close to Asant and Zeke.

"Hmm...they seem to be members of the local nomadic tribe. They are a tremendous people, certainly under-appreciated by the rest of the population." Zeke answered.

The woman and the boy turned and walked with short strides away from the golden stone gateway.

"How do you mean tremendous?" Asant pursued.

"Well, it is believed that they've managed to preserve their ancient knowledge and practices. They have a certain connection with their surroundings, with the desert, with the hidden world."

"I have heard similar things about the nomads in my country," Ismael said.

"Hidden world? What hidden world?" asked Asant.

"The spiritual world, my friend."

"Oh, I see. Well, I would argue it's not a hidden or even a separate world at all, but simply a part of our own world, a part we don't see because we choose not to."

"Yes, yes, a fine point, Asant; and, since we're on this subject, would you agree the names, labels, and descriptions we use are not as important as what the descriptions help us do?" asked Zeke.

"Do you mean, now that we have pointed to this part, the hidden world, whether or not we seek is what's important?"

"Yes. And, I'm sure you know of this part that we speak of, but are you seeking it?" Zeke asked with a faint smile. "Asant, my friend, knowing is good but insufficient alone. We need to act. We need to keep on with our search and apply what we learn."

Asant's demeanor changed, reminding him of his own attempts to learn and decipher life, and how he considered all of them as failed attempts. He sighed and looked down. "I am seeking it. I have been seeking it most of my life, Zeke. But it evades me because I'm not strong enough, because I fail when I'm tested and when I'm tempted. And to be honest, as tremendous as this world may be, seeking it is as tremendously frustrating. To be honest, I don't like the seeking part. I don't like it one bit." He looked back at Zeke, squeezed his eyes in an attempt to sway the sun's light. It was bright, and hot. He then looked around the desert, just then feeling its heat, seeing shimmering haze in the distance.

"What is it that you don't like about it?" Zeke asked, bringing him back.

"I don't like living through it. I guess I am lazy because I really don't want to do the seeking...I don't want to deal."

"Surely it is not that you're lazy. Perhaps you haven't learned yet. It is one thing to know from books and discussions; it is another to act on and live that knowledge. For me, it is not about liking or not. I like it all when I am doing my work, when I am with others, then seeking is a part of the process," Zeke turned to look at Asant, finding a face contorted from trying to reconcile thoughts and desires. Zeke then changed course. "We digress. Simply, the nomadic tribes in this area are unique."

"How are they unique?"

"Hmm, let's see. They are not as attached to the things they have. They look for little more than what they need; thus, they are not as distracted."

Other locals approached Zeke's group, looking to sell goods.

"Scarves, jewelry," one yelled in the common language, raising a scarf vibrant with colors. It flapped with the wind, displaying its colors of red, yellow, and blue, along with sparkling short golden chains at its ends.

"Best products here, come see," another said.

"Best that Kamur has to offer. Best shirts and beautiful postcards."

The calling did not escape Asant. He approached one of the sellers and asked, "Are these made in Kamur?"

"Yes, yes, they are made right here. Look, this is excellent quality, and it costs only two local coins."

Caught by surprise, Asant turned to look for the nomadic pair – the woman and the boy they encountered earlier – then toward Zeke. "Zeke, you said this is the City of the Green Desert."

"Yes. It is."

"But they just called it Kamur."

"Yes. The locals use that name."

Asant turned to find the nomadic woman and boy, now blending with the desert sand. He stared at them through the sun's haze, and after a minute or so, ventured into a run toward them.

Finally standing just behind the pair, sweat beginning to form on his forehead, he said in the common language, "Hello, hello, please forgive me."

The woman and the boy stopped and turned to look at him. Neither said anything. Their eyes did not blink. They looked at Assant, waited for him to speak, to explain himself.

"Hello," he said again, while heaving, his voice shaking with reluctance.

The woman continued to look at him, a sparkle in her eyes, somewhat curious, while her face continued to wait for Asant to say more.

"Ummm. Sorry. I know this is out of the ordinary. I simply wanted to find out more about your people, your tribe. Please don't consider this intrusive. I just wanted to ask where you are living right now?"

"I don't understand your question," the woman replied, with the boy close to her side, looking at Asant with the same unblinking eyes.

"Well, I mean where are your people right now...where will everyone sleep tonight?" he asked.

"Our tents are nearly a thousand strides from here."

Ismael remained near Zeke. However, he decided to follow Asant once he noticed that Asant was still in the distance by the woman and youngster and did not seem to be returning.

"I see. I do want to ask..." Asant continued, his voice still shaking.

The woman and the boy waited, their faces and eyes still and unchanged.

Asant searched for the thoughts he had minutes prior, when it first occurred to him to go after them. Nothing came from his mouth. He felt light steps behind him and allowed the feeling to distract him.

Ismael arrived. He sensed Asant was at a loss, that he wanted something but did not know how to acquire it. Ismael remained quiet and attempted to read and understand Asant's thoughts, attempted to learn what it was that Asant wanted.

Asant turned his face and looked at Ismael, finding familiar eyes, calm, wanting to help. He then turned to the woman. "I want to ask if I could stay with your people? To learn." He pleaded. His words followed each other without a break; his voice quivered between asking and pleading.

The woman's eyes continued their stillness, unblinking, now looking through Asant. A moment passed. "You can follow me," she said finally.

Taken aback, Ismael turned and searched one face after the other. "Where are we going?" He asked Asant.

Asant turned to look in Zeke's direction. Both he and Zeke raised their hands and waved in the same moment. "I want to stay with the clan," Asant said to Ismael while his arm and hand moved in the air, continuing to wave, hoping Zeke would receive his gratitude.

Ismael looked on, incredulous, his thoughts traversing his mind. It was his turn to have no words. Then, "I'm coming. I will stay with them too."

"I don't know if they will take you," Asant said with a low voice, then turned and began to walk in the direction of the woman and the boy. He was already paces away when Ismael called out.

"Of course they will," Ismael said, following in Asant's steps. "Why would they take you and not me?!"

The clan's tents in the desert amounted to fewer than fifteen. There were two in particular that were about three times the size of the other tents. Some animals roamed within an imaginary circle nearby; two sticks moved in the hands of two men on the outskirts of the circle. The woman and the boy with her continued to walk ahead while Asant and Ismael followed. At one of the larger tents, the woman said two words to the boy, looked at Asant one last time and walked away. The boy turned to face the tent and walked into it through its flap. Perplexed, Asant watched the boy disappear and the flap return to its original position. He did not know whether to follow or remain where he was; regardless, the boy came out within a minute's passing and motioned for him and Ismael to enter.

Unsure of what was happening, and who, or what, was inside, Asant hesitated. It also came to him that it was he who asked to be invited to visit the clan. He managed one step to take him away from the outside of the tent, feeling the desert's brightness dwindle, with Ismael directly behind him. The flap closed behind them and completely hid the sun.

Although his eyes needed more time to adjust, Asant nonetheless recognized outlines of two figures on the other end. They were laying on their sides, leaning on their elbows, their heads almost touching and appearing to be extensions of one another.

Asant felt nervous for reasons he could not place. Even though it was only a few more steps forward, his legs were unresponsive, as if he could not maintain control, as if they were not his.

As seconds passed, he was able to recognize details and differentiate the two figures. One wore numerous golden and sparkling bracelets on the wrists; the other had facial hair. It was a woman and a man. Both their heads were covered. The woman's free hand rested on her hip; the man's was occupied with something of a rosary. The three pairs of eyes met, forming a triangle, acknowledging one another, a meeting that led Asant to relax enough to manage a nod. The man maintained a hidden but clear smile. He moved to sit, and motioned for the two incomers to step in and sit to his left. The man was subtle in his demeanor and expressions. He moved just enough to reach for a narrow, long, and pointy yellow brass pot and two flat-bottomed cone-shaped porcelain cups about two inches deep. He poured what was likely coffee, black and rich in aroma, and handed one cup to Asant and another to Ismael. With a gentle move, he leaned a bit to his side and looked at the rosary, holding it with both hands and moving the beads slowly and gently one by one.

Smoke from the cups traversed the air, spreading the coffee's aroma, as if inviting them to converse. Asant and Ismael drank the coffee a sip at a time, neither perturbed by its bitterness but conscious of their every move, almost in sync with each other while unsure of the custom and etiquette. The man moved to pour them more, but Asant covered his cup and put it by the coffee pot.

"Where are you coming from?" He questioned them in his language, with a soft and low tone.

"Honestly, sir, from a far land," Ismael said. Asant turned, surprised at Ismael's command of the situation. Ismael cleared his throat, and added, "We would be most gracious sir if we can use the common language."

"Of course," the man replied.

A few moments passed. The man averted his gaze from the rosary and asked, "What do you seek?"

"I seek to stay with your people," Asant replied.

"I am told as much. There is a sense, nonetheless, that you are here in this region for a different purpose. Tell me what it is you seek."

Asant lowered his head, thrown into thought by the man's inquiry. "I seek to assist...no, sorry...I seek to alleviate the pains of war in this country. I must do this."

"We all must be of service, and we are often guided to meet our assigned role. It is not of import how you came to yours, and I will not ask," the man said, appearing to pause with more to say. He returned his attention to the rosary and continued to roll the beads one by one. "It is unclear whether or how we can in turn assist you," he continued, "but that also is not of import, because without a doubt it will be revealed in time. We are a hospitable people, and you shall be one of us for as long as you require or desire."

"Thank you, sir."

"You shall call me Yusef," replied the man with a faint smile and soft tone.

"I am Asant; and this is my friend, Ismael."

Two days into their stay, Asant and Ismael sat with Yusef and his company for the midday meal.

Yusef asked, "Asant, how long have you been traveling?"

"It has been weeks since I started. Along the way I must say I have had much help and had no need to continue counting. Ismael kindly accompanied me almost from the beginning."

"I see," Yusef said, and looked to continue with the meal, holding a clay bowl in his left hand, filling it with yellow rice, then adding steaming yogurt from a pot sitting over a gas flame. "And, if you don't mind the inquiry, how do you wish to address the war?"

The question was awakening. It brought the task to the forefront of Asant's mind, along with images of what he knew of wars and violent conflict. In his mind, he saw black smoke, growing and spreading into the air as he stood watching. The image was alive in his mind; the smoke was moving, threatening. Nonetheless, he accepted his need to act, did not move, stood his ground. He returned his attention to Yusef, took a deep breath. "I do not know, I truly thought that you, your clan, because of your ways, might be able to help."

"We do not become involved in conflicts. Certainly, we defend ourselves against a wrong; however, that is the extent of our involvement."

"I see. I really should have guessed as much," Asant said, then paused for a moment. "If I may ask then, you said conflict...what conflict started the war?"

"My words were in the general sense. A war by default is borne of conflict, of interests or conflicting interests, wouldn't you say?"

"I suppose. Are you aware of the conflict or the interests that ignited this war?"

Yusef's face changed. Although his face continued to indicate a calm demeanor, his smile now disappeared altogether, as if readying to confront a danger. "This war appears to be complicated, Asant, with many opposing sides. It appears to have in fact many conflicts, many interests. In truth, however, our understanding is that it started with one man, a conflict with one man."

"How do you mean? One man started this war?" asked Asant.

"Yes and no. No in that this man did not start the war in the common understanding of the word; however, he laid the foundation. He was the one who called the conflicts to ignite."

"You will forgive me for not understanding."

"Yes, of course. In short, the story is that the country's police imprisoned this man;" Yusef stopped mid-sentence. Asant felt discomfort at the mention of prison. He averted Yusef's gaze and focused on one of the tent's corners and repositioned himself. "They – the police – imprisoned him some years ago, before the war began. By all intents representing this people, the people of this country." Yusef continued, "he waited to be released. But when they did not let him free, he put a curse on the whole nation for not letting him be."

"How does a curse work on a whole nation?"

"From our understanding, a curse is transferring vice or dark energy from one to another. Ill thoughts can work in this fashion, to a lesser extent than intentional deliberate placement. For Siljap, we believe the fighting began between this man and the nation. The man perhaps fought back in the form of energy.

"All things have a root, dear Asant. And so, if you wish to stop the war, to alleviate its pains, I believe you must start with this one man. He may or may not be the root of the conflict itself. Such violent conflicts have deep roots, ones that go far into our past. This man, however, appears to have had a hand in igniting the conflict into what it is today. And so, he is where I suggest you start."

"But even if he is the source, or ignitor, of this humongous and complicated problem...well, could one person truly wish so much pain on so many people?"

"That is a good question. Possibly, yes. Or, he did not know what he was doing. Just as a possibility, he did not believe in the power in him."

"Forgive me Yusef, if I have a hard time...kindly allow me to take it one step back," Asant stopped and looked at Yusef, waiting for permission. He continued when he did not sense an objection. "Why do you believe it started with one man, with this man? How did you come to this, as you say, understanding?"

Yusef's face remained blank, his smile still evading his face. "It was pieces of stories, and perhaps a little from the stars."

"The stars? Do you mean the stars foretold of this war?" asked Asant.

"No. Not exactly. We saw from the stars that a change was coming, but it was not available to us—the direction of that change. We interpreted this as a prime opportunity, possibly for order or for chaos such as suffering or cleansing."

"Truthfully, I'm not sure what you mean."

Such knowledge was inaccessible to Asant. In turn, the lack of understanding was frustrating him. He thought about the stars. Perhaps they somehow played a role in foretelling events or describing the world, but he did not see any connection to actual events or conflicts, and even more so personally, when it came to hunger and pain. He trusted his teacher, and now Yusef, but how to use the information he was receiving was not privy to him.

"Both were knocking at a door... and waiting, if you will. The change was going to happen, a door was going to open, and allow this change to happen through either order and good days or through chaos. After we heard the stories about this man, we concluded that how the country's government and that man resolved the conflict between them would determine which door was to open. Their actions would determine whether they invite order and peace or chaos and conflict. We believed it was an opportunity to shape the nation's future."

"Very well. I hope you can forgive me Yusef, I believe I will need time to understand."

"Granted." Yusef smiled.

"Can you tell us the stories you heard?"

"The man spoke of the country's possible suffering, that it was not good for the country to steal his freedom and choice in his path."

"But that says nothing," Asant said with a higher tone. He stopped, averted Yusef's eyes and looked away, even though Yusef was not looking at Asant. "Pardon me Yusef. I am your guest."

"There were other threads," continued Yusef, his eyes on the still rosary. "A prison guard who claimed to be a medium, well-versed in soul and energy matters. Other guards claimed this same prisoner, this man, would not sleep at night but instead sit crossed legged night after night muttering indiscernible words."

"Even if any of this had any bearing, why didn't anyone do anything? Why didn't these guards do something? Or even your clan?"

"We do not become involved. As for the guards, you can imagine none of this was expressed, and certainly no one connected these threads to any conflict or issue until the war had gripped the nation and was beyond anyone's control. The events began just as a storm would, distant and not a threat. It inched closer and closer, and even when its edge reached into Siljap, no one was the wiser. At one point, there was hope, a shimmer, by chance, that this person, by then free, had it in him to change the course of the nation. There were few who knew of his power. Alas, this did not come to fruition. He made other choices, and, once the nation delved into a war with itself, there was no going back. The choice was made; the change had begun. More importantly, no one was at the helm to rein in this change. No one was capable of leading the nation and its people."

Asant stared at Yusef. He had no words. For him, Yusef's story was illogical, and did not offer possible solutions. Questions overwhelmed him, leading to too many confusing thoughts. He shook his head, brought his right hand to his face to hide, even if only for a brief pause.

"Son, I imagine your task appears insurmountable, regardless of what story or reasons you believe; nonetheless, the task is yours, and since it is so, it is also true that you must already have what you need."

"Yusef, it appears more than insurmountable. There is no place to start. I do not even know what I can possibly do to change anything. And the story you tell is too strange and unreal to simply accept," Asant replied, thinking of his teacher and their last meeting, remembering the feeling of having to choose in that instant. Still etched in his person and his mind was that feeling of the weight of life collapsing on him, as a result of one decision.

"Anything imaginable is possible, Asant. And you must move forward since you already chose to take on this task."

"I understand." Asant nodded. "The story you speak of is related to how it all started. And while it is perhaps beyond my comprehension, it maybe true. However, my focus must be to help end the conflict, Yusef. Do you believe this one person he can help me in that regard?"

"As you said, he had a hand in starting it. As such, our teachings instruct that he would have the key to ending it." Yusef then turned to Ismael. "It is easy to feel overwhelmed, Asant. Even more so with stories and recommendations that defy logic; nonetheless, you have a dear friend to help you. That alone is more than many of us are granted. For now, perhaps it would help to trace the steps that unleashed these events, beginning with the stories we eventually accumulated, and the persons behind each event. After that, you might be able to decide what is true, what you need to do, and whether you should seek the person of whom I speak."

"Do you know any of these individuals?" asked Asant.

"No. But, as long as we maintain our non-involvement in the war itself, we might be able to assist in locating any one of them, if you wish."

"Who? Even if we assume this is in fact how it all unraveled, how do we make sense of what or whom to look for?"

"Starting, somewhere, anywhere, is what matters. I recommend we start with some detail, to help you decide for whom to search or how to approach your task. Let us meet with two of our elders in two days. They are a short distance from here."

The two days were slow to pass. Asant's squeezed eyes and crunched face exhibited his anxiety. Ismael accompanied Asant as would a guard, aiming to be helpful, to be a friend, at the minimum a trusted companion.

The meeting with the elders revealed only some details, but no comforting or illuminating facts. They spoke of the universe, of balance, of inevitabilities, and of powers all individuals have. They did not make any mention of justice, truth, or peace. In the end, Yusef, after his own discussions with his companion and the clan, recommended that Asant and Ismael find a person by the name of Kadir, an accountant reputed to be from the city of Lamania, about a month's journey from Kamur by foot. Kadir, they said, was known in his community to be an intuitive and kind individual. He was the first person to have encountered the person of interest, and the one to hear that person speak of the difficulties the country would face if the police continued to keep him behind doors.

Kadir, they said, may have helpful facts about that person's articulations, and about his whereabouts, if Asant chose to pursue this thread.

Part V – Kadir

LAMANIA SURPRISED BOTH ASANT and Ismael. The city was a contrast from the oasis of Kamur. Lamania was a major port, colored by small buildings, interrupted by craters, downed buildings, and darkened concrete ruble. Nature persisted to make its presence, surrounding the city by a sea, a beautiful flat blue surface, in one direction and green mountains in another. It was also the city's size that left them caught off-guard or perhaps even more dismayed.

On foot, coming from Kamur, they had ascended to a mountain's peak and stood looking down at the city's streets, some leading to the sea at one end, others toward the mountain on which they stood. The mountain itself was inviting in its own way. A breeze going through evergreens, a few fruitful trees and vines.

They decided on a spot for the night. They would venture into the city after some planning.

"How will we find him, Ismael?" Asant asked.

"It will happen, friend, just as we somehow managed with food. We cannot doubt that we, you, will also manage finding what's needed," Ismael replied, then added after a pause while appearing to admire the city below and beyond. "Perhaps the city's center is a reasonable start."

"Ismael," Asant began. "I must tell you I am glad you insisted to accompany me."

"Ah," Ismael smiled. "You see, Asant, I know a thing or two."

"You know more than a thing or two." Asant sighed. "You know, Ismael, I feel I've aged ten years since we crossed that first border."

"I would say you have grown, not aged."

Asant smiled. "I saw my teacher last night, in my sleep."

"Did he say anything?"

"I was afraid, worried. I wanted to say as much. He smiled. That is all I remember."

The city's center was more than one simple location or street. It seemed to be a city within a city. The former was lined with shops and old buildings, most appearing to be either deserted or crumbling. Beaten and defeated concrete was ubiquitous and a consistent view.

The city's center was an ancient city—a business and residential area, with shops lining several streets, mostly under tin roofs, and countless small buildings half toppled, with few remaining as they once were. The old city's walls – now mostly imaginary, victims of centuries-worth of erosion, conflict, and fighting – now created a border of sorts, separating the old from the new.

The two walked these streets looking for an accountant. "How do you think we can find where he works, if he's working around here? How does one find an accountant?" asked Asant, more to himself than to Ismael.

"Let's ask, let me ask," replied Ismael, while turning and walking towards the closest shop. "Hello. A quick question if you don't mind. Is there an accountant or a business of that sort nearby?"

These questions sent them to several parts and corners around the old city over their first few days, but to no avail. As they walked near an outer part of the old city, leaving the last shop behind them, a person sitting on a lonely piece of rock walked to them and asked for money.

"Please young man," she said to Ismael, "one coin would go a long way. One coin please. Have heart."

"I truly do not have anything to give you," replied Ismael.

"Wait," Asant interjected. "We cannot provide you with coins, but perhaps something to eat or drink. May I?"

"Yes, that would be good. A sandwich or a drink from that restaurant," the woman said pointing back to the street they had just turned from.

"Sure, I think I can get you one of those, what would you like?"

"Juice. Juice would be good."

In the restaurant, Asant grabbed a drink and took it to the cashier. "Hello, is the owner here?" Asant asked.

"No, I manage the place. What do you need?"

"I would like to take this drink in exchange for work."

"Work? No. Money. Money for drink and food. Only money."

"Sir, please. I promise good work so you don't have to do it, and you can attend to more important matters."

"Look man, I need money to fix this place, not a dishwasher or a cook."

"Great. I can fix things. I can help you fix this wall and paint it. Whatever you need."

"Fine. Fix the sink in the kitchen."

"Very well," replied Asant, "but my friend takes the drink now."

The manager led Asant to the back for supplies and pointed out the sink on the way, then pointed away and out of the kitchen. "Tools are just outside that door," he said, and walked back to the store's front.

Asant turned to the sink, looked at it, then at a puddle in front of it. He turned the faucet. Pressure streaked through the pipes, eventually whatever little water was still coming through the plumbing began to trickle and drip through one of the pipes below.

He shut it and went for the tools.

Just outside the kitchen, on the other side of the door, an individual was looking at electrical meters and cables.

"Hello," Asant said, surprised, becoming excited.

The man nodded but did not turn to look at Asant.

"Hello, my name is Asant." He waited, wanted to think. It seemed to be too quick to happen this way, too lucky, too good to be true. "Umm," he decided to continue nonetheless. "I'm looking for someone, and really, it's fortuitous that you're here, maybe I can ask you, if you don't mind."

The man remained still, looking at the meters and the wires, while Asant waited.

"I really don't mean to bother you, but if you would just let me know if..."

"Yes. I know. Kadir. You want to find Kadir."

"What?" Asant asked, again surprised, caught off guard. "Um. Yes. Yes. Right. How did you know?"

"Let's just say you're not the first person to ask us accountants in this city about Kadir."

"I see. I understand, and I hope you can forgive me, it's just important that I meet Kadir. You're not him, are you?"

"No. Obviously I am not."

Asant waited for the man to provide some information. "Please, would you point me in the right direction?" he asked.

"Well. I can tell you he worked for the government just like I do now."

"He does? So do you work together? Are you co-workers?"

"Like I said, he did. They let him go, or maybe he left, I don't know."

"Can you tell me where I can find him?"

"No. No idea. He's probably in the city."

"Do you know where he lives?"

The accountant gazed at Asant with a tense and disgruntled look. "He used to live in the Hezb neighborhood, not far from here," he said, and returned to his work. Asant waited for more. When nothing came, he took a step back, looked down and stared at the tools.

It was another few days of similar interactions before Asant and Ismael managed to find Kadir in a nearby village. Situated between the mountains, the blue sea, cedar and other evergreens, the village presented quaint and quiet living, insulated from an otherwise ubiquitous conflict. In spite of their fragility, the simple but still standing huts and tents created an impression of immunity from destruction.

Kadir was sitting by one such hut, leaning on its sea-facing wall, a knife in one hand, an apple in the other. Asant and Ismael walked up through one of the mountain's rising slopes, and, just as they rose above a line, they saw him to their right. The sun was high, only minutes before noon. He did look up and offered a welcoming smile. A quarter of an hour's time later, they were sitting on mats with light food between them. Bread, olive oil and salt.

Asant was quiet. Kadir noticed his gaze and light smile, sensing hesitation and choosing to enter into the subject. "I suppose people told you about me?" he said, "Or rather, not me, but my experience and those I met. You know, this," he said with a smile, pointing to the food in front of them, "This was a luxury. Sometimes they used luxuries like this to bribe us. After leaving, after they let me be, I stuck with these simplicities. It's really more than enough."

Ismael looked away, then back at Kadir. With many questions in his mind, he felt more anxious than his normal self. He cleared his throat to announce he was about to say something, "Why did they take you?"

"Well, it was appropriate really. I cheated on the meters. I knew it was not right. I did it only twice, but that was enough."

"I'm sorry!" exclaimed Asant.

"It's okay. It was harsh, a harsh price, but I shouldn't have done that. I shouldn't have succumbed," Kadir focused his eyes on the mats, avoiding eye contact.

No one said anything, allowing the moment's severity to pass.

"Was it bad inside?" Ismael asked.

"You know, not really. Everyone I met was kind. Everyone who was with me. The guards were rough at the beginning. But the guys they placed with me were kind and innately happy people, just facing a rough time in life, you know?" He continued to look at the mats. "I met some of the best people I have yet to meet. At first, it was just one other guy; much better than being alone. We kept the place clean, learned to share food, chores, jokes. The jokes were the most important. The jokes helped us stay sane." He maintained his smile as he turned to the task of cutting the apple.

The three were silent again. This time, however, Ismael moved himself a bit, expecting more information and feeling impatient. "Was this the person?" he asked.

"What? Oh, Yeshu. No. This was not Yeshu. About two weeks after they put me in, they put Yeshu in the same cell as us. Sometimes they move people from cell to another. But with him, it was clear he had just arrived. He looked shocked. I suppose everyone is shocked when it's their first time. Still, that black metal door slammed."

"The lock turned. And he stared and stared. Suit jacket on, belt around his waist. He didn't belong there. They probably only wanted to scare him so he would give them information. They didn't bother to take the belt from him."

"Yeshu? Is that his name?" Asant asked.

"Yes. Yeshu."

"How long did they keep him?"

"All together I don't know. It seemed they changed their plans after those first couple of days. Something happened. I think they were going to let him go, but instead they took him away and put two others with us. They brought him back a few days later, roughed up and even more shocked than before."

Both Asant and Ismael remained still, waited, maintained their gaze on Kadir, expecting to hear more.

"Then, after another week, it was Jared. Jared was very funny. Actually, he had big downs."

"Jared?"

"Yes."

A boy of perhaps around six years of age walked toward Kadir, sat in his lap, looked up at him. "Can I have olives?"

"Of course, my friend," Kadir replied, a smile reaching his ears, marveling at the boy. "Our young man here cares for olives almost more than for sweets."

The boy chuckled, took one olive after the other.

"Wash your hands!" Kadir instructed.

The boy jumped out of Kadir's lap and walked toward a square platform with a few buckets.

"The children are the biggest victims," Kadir said, his eyes following the boy.

Asant and Ismael both turned between the two and observed the boy with Kadir, reminding them of their childhood. Asant then averted his eyes, then turned to Ismael. Neither said anything and without words decided together not delve into the topic.

Kadir sighed. "Let me come back to our talk. Ah..." he thought for a moment. "Jared, correct?"

Asant turned to Kadir, caught in the moment, his mind blank, working to return from his memories.

"Yes, yes," Ismael said, himself waking from a trance.

"Jared was good to have," Kadir continued.

"I meant to ask," Ismael interrupted. "Was he related to Yeshu, or did they know each other?"

"No, no. They had never met, didn't know each other. Anyway, Jared would cry and cry, then snap out of it, joke around, exercise, more jokes, then cry, and cry. He wasn't in for long. They let me and him out together that last week." Kadir stopped for a moment. "But I suppose you want to know about Yeshu. Most people want to know about Yeshu. He was different, a special person. I knew it the moment I saw him. I think they...they had him in that room alone when we left."

"Who? You mean the guards?" asked Asant.

"Well, the officers really. The guards were just there. The officers made the decisions. It was an intelligence holding."

"I see."

"You know intelligence holdings are the worst. Nobody knows where you are. You disappear until these officers decide to make you reappear on the streets, in life." Kadir pursed his lips, shook his head.

"I'm sorry!" Asant said, sensing a guarded anger and disbelief.

"There is a reason for everything, wouldn't you say?" Kadir exclaimed.

"I suppose, but that goes both ways, wouldn't you say?" Asant asked, almost stating rather than asking.

Kadir moved his head to look at Asant, then looked away towards the sea. "Of course. You are referring to Yeshu. That perhaps he was there for a reason."

"I am."

"Right." Kadir looked at Asant again. "I can estimate what you heard but have to tell you that I did not witness any of it. Yeshu was a special person, unique; but the rumors you heard about what he may have done or his role in what's happening, that was after they let me go."

"I understand," Asant looked at Kadir, and acknowledged. He needed more. "I am curious, though. You said he was special, can you tell us how, or what you mean?"

"Honestly I'm not sure he knew himself. When they first brought him, with his jacket on, loose, yellow dress shirt underneath it. You know they never leave a belt on anyone. It was as if they planned for him to be there only for a few hours." Kadir stopped for a few seconds, regarded Asant and Ismael and nodded, waiting for agreement or affirmation from them.

"Right, you said that earlier. It does make sense." Ismael said.

"That moment alone was different," Kadir continued. "The moment they brought him in. We stood up when they started to unlock the door. We always stood. It was a rule, otherwise they would yell at us. We were attentive. They opened the door, and he took two steps in. The room changed in that instant. I can't describe how, I just felt that he was too kind, too special to be in there, to be where I was.

It was like locking up light. How can you lock up light? Then again, I guess we do it all the time, we simply build walls."

"Did he know why he was there?" Asked Asant.

"I didn't, still don't. Maybe in that moment he didn't either. He looked shocked," said Kadir. "The first few days, he almost said nothing. We helped him flatten and clean a slab of sponge for sleeping on and gave him a couple of brown blankets. He used the sponge but not the blankets. He slept with his jacket on and did not take it off for days. Spoke very little, if at all, during the first few days."

"Did he use the common language when he spoke with you?" asked Ismael.

"No. He used the local language, but he had a strange accent, not foreign, but not local, almost like a child's accent."

"Did you try to talk to him?"

"Of course."

"What did you talk about?"

"Well, first I tried basic things. I explained that it was important to keep our space clean. It was important to me. I showed him how to clean with the little that we had. We talked a little about his work, my work, where he was from. He generally gave short answers. He really didn't relax until toward the end of his first week. It was as if he needed those few days to accept the fact of where he was. It was really the case for most of us."

"It was normal that he was shocked when he first walked in?" asked Asant.

"Sure. Most of us find it shocking the first time. It is shocking."

"What do you think helped him relax?"

"I think he trusted us. He trusted me," Kadir said with a softer tone.

Asant looked into Kadir's eyes, finding comfort and honesty, imagining, wondering how he and Yeshu related to each other. Strangers forced into each other's lives.

"Was anyone else in the room that week?" asked Ismael.

"Yes. There was one other person. He and I were there together from the week before, but to be honest I don't remember his name any longer. Around the end of Yeshu's first week, they came to ask Yeshu for his address. I think they were planning to release him. The poor guy blanked, could not answer." Kadir chuckled, while his eyes looked through the air, telling of a different emotion. "It was as if something blocked him. Little came to him in that moment. He mentioned a city, then changed his mind and said another." Kadir stopped, stared at the olives. "They needed an address. Papers and reports I suppose. They took him out to call a relative. Something happened while they had him with them, because the next day they took him out and we did not see him for the following two nights. When they did bring him back, he was different. In one way, he seemed violated and defeated; yet, in another way, determined and confident. It was strange."

"Did he talk more?" Asant interrupted.

"No, it wasn't that. It was more his demeanor. It seemed the officers had interacted with him, because the day after they brought him back, three guards came to the door. Before we even had a chance to react, they yelled at us to stand, and announced that the lieutenant was coming in.

They unlocked the door, and the lieutenant marched into the room, took notice of the space, then went into the bathroom. It was not much of a bathroom. There was a hole in the floor, a sink, and a shower head that trickled freezing water. He shone a light and looked around. He was inspecting the place. It was obvious. They never do that. And for sure it was not for our sake. They did not care...probably still do not care about the people they keep. It was for his sake. For Yeshu. That lieutenant needed to protect himself. He seemed worried."

"Then what, what did he do after that? Did he just leave?" asked Ismael.

"No. Not immediately anyway. He first came and walked in between us. We all were looking down, avoiding eye contact – except Yeshu. I could not see Yeshu directly, but he was standing next to me and I could tell his head was up. I even felt his defiance. The lieutenant then said that they had the power and that others could not intimidate them. Then he spoke about Yeshu without mentioning his name. He said that they were going to keep him for another week..."

"Did Yeshu say anything?" interrupted Ismael.

"No. He did not have to. It did not affect him, but it was clear to everyone there that the lieutenant intended to reach Yeshu's fears. After they all left, Yeshu paced the room for a bit, then said, it will not be good for this nation if they keep me.'"

"What? What did he mean?" Ismael asked, surprised, his voice raised.

Kadir's eyes searched Ismael's face.

"What did you think he meant?" Asant asked.

"Well, at the time I had no idea. I wasn't sure. I did not think that much of it. Still, I was perplexed, surprised, and believed him all at once. Because I didn't know enough about him, I didn't know his background or where he was from exactly. From the lieutenant's behavior, I thought perhaps someone or some group supported him, but I had no clue as to who or what group that could be."

"Umm," Asant cleared his throat and moved in his spot. Impatience was itching him. He wanted more helpful detail. "What do you think now?" he asked.

"I don't know. I don't even know if he had a clear vision of what he meant. A part of me now feels it was like a prophecy – something we don't know the meaning of until it becomes reality. Another part of me feels it was his confidence, his anger and his defiance when speaking."

"Was anyone else with you?" asked Asant.

"The day before they had put Jared with us. But he didn't think much of it either. I think he thought that Yeshu was blowing off steam. As it was, Jared was too occupied with his own troubles, alternating between crying spells and laughter and humor to cope."

"Anyone else?"

"No. That week it was just Jared, Yeshu, and me."

"If I may," Asant began, then paused. "Do you remember what happened next? Perhaps the next day?"

"They released us."

"All of you?" asked Ismael, eyebrows raised and voice higher. He was again surprised.

"Me and Jared."

Loud noise traveled through the air, through the sky, gradually overwhelming the three of them. Two fighter jets approached the sky above Lamania, then the village. Asant and Ismael turned and followed the planes with their eyes; Kadir shook his head slightly in dislike. The planes continued on along the shoreline; seconds later explosions accompanied black smoke towers in the distance.

"It is horrific. Saddening. Even though they do this a lot less often now. Only a year ago it was almost every hour," Kadir said.

"Bombings?"

Kadir nodded. Asant and Ismael watched the smoke persist and linger. Minutes passed, only giving it time to spread and move toward the village.

"It does not stop. And it's everywhere!" Ismael exclaimed while staring through the air. "But we cannot simply watch. That does not work."

"I'm not sure what works," Kadir replied.

Ismael looked back at Kadir. "It might help to return to our subject. If you would allow us, Kadir?"

Ismael cleared his throat. "What happened to Yeshu?"

Kadir drew in a breath. "I don't know exactly. It was clear that his defiance was complicating his matter. I think the lieutenant was running out of time. I heard that they kept Yeshu a couple more weeks and then transferred him to the headquarters."

"He was alone for two weeks?" Asant asked.

"No. It seemed he was alone for one week, then they put another person with him."

"Do you know who that was?"

"Fareez."

"Fareez?"

Kadir nodded gently.

"Who is he?" asked Asant.

"Another person who was struggling to survive, needing money," replied Kadir.

"I mean, do you know him?"

"I didn't know him before my incarceration, but he and I met and spoke a few times a couple of years ago after the events in the country worsened and persisted." Kadir fell quiet for a moment, was still, seemed deep in thought while gazing at the bread and the olives.

Asant moved slightly forward then remained still, again anticipating more. He waited a few seconds, then interrupted Kadir's stupor with a question.

"Can you tell us what you talked about?" He asked.

"With whom?"

"Fareez."

"About life. About our experiences."

Another quiet moment ensued. By then the black smoke was moving over the village.

Kadir finally said, "I can take you to him, and you can talk to him if that helps?"

"Yes, absolutely, that would indeed be helpful," Asant replied.

"Sure. You're welcome to sleep here tonight. I will send a message to him and we will plan on heading to the city tomorrow afternoon."

They ventured out late next morning.

"Where in the city does he live?" asked Asant as they walked to a bus station.

"In the old city. It won't be much longer from here."

"*In the old city,*" thought Asant. "*Maybe even a place we passed.*"

Some minutes later they sat in an otherwise empty minivan. It jolted and maneuvered around massive potholes in the road, at one point passing a burned tank with half its front teetering over a crater's edge. Asant looked through the window to his left, mouth agape, while the driver worked the scenery as if it was normal.

The van stopped every few miles, allowing new passengers to enter. It wasn't long after that the three of them had to cram into the same row. The driver put out his arm and hand toward the row behind him, requesting payment, as his other hand moved the steering wheel half circles.

Kadir dropped a few coins in the driver's hand. "This is for the three of us," he said. "To Hezb please."

"Hezb neighborhood?" asked Ismael. "Fareez is in the Hezb neighborhood?"

"Yes. Are you familiar with it?" Kadir asked in return.

"Not really. It's just that someone sent us there when we were looking for you," Ismael replied.

"Ah, yes. I used to live there, before I was taken in," Kadir said. "It is funny, curious."

"Why is that?" asked Asant.

"Most of us know each other in these neighborhoods; yet, I never actually met Fareez until all this happened."

Kadir did not say anything for the remainder of their ride. Fifteen minutes later, he put his hand on the driver's shoulder. The van came to a halt and the three made their way out onto the curb.

They traversed what may have once been a sidewalk, passing charred exteriors of shops. A few yards in front of them, a child – a barefoot girl – was sitting cross-legged on rubble. Her back was leaning on one of those walls and her head was down. As they drew closer, they saw her feet and hands dark with mud. Her clothes were torn in several spots. Kadir stopped, leaned down, patted the girl on the shoulder and held her hand.

"What is your name?" he asked in the local language.

"Sonja," she whispered. Her head was still down and she was almost inaudible.

"Sonja." Kadir waited a second for a sign. "Hello Sonja! I would say you're about nine years old," he smiled. "Am I right?"

"Eight."

"I was close," he said, smiling. "You know, I am going to my friend's home. He and his wife might be able to help you with a bath. What do you think?"

The four approached a building's entrance about ten minutes later with Kadir leading and Sonja's right hand in his left. Kadir led the others up a narrow and dark staircase to the second level. Some remains of light bulbs protruded from electrical sockets. At the top of the stairs, Kadir turned and faced a thick-looking wooden door. He stood still in front of it but did not move to knock or ring the bell.

"Is this the place?" asked Asant.

Kadir remained still, did not respond, his grip tightened a bit around Sonja's hand.

"Kadir, are you okay?" asked Ismael.

"Yes. Yes, I am. I need a moment, though. It is not easy bringing back those experiences."

"I can imagine, Kadir. I am sorry that we are... that I am doing this to you," Asant said.

"You have good reasons, and we in this country need help these days." He looked at Sonja, now smiling. He hovered his hand over the bell to the right of the door, breathed in, then pushed the button.

The bell did not make a sound. The three men watched one another as if to ask what they should do. Sonja, her hand still in Kadir's, looked up at him and smiled.

Kadir repositioned himself, moved closer to the door, and knocked on its dark-stained wood. The four of them stood looking at it. After a few minutes they heard faint footsteps approaching. The door knob creaked as the door swung open.

They were greeted by a plump man shorter than the other three he faced. He had disheveled white hair on his face and head. He stood facing them, holding the door with his right hand.

"Kadir. How are you?" he said.

"Fareez, my dear."

"It's good to see you, my friend."

"It's good to see you too. It has been a while though," replied Kadir. "I trust you received my message. This is Asant and Ismael. And Sonja!"

"Yes, I did," Fareez replied, smiling. "Welcome! Please come in," he turned to make way for them and motioned with his right arm. "Hello Sonja."

"Fareez, she was outside. Do you think you or your wife can help her with a bath?"

"Of course. Of course." He looked down to Sonja. "My child, you know you are a gift to us, to all of us. Come, let me show you where you can clean up. My wife is going to be very happy to see you."

Fareez returned, then showed them into his home. It apparently was typical of houses in the area. Glossy white paint covered the walls, albeit brushed with dark dust in some spots. Floors were tiled with white marble, rugs covering parts of it. The furniture was ornate with carvings on the wood and intricate designs on the upholstery.

"Please make yourselves comfortable. I was preparing coffee. It should be ready shortly. Please be comfortable. Please!" Fareez walked away. A few minutes later, he came back with a large tray filled with cups of coffee and a bowl of nuts and some sweets.

"I went out and bought water this morning. Luckily it should be enough for Sonja too. Half the neighborhood doesn't have water." Fareez put the tray on a table in the center of the room. "How have you been, Kadir?"

"Not bad. Thanks to the One. I've been good. It is good to see you, Fareez," Kadir replied while Asant and Ismael sat quietly, unsure of whether they should say anything.

"Where have you been? Still in your home village?" Fareez asked.

"Yes. Just as we last spoke," Kadir said in a soft tone. "It is the right place for me."

"I understand my friend. I understand."

"How about you? What are you doing these days?" asked Kadir.

"I am trying to make a living, and as always, I'm looking for ways. You can imagine it's not simple in the cities." Fareez said. His mouth shaped into a smile that did not last. "Truly, years ago, it never occurred to me it could be more difficult to make a living than at that time," he added, then paused. "Back then, I found it difficult; now I know the value, and precariousness of peace. Nonetheless, I have been honest, in spite of how difficult it has become."

"I know. I understand," Kadir said, nodding a few times, and then sipping from his coffee cup." Fareez, our friends here, Asant and Ismael, have come a long way from another land," he paused while looking at Fareez, then rested the coffee cup on a table by his side. "They have come in good faith to learn about Yeshu," he stopped again, took another sip of his coffee and let a moment pass to allow Fareez a moment for his thoughts. "I can imagine you are likely bombarded with questions about Yeshu, from the friendly and from the not so friendly."

Fareez took a long breath. "Yes, but no matter. You are different. You, of all people, Kadir, are entitled to this time. I trust you."

Kadir felt some discomfort. His humbleness prevented him from more of a response, but he managed a gentle nod. He cleared his throat again. "I spoke with them about my encounter, as much as I remember. I think it's a lot of information. It is hard to forget such things."

"True, true. I have to say; you and I have recounted these memories time after time. Perhaps for the same reason."

"Perhaps," responded Kadir.

Asant and Ismael looked from one man to the other, each curious about the subtexts of the exchange, but chose to remain silent. Asant sought a brief distraction as he took his cup of coffee, noticed its aroma and felt it work its magic. It was sweet in comparison to the cup he had with Yusef in Kamur. He took a sip, looked up at Fareez then Kadir and waited, deciding it would be best for Kadir to choose the direction of the conversation.

"Fareez, do you recall the time when they first put you into that space?" asked Kadir.

"I do. A person cannot forget such a moment. I'm afraid, however, what I remember from that first day is all about me. My fears for myself and for my family. Having Yeshu there from the beginning was more helpful than I could have asked for."

"What do you mean?" asked Kadir.

"From my first day in the cell, he was calm and confident. Maybe even happy to see me. For the rest of the week I was there, I appreciated him and his presence. I shared everything with him. My experiences, my life, and whatever reached me from my family. Some food, clean clothes, a towel." Fareez stopped and breathed a long breath. He appeared to revisit a memory in his mind and smiled. "You know, he was even helpful when I cried, when I was in despair. He helped me occupy my mind with the simplest of games with olive seeds. Never complained about my snoring." Fareez chuckled. "Also, I didn't recognize the significance then, but they asked time after time why he would stay awake at night. I told them it was probably my snoring. I think they allowed me to have the food and clothes my family sent because they wanted me to get information from him."

"Fareez, can you tell us what you talked about?" asked Kadir.

"Well, many things. We talked about religion, about The One and Only, how He loves everyone and all that has been created without differentiation. About our families. He told me to pray for them. For all of them. He prayed too. I think he prayed while walking. Kadir, you used to walk in that small space too, no doubt, for exercise. We did the same. I would say you taught him well." Fareez paused, managed a faint smile and drew in a breath. "Haa," he said while shaking his head sideways. "He prayed while walking, usually silently, but when I heard him, it was in a different language. I asked him about it once. He told me he was praying for his family, and then for everyone he knew."

"Yes. We walked plenty. Exercising. Thinking." Kadir looked toward Asant and Ismael and motioned in their direction. "Fareez, if you would allow me, Asant and Ismael here wanted to know about him as a person, and also about what he thought of our country."

"This country I can tell you he loved," Fareez said to Asant and Ismael. "I think by the time I met him he had become resigned to being there, inside, but it did not change what he felt for the country, for its people. It did change, however, what he wanted for it."

Asant moved in his chair. "If I may, Mr. Fareez, can you elaborate? What do you mean from that?"

Fareez turned his attention to Asant. "I cannot say what was happening in his mind. He never told me. I can only say what I thought based on other things we talked about and what I saw in his face. For example, he talked about how precious everything and everyone is—rocks, flowers, butterflies, all humans. But he avoided any talk about the guards or why he was there. When they took him for questioning, he came back with more determination on his face and still would not say anything about why he was there." Fareez leaned forward, "You know what else, Ismael, Asant?" He asked while looking at them, "I felt they were scared of him and that he knew it. He cared about the country but did not like those with authority. Perhaps it was about being controlled by others."

"Do you think he worried them, or was it, as you said, scared them?" asked Asant.

"Both. Yes. They were both worried and scared. I could tell when they asked me about him being awake at night. Sometimes they brought me out only to ask me about him. They treated me well so that I would tell them everything I learned about him."

"What do you think worried them?" asked Asant.

"I don't know. One might think it was pressure from superiors," Fareez stopped, then shook his head. "No. It wasn't the pressure. There was pressure, I'm sure. But what worried them was his confidence. He did not care what they did. He exuded an attitude that they could not hurt him. His confidence made it only worse."

"Made what worse?" asked Asant.

"The tension between these two sides, between him and the lieutenant, the lieutenant of the branch," answered Fareez.

"What about being awake at night, did you ever see him? Would he walk and pace?" asked Asant.

"I saw him only one time. I woke up briefly. He was sitting with his eyes closed."

"Was he saying anything?"

"No. Nothing."

"Do you think he was awake? Or was he resting or sleeping somehow?"

"His back was upright and straight up against the wall, and his legs were crossed. This posture informed me he was aware – awake for sure."

"I know this may be strange to ask, or maybe not, considering you know how far Ismael and I have come. We would like to meet him. Do you think that's possible? Do you know whether he is in the country?" asked Asant with his lips pursed, reminding himself and the others of his purpose. He turned his head to look at both Fareez and Kadir.

"I don't think it's strange," Fareez said while shaking his head. "What do you think, Kadir?"

"Of course, it's understandable. But it's more whether he wants to be found," said Kadir.

"Have either of you seen him since?" asked Asant.

"I have not," said Fareez.

"I have not either," said Kadir. "I expect that would be part of the issue, that he would know how not to be found if that was what he wanted."

"If I may, have you looked for him since you left?" Ismael chimed.

"I must admit, I have not," replied Kadir.

"I have," said Fareez. "They let me out a few days after they took him away. I learned as much, but didn't know whether they set him free or took him to another location. Nobody ever knows their fate or the fate of other inmates. After a few days of being out, and being with my wife and family, I decided I wanted to see him. I asked about him. Eventually I found out from an officer friend inside that he was transferred, but I could not find out to where. I think he was freed long after, after the upheaval began, but I would arrive at dead ends whenever I tried to find him. After a while I decided I would see him if he wanted that, or if it was meant."

"Can you tell us where we can start looking based on your initial attempts?" asked Asant.

"I remember him telling the guards one time that he has family in a town thirty minutes from here," said Kadir. "This could be helpful – reaching out to his relatives. But I don't know his last name. A possibility would be to find one of the guards and ask for the last name."

"Are you sure talking to one of the guards is a good idea?" Ismael interjected.

"The guard I'm thinking of is a good man. He saw something in Yeshu," Kadir replied.

"What do you mean?" asked Asant.

"All of the guards treated him differently from how they treated others. They were kind in general, it seemed they were acknowledging among themselves that he had some power or influence. Maybe it was the people who were attempting to find him and attempting to contact authorities in the country," Kadir said. "Still, though, this one guard seemed to respect him even more, in subtle ways. I think he saw in him what I saw."

"Forgive me Kadir, we haven't talked about that. Can you tell us, can you describe what you saw?" asked Asant emphasizing the latter part of the question.

"I probably alluded to it before," started Kadir. "He had an aura about him. Maybe similar to what Fareez was describing. It was what gave him the confidence, something like knowledge the rest of us generally do not have. Perhaps faith. I'm not exactly sure, it's just hard to describe with words."

"Understood," exclaimed Asant.

"I will send word. Perhaps we can make arrangements for some time in the next day or two, if we manage to reach that guard."

"That is as good a plan as any," Fareez said.

Kadir looked at him, smiled. "Thank you Fareez. Will Sonja be alright?"

"Yes. Do not worry."

Kadir pointed with his head and chin to a tall person walking with slow and short steps. The man was inside a park. He seemed to be on a stroll. His head was down, and he seemed nonchalant and unconcerned with his surroundings. Short shrubs and sparse narrow trees populated the park and the surrounding area; a couple of the trees were burned and charred, their lives cut short. Fareez did not accompany them to avoid more suspicion than necessary. The three continued in the direction of the tall man, entered the park, strolled passed him soon thereafter.

"Let's walk toward the two benches up ahead," announced Kadir in a quiet tone. "I want you, Asant, to depart from us and sit on one of these two benches. Ismael and I will continue walking. This man will come and sit across from you on the other bench soon thereafter, but don't look directly at him at any time. Not while he's walking and certainly not while he is sitting. Ismael and I will just continue walking on this path."

"Will you stay in the park?" asked Asant.

"No. We will walk for a bit more then leave about ten minutes later. You can meet us on the street two blocks east of the park entrance. The one we came through fifteen minutes ago."

The tall man – the guard – continued on with a brisk walk. He made a gentle turn toward one of the benches and then sat across from Asant, as Kadir had said. Neither said anything for a few minutes. Asant was unsure of whether he should begin with a question. The guard looked into the distance through the air at nothing in particular. He still seemed unconcerned and his face expressed little. His eyes, forehead, mouth, were all neutral, revealing no emotion as he remained consistent with aloofness and indifference even while sitting.

"He was different. He is different, I suppose. A special person," began the guard, his face now focused on a tree in his line of sight near the park's entrance. "You see, I meditate. It helps me maintain my intuition, the gift. Perhaps everyone has this as a gift but most don't know of it. For me, I saw that he was different from the beginning, but I could not help him aside from trying to make him comfortable and spreading the truth that he was not a threat."

The man moved his head to look at another tree, accentuating his indifference toward Asant. He allowed some seconds to pass, then continued. "He was royalty to me. He demanded respect without asking or fighting for it. When that happens, those who are stubborn become angry and attempt to be abusive, while others become kind and helpful." The guard stopped, stretched and rested his right arm on the back of the bench; then turned his head away from the tree to another angle in the park, his eyes hazy and occupied with thought, again focusing on nothing in particular.

He breathed a slow breath, then started again. "I even wore a purple shirt every day I was there, hoping to let him know that I respected him. I say this because I regret I did not do more to help him. I knew he had a mission. Those who do not help one of his kind – one with such a mission – will suffer, in a way similar to how many of us are suffering today, trapped in a war that did not have to be," the guard paused again and pulled in a deep breath. "After they noticed the green ring he wore, as innocuous as it looked, they became too suspicious. By then, I was no longer able to help, and managed nothing for him." He stopped again and sighed. For the first time, he closed his eyes and struggled to maintain a neutral and expressionless face. "No matter. Perhaps it is your turn, so I will attempt to help through you. The uncle's full name is Blessed Wolf. Strange but fitting really. You might find him in Tannis. He's lived there for at least forty years, I can't imagine he would leave now, even with the incidents and the fighting. It's the town south of here. A small town, everyone knows one another, so you should have no trouble finding him. I think the uncle will let you know where to find him, if it is a possibility."

"He said to find the uncle," exclaimed Asant some fifteen minutes later.

"Whose uncle?" asked Ismael.

"Yeshu's," replied Asant. "He gave me the name, the likely town, then he stood and walked away leisurely," Asant paused, "as if his work was done, or maybe he was done with me."

"It's his way, Asant. I think you will be able to find him if you need him."

"He said some strange things, Kadir."

"Like what?" Asked Kadir.

"Well, like wearing purple around Yeshu. But not just wearing purple as in clothes or favoring a color; rather, wearing purple to send a message, a comforting message, essentially to communicate. And he said the uncle's name is Blessed Wolf. I mean even I know that is not a name for any person from this area."

"Yes. Yes. It is a code name, so you would have to be careful whom to ask. I will of course help – if you want my help that is. As to the color, well, it is not so far-fetched. People have abilities, traditions, practices. Sometimes, in a country such as this, it is better to be careful and not talk about your ways, about your beliefs and practices. In turn, traditions and possible abilities easily and quickly become less known, and people resort to uncommon methods and to speaking in vague terms."

"I know. I should know. I suppose not being able to talk to him, not looking at him, likely threw me off, along with his physical size. Maybe there was too much that intimidated me and did not allow me to understand."

"It's plausible enough...nevertheless, we, certainly you, should focus. Aim for objectivity and focus on your goal. Did he tell you where you could find the uncle?"

"He mentioned a town south of here."

"Tannis?"

"That sounds it, yes."

"Good. We will talk more tonight at my place, over a meal. I'll send word among friends that we would like to visit him, and we'll plan a trip to poke around tomorrow. Tannis is not far from where I am. In fact, my place is about halfway between here and Tannis."

Tannis' town center had two main roads, almost parallel, each sandwiched by a long line of two-story buildings with shops. The two roads ran for about a mile, then converged, became one, and continued on raised land by the shore's edge. Traveling in the customary mini-van taxi, Asant, Ismael, Kadir, and Fareez first passed some of those shops on their left and their right, then found themselves looking at an expansive view of the sea. Unknowable, precarious, and mysterious, it reflected Asant's feelings – being in a foreign country, where anything could happen, and all while continuing to have no indication of the next personality he was to meet.

The van stopped at a checkpoint. A soldier, in heavy olive-green gear and a bullet-proof vest, knocked on the driver's window with a semi-automatic. The two spoke for a moment. The soldier looked into the van, at the three in the back. Another soldier looked in from the opposite side. Asant labored to pace his breathing as he regarded the soldier nearest to him. His eyes rested on the machine gun as the soldier held it above his waist, in front of numerous pockets full of the unimaginable. Kadir and Fareez both nodded at the soldiers as a common greeting. Then both stepped back, and motioned for the driver to move on.

Fareez stopped the taxi after another half mile. As they left their ride behind, they turned their backs to the water and walked into the residential area of Tannis.

They walked up a paved hill on a sidewalk for another twenty minutes. The same monotonous two-story buildings stood on both sides of the road. They all had the same architecture as those housing the shops. The one difference was these stood behind fenced and painted metal doors, revealing that they were family homes. Some fences were dented, others broken. Asant looked at each building they passed, most were gray unpainted concrete. A couple had clothes hanging out some windows, likely to dry; some windows had potted plants on the edges. One building was naked concrete all together, unfinished, bullet holes lining its walls. In clear contrast, its neighbor appeared as if it had been painted days before, showing life, with evergreens by its side and separating it from the next building.

They continued walking up the same road until they reached a break from the fences and found an open shop.

"Let me go in alone and see if I can learn something helpful," Fareez said as Kadir nodded in agreement.

Fareez came back a few minutes later. He pointed to his left, in the direction of the hill. "I think he lives nearby; I mean the uncle," he said to the others. "A couple of turns from here. It's a small single-story home, with an orange tree and a pear tree next to each other, by a green gate."

They resumed to walk for a half mile or so; turned right, then a slight left to merge onto a curved road. The styles of the buildings change a bit. Now a few single-family homes faced them as the road curved only to surround a larger apartment building to the right of the sidewalk.

"From the shopkeeper's description, I would say it's in the middle of this road, by the first intersection," Fareez pointed again.

Anticipation grew in each of them, albeit for different reasons. Asant felt optimistic that this could be a step forward; while Kadir imagined hearing news of Yeshu.

It was a lone green-colored gate between two concrete walls rising to about their shoulders. It was the only gate of its kind on the block, unique in that it was adorned in the middle by two peacocks that faced each other with expanded metal tail feathers. The rest of the gate had a few horizontal bars with the space of about an inch separating each.

Fareez found a bell. It was hidden and halfway behind a few ivy leaves. A few bullets seemed to have missed it, leaving holes next to it.

After a couple of minutes, a woman walked out of the home's doors and down the steps toward the green metal gate and toward them. She was a stout woman with short but full salt and pepper hair, possibly in her sixties.

"Yes?"

"Hello ma'am. I'm Kadir Easty, from Lamania. I imagine we have surprised you. We are here to visit your husband, he likely is expecting us. Is he home?"

"My husband? And who are you?" the woman asked with quick words and a high tone, exasperation and impatience in her voice. She looked from one man to the other.

"Yes, of course. I am Kadir Easty," Kadir said again in attempt to avoid a negative encounter. "This is Fareez Shamus from Hezb, and our friends Asant and Ismael. Suffice it to say they are good people and have come from afar and traveled long to meet your husband, and nephew."

"I see." The woman's eyebrows squeezed toward each other, her forehead lines became accentuated. She seemed to absorb the subtlety and implication behind Kadir's response.

Kadir was unable to discern her thoughts, and whether she was now determined to avoid the encounter. "We have sent word, but we can certainly return another time if now is not convenient for either yourself or your husband."

"Stay here please," she said, her voice plain and linear. Before she turned back to the house's doors, she looked at the lock on her side of the green gate – partly visible but inaccessible through the horizontal bars from the other side.

The house was surrounded with metal fencing and some concrete columns. Plants rose above the fence; orange and pear trees leaned on and spread over the concrete columns. The four men waited at the green gate for what may have been ten to fifteen minutes. They said little as they stood on the sidewalk, each looking at a different branch that hung over.

A middle-aged man who looked much like the older woman – with almost the same short hair and rounded face, eventually came to greet them at the gate. The older woman behind him holding a couple of folding chairs.

"Forgive us for making you wait," the man announced while unlocking the gate. "My father is on his way."

He shook hands with Kadir, then Fareez.

"You must be Sam." Fareez stated.

"Yes. We must have met some time ago. Your face is familiar."

"Yes. Thank you. Thank you for welcoming us."

Sam closed the green gate behind them and led them to the porch near the house's wooden doors. "Please be comfortable," he said as he turned and entered the house. He returned with more chairs and a table.

"It is nice to have you."

"Thank you, Sam. Forgive me. This is my dear friend Kadir Easty from Lamania. Asant and Ismael are visitors from another land." This time it was Fareez doing the introductions.

"It is a great opportunity to meet you," the man said, nodding to each of the three. "Can we get you coffee or tea?"

The four visitors looked at one another. "For this hour, tea would be great, if it is not an intrusion." Fareez responded.

Sam left them, and shortly thereafter returned with two trays of pastries - each pastry cut in half. After another trip, he came with several small and curved clear and intricately designed glasses and a large pot.

The older woman reappeared in the doors' frame. Her right arm was holding on to a man almost hidden in the house's shade behind her. The two crossed the frame's platform. The woman led the way, while the man, who was at least in his eighties, kept his free hand on the wall to his right, a rosary hanging from his wrist. He advanced with one slow step after another, head down all the while. The woman guided him with her arm and words to a chair.

The visitors looked on, smiled in politeness, without saying anything. They watched the man search for and find some comfort in the chair.

"Diabetes. It has reached my eyes and feet," he said, after minutes of silence. He bent towards the table and found a pastry. "But I can still find good things. Please help yourselves," he said with a smile as he brought the pastry to his mouth.

Sam rejoined them. Another moment of silence passed. Fareez reached to the table for a glass. The other three followed one by one.

"It is nice to have visitors," said the man. "These days it is mostly my sons and their children. It is a blessing. They are a blessing."

"Of course. It is a pleasure meeting your wife and seeing your son Sam," Fareez said.

"Thank you. Thank you," the man said, maintaining the same smile. "Fareez, is it?"

"Yes. Yes sir. Fareez Shamus from Lamania."

"Of course. From the Hezb neighborhood. It has been a while, but I spent enough time there. I have many friends. Many friends in Lamania." The man turned his head just a little, away from Fareez, changing his focus and looked in the direction of the trees in the yard, perhaps to recall a memory, or to reminisce. He then turned back. "Shamus, you said? Your parents and grandfather are from Lamania. If my memory serves me, your great grandfather moved to the area from a village next to Arapali, some two hundred miles south."

Fareez laughed. "Your reputation does not do you justice, sir. You know more about my heritage than I do. I do not recall my father mentioning this, and it has been years since I visited that area, certainly not in the past year considering the current situation in our country. But, come to think of it, it fits. My grandfather spoke once or twice of a village that far south, where Arapali stands today."

"Today Siljap and Vant are separate countries, but they were one back then, and it was much easier for people to move between cities and villages." The man turned his chin down and smiled, continuing to move the beads of the rosary.

"May I ask you sir about how you acquired your nickname?" asked Fareez.

The man's smile widened. "To be honest, you may well know more about that than I, and it might be your turn to tell me something I don't know," he replied.

"I doubt that. We only heard of the name, and even then, it was only in these past couple of days."

"I see." The man fixed his eyes on the rosary, for a few seconds appeared to think through it. "I am not sure it is deserved," he said. "Years ago, for a short while mind you, I was a rebel. I was against torturing people for information. As a result, one person happened to benefit, completely by chance. I had asked the authorities at the time about him, and I requested that he not be hurt in any way. I explained that he was a kind individual, not involved in anything but his farming and music, and that even if he knew of any useful information he would relinquish it simply by being asked for it. I am guessing, and it is only a guess, this man, this old friend, bless his soul, used that name to describe me while among a circle of friends, perhaps in song. He was talented, sang well." The man smiled again and refocused on the rosary.

The four guests listened intently, and admired the old man. Asant observed the connection the man seemed to have with the rosary. The others sipped more of the tea. Silence ensued.

Then, Fareez cleared his throat. "Sir, if I may discuss the reason why our visitors and I sought you out...you see, they came asking about your nephew."

"I see. What about him?"

"Perhaps, if it pleases you, I will leave it to Asant to explain. In short, I would like to send your nephew my regards and appreciation. But truly it is more Asant that has come a long way to speak with him."

"He may well be outside the country. You must know that I am not privy to his whereabouts."

"I understand, of course. I am not aware of the extent of your contact with him, if any. In fact, I know little. Nonetheless, if you allow me to ask, are you able to pass to him a message?"

"I suppose I can try. In all honesty, we speak only when he calls, and he calls once a year or so, but I can try." The man repositioned himself, coughed twice then cleared his throat. "What word would you like to send him?"

"It is not me, sir. As much as I would like to speak with him – and I have no doubt Kadir feels the same – we must give Asant priority, in the interest of brevity," Fareez said, opening his palm in the direction where Asant was sitting.

Everyone sitting on the porch, turned to Asant, and waited. Asant looked from one staring face to another. He was caught off guard and did not have any words ready. He cleared his throat. "Thank you, sir. It is kind of you and your family to welcome us. It is simply that I would like to speak with your nephew."

All present remained focused on Asant, expecting more. They waited for more, for him to explain the substance of his purpose and intent.

Fareez decided that Asant's reply was insufficient. He turned his attention to the old man. "What Asant means, I think, is that he came a long way, heard about your nephew from afar. Asant of course can explain his intention better than I can, but I believe Asant is looking to hear his story, your nephew's story."

"What story is that?" Sam interjected.

Fareez noted Sam's sudden tone. He extended both arms toward Sam and held his palms open and facing up, wanting to show agreement and understanding. "Yes, of course, it is a sensitive subject."

Kadir also sensed the need to acknowledge the subject's sensitivity. "I agree," he offered in a low and soft tone. "It is a delicate subject, in particular considering that our country is in such a violent and fragile state. But please know, sir, no one here wishes your nephew, or anyone in your family, any harm." Kadir wished to avoid the tension that was attempting to enter. "If I may, you know us and our families. You must know of our peaceful nature, mine and Fareez's. We certainly would not support anything but peaceful conversation. Asant, it is true I met him only recently, and he is from another land, but I assure you, he is not a person of ill will. The same with his friend Ismael. I have already spent several nights with them. They have been my guests in my home as well as in Fareez's."

"I am aware of your work Kadir, and I know of your family; and yours Fareez. Your guests are welcome any time. We do not suggest any feelings of ill will from our visitors; however, if there is to be some message, then there must be a message, something with an indication of...substance."

One by one, four pairs of eyes again turned their focus to Asant's. Ismael fought to hold back his doubts. He consciously desired to maintain his commitment to Asant's cause. He moved his body ever so, feeling a bit anxious, wanting to support his companion in some way but unsure how.

"Sir, thank you again for welcoming us and for your kindness," Asant began. He cleared his throat again. "Sir. It is now well known throughout the world the troubles this nation has come to see over the past few years. I cannot imagine what any family in this country, including yours, has endured. To that effect, my teacher sent me – no, forgive me – my teacher showed me that I must help bring peace back to your nation." He stopped, looked away, found a tree to help him regain his focus. "I imagine it likely sounds strange. Nevertheless, I have taken it upon myself. As for your nephew, my teacher indicated that I am to work with him to effect peace."

"What? You know you sound crazy, right?" Sam stated. "Not for anything but my cousin is not involved in this whole conflict whatsoever. He has not even lived here, it has been years. And, he does not live here now. Nothing you say makes sense."

"Sam. Son. Please."

"Sir, Sam, I know, it does sound crazy," Asant said. "But please know, I trust my teacher with my life. He has been my teacher for many years. He has helped me see the truth many many times, and I have learned not to doubt his wisdom, certainly not his intentions. Over the years, I have learned that he sees what most of us do not. I must go through with this. With this task."

"No."

"Sam. Stop." The old man reached over and touched Sam's arm.

"Sam, I understand," Asant said, looking at Sam. "I reacted just about the same way the morning when my teacher told me all this." He stopped and looked away. "But, please...think about it, and the fact that I have come a long way. I carried nothing with me and have come with only one companion. Think about it. What harm could I do? What harm would speaking with your cousin do? If there is a chance of doing good, we must at a minimum try."

"There is in fact a chance of doing harm. To my cousin. To my family. To my father. You don't understand. The city was under siege barely two months ago. I am sure they are still watching and surveying. We cannot risk asking strange questions." Sam turned to his father. "Father, we cannot take part. Even now, we may have done harm to ourselves simply from sitting here. Father, please."

Asant's thoughts carried him into his past. He recalled the fears he felt when faced with possible imprisonment and violence, and he understood Sam's resistance and misgivings. In the same instant, an image of his teacher came to him, reminding Asant of the task he had chosen, helping him refocus, perhaps even gifting him with a bit of courage and the right words to speak.

"Sam," Asant began a second attempt, turned to the old man, "Sir, I believe in doing good, I believe in making an effort. There is a chance that we will do good here; and even though, I admit, I do not know the intricacies of this war, this conflict, and I do not even understand the history of this land and its people – I only wish to do good. I do not wish harm to anyone. Kadir and Fareez, your countrymen, can attest to that."

Sam leaned forward, then sat back in his chair. "Harm may come regardless of your intentions, regardless of your motives. Even if it simply raises a flag in some official's mind. It is not in your hands...there are too many variables – too many unknowns."

"That may be. I do not dispute the need to be cautious; however, it is our responsibility to act when given the vision. We must act on the idea, else we permit chaos to prolong its stay. I have no doubt that everyone here is aware of our responsibility, of how we can change our world for the better. I would be doing the work, and I am only asking that you allow me to."

"Father!" Sam exclaimed.

The old man looked at the rosary between his hands. "I will think about it and will send word to Lamania of my decision and of any action on my part." The man looked at Asant and smiled. "Now, let us talk about your land and what you've seen along your journey."

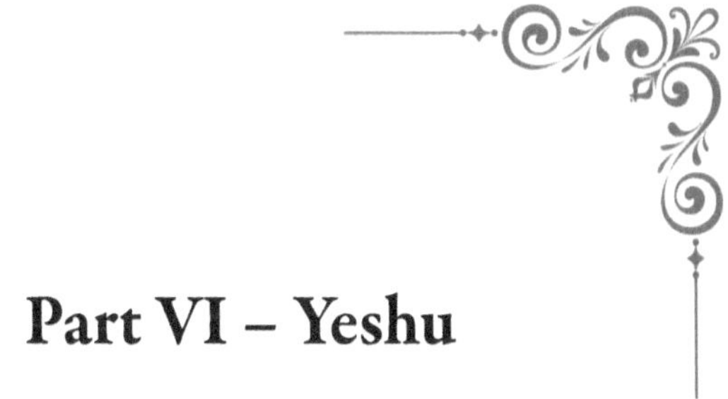

Part VI – Yeshu

A WEEK PASSED BEFORE there was any word from the man, the uncle. Asant and Ismael first stayed with Fareez, then with Kadir. All three visited Fareez just about every other day.

A young man came to Fareez late that week and stated simply that he needed food, that he had not eaten in days. After receiving bread and cooked beans, he added, "He will be at a seafood restaurant situated directly on the water, about twenty miles south of Arapali around eleven on Thursday, a week from now." Unexpected and conspicuous. It was the message.

The following day, during their stop to see Fareez, Kadir discerned that look on Fareez' face – unattentive to the usual greeting, eyes eager, ready to say something. Fareez, for his part, held back and waited a few minutes before speaking of the arrangement.

"Asant, Ismael," Fareez said after conveying the message, "I can go as far as Tannis. I imagine it's a similar situation for Kadir. But I will arrange a ride – a taxi – all the way to Arapali. I would like to do that for you. The driver will help you navigate the border, its security, its mess, and probably, hopefully, a ride from the border to the restaurant. Please allow me this deed."

Fareez did not understate the conditions at the border. It was yet another stark difference from the experience Asant and Ismael had along the route with the caravan on the opposite side of the country. With the caravan, and Zeke, it was a path through a desert largely devoid of humans, devoid of any paved roads or man-made markings. The road leading to Arapali, on the other hand, passed between demolished buildings, burned and abandoned military equipment, broken road instructions, charred trees, and frequent breaks in the pavement.

They drove from Lamania, through Tannis, then south towards the border. Asant, sitting in the backseat, looked through the side window and watched the opposite side of the road to their left. They passed a lone tank. Odd enough, it did not look broken down. Then there was another. And another. It was a line of tanks, one in front of the other, taking over what remained of that highway. Asant thought it was a few too many. The line did not stop. There must have been tens of them, perhaps more than a hundred. Their presence imprinted an image of despair in his mind.

"These are probably from the siege on Tannis. I suppose they're off to their next spot."

"Can we stop?" Asant asked, overwhelmed and feeling lightheaded. He brought his head to his knees, covered his face. "I think I need some air."

"No. They will shoot us. We will be destroyed in seconds. Here." The driver rummaged in the center compartment and handed a plastic bag to Asant.

They passed several military checkpoints before arriving at the border. The soldiers focused more of their attention on the other side of the road, the opposite direction. One group of men dressed in jeans, sweatshirts, ordinary jackets could have passed for a group of civilians were it not for the machine guns and strings of bullets hanging off their belts around their shoulders and waists.

"Before it all started," the driver said after the fourth and last checkpoint, "weapons, guns, bombs, were getting smuggled into the country from everywhere. Border soldiers caught some of it; and, even though they caught only a small portion, it was still noticeably more than usual.

It led the intelligence forces to realize something was going on so now they check and record everything. Names, records, cars, boxes, you know – just like before – except now it's multiple times, from all kinds of government offices, ministries, police, military, intelligence. Every kind of government office you can imagine is now involved."

"Then, as the conflict began, all kinds of people were crossing through our border, from all kinds of countries. It's a strange world."

They passed the first sign pointing to the border. "We will miss you!" one sign proclaimed, hanging loosely off a bent pole. "Return safely!" another pleaded. "Arapali – 35 miles."

There was a change in the road ahead. It looked blocked, destroyed, with an abrupt ending to the pavement visible from where their vehicle was in that instant. Rubble and remains of a few buildings stood to the right, contrasting peaceful-appearing mountains to their left, covered in green, giving the appearance of unwavering trees.

The driver downshifted. The car reduced its speed, turned away from the paved road, onto dirt, and gradually came to a halt behind a line of other cars, near enough to another sign. "Border Security Checkpoint – 1 mile," and in smaller print, "Have your passports or identification documents ready. Buses, commercial vehicles to the left. All others, cars, to the right."

"Which direction will we go?" asked Ismael.

"Left. They consider me, us, commercial. We are registered. Our cars have to be stripped, as you can see, so they can be easily inspected and searched."

"Will they give us hard time?" Ismael asked.

"I don't know. Maybe yes maybe no. You are from another country, but really, as far as I know, no foreigners from your country have been caught here, so it's not so suspicious." The driver drew a long breath, tilted his head to the left and leaned on his left arm. "Then again, nowadays they think everything is suspicious," he added as he gazed through the vehicle's glass. His free hand shifted the gear to inch forward, then downshifted again. "I don't know my friend. I really don't know."

"You. Get out. Now." They heard a soldier on the other side of the road yell through a van's open window, machine gun pointed. A row of soldiers lined up on each side. "Where are you going?" the same soldier yelled. The man from the car was now standing next to him, looking at the pavement.

"Don't look," the driver told Asant and Ismael as he shifted again and moved the car as much as the space allowed.

Twenty minutes of standstill passed in what was now a one lane road. There were some cars ahead, in their direction and before the fork, along with two groups of soldiers questioning occupants from different vehicles. Three German Shepherds on leashes spread out and circled the vehicles. Farther yet, on the left side of the fork, passengers exited a bus, one by one, through soldiers on each side of the bus' door. The driver was the last to exit. Two more soldiers and another canine stepped up and into the bus.

"What are they afraid of?" asked Ismael.

"Bombs," the driver said. "Smugglers want free access to this road even in its current condition, so they would want to clear it. It's a major entry point."

"Have they done that before?"

"Oh yes. Several times around the beginning. The rebels had control of it for a while. It's war, my friend. This is what the fringes of war look like. Indications, signs, intelligence, then lockdowns; everyone becomes a suspect. This is not where the war is now, but it is part of it still." The driver looked on; then, without turning to look at his two passengers, continued. "By the way, you're simply visitors, visiting the region, the two of you are friends visiting the region. You don't know anyone here; you're not looking for anyone."

Asant looked ahead at the next group of soldiers and as if woken by the driver's comments, asked, "How did it start? Did the violence start suddenly or has there always been conflict?"

"Tough question. Really, this country was, for a long time, stable, with little conflict, compared to many other countries around the world. There was a price for that though."

"What price was that?" Ismael asked.

"For that stability and security...I'd say it was the lack of freedom. The stability was ensured by a massive intelligence force, probably the size of an army in itself, plus martial law. Martial law has always been excessive and unreasonable, but it gave the government an excuse to do its thing."

"What happened? What changed?" Asant asked.

"That's the question. It's really not simple. Or maybe it is. I don't know. First an oppressive government like that is just not sustainable. People will get fed up sooner or later. Plus, eventually, other countries wanted a change in the regime, politics, special interests, so they supported smugglers, including our neighbor, Vant – the country you want to visit. The smugglers were at it for a long time. They built up their numbers, then found enough support from other parts of the region. In response, different countries came to support the regime. It all got mixed up."

"It doesn't sound simple," exclaimed Ismael.

"No. Then again, it's just people against people. People in the country want to do away with the oppression. People outside the country want...I don't know, something, maybe land, maybe resources, they want something."

"It's still not simple, especially when other countries get involved."

"It's simple in that being good to your people along with strong relationships with neighbors all translate into a strong foundation. A foundation strong enough to withstand greed and chaos." The driver, elbow still on his window's base, leaned his head on his left arm again. He looked up after a few seconds as if with a new thought. "Don't get me wrong. This is a great country. It is my country. I was born and raised in Tannis and have driven across most of the land. It is incredible. Beautiful land, mountains, beaches, history, great food. Beautiful, generous, kind people. Diverse with so many cultures, many languages, people from different backgrounds and histories living together, even loving each other. But the ruling people were not kind to many. That, along with outside interests, spelled trouble."

"Was there violence in Tannis?" asked Asant.

"Oh yes," the driver replied. "Tannis and Lamania, saw some of the first waves of the war. The smugglers wanted to control this whole region because it was full of government backers. Battles were unrelenting for weeks. People shooting at each other. Tanks and fighter jets followed, then checkpoints around both cities. Other cities soon after succumbed to the violence and the fighting. The worst is the not so obvious. The children, and how it is affecting them. A whole generation simply lost. Thousands and thousands without their families, without a home, no education, no food. No future. I don't understand how we reached this depth of evil, how we can be so blind and capable of destroying our own future." He stopped, fell silent, leaned his head on his hand again, and watched the car in front of him as their car stood idle. Soon, he turned off the engine.

Another twenty minutes brought them to the first group of soldiers and canines. Then it was questions, stares, passports, more stares, doors opening, trunk, hood. The car was in its metal skeleton, on four all-rubber spare tires, bearing little aside from the thin cushions.

One soldier, perhaps the captain in the group, held the three passports by her side and held a prolonged gaze at Asant and Ismael. She passed the passports to another soldier, who walked away and into a make-shift small square building. The first soldier turned to the driver, asked another question using the local language. "Arapali," the driver said. The soldier walked around the car another time, opened each door again and peered in. Seemingly satisfied, she stepped back to the driver side and waited. Another ten minutes passed before the second soldier walked back toward the car and returned the passports. The soldier raised her passport-holding hand toward the driver, and motioned them forward.

"Thank you," Asant said.

"Not yet my friend. We have another point, then we will need stamps in your passports."

"Will we need to go in ourselves?"

"No. I will go. I will take your passports and apply for the stamps."

Back on pavement, they soon passed another sign. "Welcome to Vant," the words declared in front of a eucalyptus tree.

The road to Arapali was clear, at least in comparison to that on the opposite side of the border. The first two miles or so after crossing were in particular a clear indication of being outside the conflict. It is strange how conditions and behavior can change and be so different on different sides of one line.

Another contrast was the difference in the vehicle. The driver had pulled into a parking lot full of yellow and red taxis. He went into the office, then returned with another man by his side. "Friends, this is Mo. He will be your next driver."

From Arapali, it was a well-cushioned car, a luxury at this point. They drove between the same lush green mountains to their left, and sparkling blue water to their right. Earth's beauty, and peace, were inescapable. It was all but thirty minutes when the vehicle slowed and turned right, giving Asant and Ismael the feeling that they were going to drive into the water. The pavement led them down then a slight left. Ahead, they now saw a one-story building, covered by a flat roof and spread out over large rocks forming a sort of a cliff. The building stretched out beyond the rocks and over the water for a few feet.

"Is this a restaurant?" asked Ismael, thinking it did not look like one.

"It is a great restaurant, dear friend!" replied the driver.

The vehicle entered a parking lot, rolled toward a slab of concrete then came to a stop. The driver moved his right arm to the passenger seat headrest and turned his head.

"This is it my friends. This is where I leave you."

From the back seat, Asant and Ismael looked at the driver as he spoke to them, questions in their eyes, perhaps unready for the next stage.

"I wish I could give me you something, a tip..." Asant started saying.

"Oh no, not to worry," the driver interrupted. "Taken care of," he added smiling, right arm still on the headrest. "Take my card," his arm hung in the middle behind his seat, between Asant and Ismael. "Contact me when you're ready for a ride back."

"Thank you."

Asant's mind alternated between thoughts of why he was yet in another country, the kindness he has received, and what might follow. It was beyond his mind's imagination. He looked at Ismael, searching for a reminder that it was real and that he was not alone. He then turned to the door to his side, and moved to exit the vehicle with reluctance, at first pulling the door's handle with less than the necessary conviction. Ismael followed suit, and a minute later the two stood about six feet apart, watching that same car move in reverse and leave them behind.

Asant saw a set of steps, in part hidden at a light, right of where he stood. "Alright," he exclaimed, breathing in, and started walking in that direction.

He and Ismael walked through clear plastic doors swinging on a brown plastic frame and into a lobby. They could see the interior of the restaurant from where they stood; its tables and chairs spread out in a predictable scheme. It was one hall with an open scheme, and with windows surrounding it allowing the light in from the sea.

A man in a white shirt and black pants approached them as they stood in the lobby. He said something using the local language. He waited for a response, allowing him time to observe their facial features – both had chiseled faces, with pronounced cheekbones and narrow noses, common among those from the region.

The man then decided to repeat himself after taking in his patrons' foreign appearance. "Good morning sirs, almost good afternoon. I can show you to a table in a minute. If you are expecting to have seafood, you can see some of our fresh catches in this box," he concluded pointing to his right, smiled, then turned and walked away.

Asant looked at Ismael, his face asking, "*What should we do?*" then followed Ismael's eyes and stepped over to the ice box.

It was full of fish, some red, some gray, some thin and long, others wide and short, all with surprised, piercing eyes.

The same man returned and looked at them hanging over the box's left side. "That would be a good choice," he said, hand close to a group of red, long, and thin fish. "It is almost exclusive to this area, because of our rocky and protruding shores. This fish just likes this environment, and the temperatures."

Asant hesitated. "Very well. But let us wait for a few minutes until after we sit. We are expecting to meet here with a friend." He cleared his throat. "Can you seat us for now, and give us a few minutes before deciding?"

"Absolutely. Of course. Of course. Please follow me." The man began walking through another set of clear plastic doors and turned right toward the corner of the restaurant.

"Would you like to sit outside, on the patio?" he asked after taking a few steps. "There is a pleasant breeze, you would have a better view of the water, and it is not cold." Asant nodded.

The restaurateur walked ahead to the patio. One behind the other, they passed through two lines of tables. One person was sitting alone at the end, at the corner table on the right side, facing the water. The restaurateur led Asant and Ismael through but stopped before reaching the end, two tables before the other patron, and pulled two chairs out of their position. "Please be comfortable."

Ismael took notice of the other patron before he turned and took hold of his chair. It was a man, with a shaven head.

Asant sat across from Ismael, his arms resting on the white cloth.

"What do we do now?" Ismael asked in their language.

"What do you mean?"

"I mean food. This is a restaurant. Are we going to eat here? And pay for it? Or are we going to wait for someone to come?"

"Yes. Right." Asant's eyes adjusted their focus away from Ismael, to the table at the corner where the other patron was sitting. "I don't know."

"Asant, do you even have money? We can't barter or exchange something in a place like this."

Asant, now looking at the man's back, motioned with his right hand, "*Wait.*" He said, in a lower voice, "Hold on Ismael, that man turned in our direction for a second."

Asant moved himself and his chair back away from the table and stood up. Ismael stayed in his place but turned his head to look at the corner table. The man was already standing, and approaching them.

"Hello. I heard you speaking in a foreign language. I would love to join you, perhaps give you a tour of the area?" he asked. "Please allow me."

Asant started to respond, "No, please, you don't have to, we are expecting a friend to..."

All three turned their attention to the door. The restaurateur was walking toward them, tray on hand facing upwards.

"Laten, they are my guests," the bald man announced. "Can you please give us a round?"

"A round? No, please. I do not drink alcohol," Asant said, now standing between the two men.

"Very well. Bread and oil then. I hope you gentlemen like fish, local fish is a must." The patron waited for a second, then added to the restaurateur, "The Reddened Snapper would be great. Laten, please."

The patron sat himself next to Ismael. "Is this your first visit to the area?"

"Yes, yes...it is," Ismael responded. "Are you a local, born and raised?"

"No. Perhaps strange, but no, not a local, a visitor, long-term visitor if you will. I like the area. I like the region. The whole region. Mind you, I am originally from the region."

Asant and Ismael, both puzzled, looked at the man trying to find more clarity from his face, attempting to understand what it meant to be a long-term visitor but also to be originally from the region. The man's response left them without a thought of what question to pose.

"Right, not exactly a local but I know plenty about the area. I hope you will allow me to give you a tour."

"Sir..." Asant started to say.

"You don't have to answer now. I'm sure you have your schedule. Let us have something to eat together. You can decide after."

"I really don't know sir," Asant said, now on guard, uncomfortable with the man's forwardness. "We do have our schedule, like you said."

"No doubt. Of course. Let's have lunch together. You are guests here, it is the least I can do."

"With all honesty, we are expecting lunch with friends," Ismael said.

"Oh sure. Here, in this restaurant?"

Asant looked at the man but did not reply. "Yes," began Ismael, "yes, here."

"Great. How about we start with something light until they come, and if they don't, very common for people around here, they just forget or get interrupted, then we can go forth with our meal."

"We just, we don't want to impose..." Asant replied and attempted to further explain.

"You would not be. It is my duty, even though I'm not local to this town, I am originally from the region like I mentioned, from the area really. It is my duty to welcome and take care of visitors. Also, it is I who invited myself to your table, so it is I who would be imposing. Plus, I am looking to gain from a conversation," he smiled.

Asant and Ismael both had too many questions and did not manage to form coherent thoughts. Neither replied. The man continued, "It would be tremendous to hear of your experiences, your travels, what brought you here. Since we will be here, you won't miss your friends once they arrive, and..."

The restaurateur returned with three glasses and a bottle. It looked to be full of water, or at least some clear liquid. All three looked at him.

"Thank you, Laten. For the fish, all three of us will have the Redden."

"Oh, forgive us, but we do not eat meat or fish."

"Very well. Then your two special salads, Laten, two for each of us. And the usual appetizer dishes."

"Good. You will very much enjoy our salads. And I will make sure they are prepared on clean boards untouched by meat," the restaurateur said smiling.

Ismael held his glass close to his face. "You must forgive us again, but we do not drink alcohol either."

"Ah. I understand. It is admirable. To be honest I do not either. So, it is all good. But, I still like this drink, even if just to have it around. Its aroma, by this salty water, by the waves and the breeze, make for a breathtaking combination." The man turned his head just enough to see the water, his eyes gazed across its surface and reveled in it. "It reminds me of the places my father used to take us. Restaurants by beaches, some on mountains. Eating in open spaces, near water just like this, sometimes between trees. This, new friends, is an experience that must be cherished." The man raised his glass.

"Please, we can have good wishes even if we do not partake in the drinking. To your health."

Asant and Ismael took their glasses, Asant looked at his, and through it. It was about twice the size of a shot glass, with three gold rings evenly spaced starting on the rim, clear liquid inside, strong aroma spreading among the three of them. The drink's aroma pervaded their space, becoming a member of their company.

The glasses clinked. The man smiled. "This is good. Thank you both." He put down his glass, then took the other glass in front of him, full of water, and drank a sip. "So, tell me about your country...I hope you don't mind my curiosity, my intrigue."

"Well," Asant began, then turned his head and looked at Ismael.

"You know, does it have mountains? Does it have tropical forests or does it see snow? How about the people, and favorite pastimes?"

"The mountains are to the north, they are spectacular. The ocean is to the south, and there is everything in between, parts that are dry, parts heavy and thick with trees." Asant looked at his lap. "It is a beautiful country."

"Of course, I'm sure," the man said. "I suppose every country is beautiful in its own way. The planet, the whole planet, is beautiful, all that it offers and provides. Every inch of it. I'm sure you know from your travels."

Asant smiled and nodded.

"So, what brought you in this direction?"

"Oh." Asant perceived the man to be too direct, perhaps because of the unexpected acquaintance. He moved in his chair and avoided eye contact. The question, and the man's self-invitation and presence at their table caught him off guard, he did not feel ready to divulge his reasons.

In spite of his candor with Yusef, the nomadic elder, and with Kadir and Fareez, Asant considered the circumstance now to be different in that with them it was Asant who sought them. Now, it was the man who initiated contact, and seemed inquisitive without sufficient reason.

"To be honest, sir, I'm not comfortable talking about my trip," he replied.

"Why not?"

"I do not know you. We do not know you," he said, moving his left hand in Ismael's direction.

"But why should that matter?"

Asant watched the man for a moment. "Like you said, it's a foreign country for us, we don't know whom to trust."

"That means your reasons require trust." The man's words were plain, his tone flat, and eyes kind and fixed on Asant.

"Not necessarily," Asant replied.

"Please explain."

"Insecurity on my part. I am not ready to confide in you because I know nothing about you."

"So, trust it is," the man said while observing Asant. He then looked down at his wrist watch. "I lost track of time. Please do allow me to provide this lunch and the drinks." He smiled and stood up, ready to leave.

Asant snapped his head back, his eyes blinked. He was again surprised. "Wait, please," he said, standing up. Ismael followed. "Please forgive me. That was rude of me. I am a guest here, but coming from Siljap, seeing war-demolished buildings and neighborhoods, then going through the border and its checkpoints, it just all led me to be afraid and to be overly and perhaps unnecessarily cautious."

The man looked at Asant for a few seconds. Neither said anything.

Asant cleared his throat and continued. "Can you stay, at least for a bit until our friends arrive? Please!"

The man continued to observe Asant, while his face remained relaxed and hard to decipher. It was not discernible whether he was considering Asant's appeal.

Asant looked away for a short moment. "It would be good and a privilege to talk with you, and of course to learn more about the area."

Now Ismael seemed unsure. He turned from the man to Asant, an inquisitive look in his eyes, questioning if that was wise. Asant sensed the insecurity, made a slight head-turn, smiled, then turned back to the man, eyes pleading.

The man smiled. "Why not, it will be good to talk some more," he replied, maintaining his smile, moved in front of the chair, sat down and pulled himself toward the table. With elbows on the table, hands in a gentle clasp, he said, "So, what would you like to talk about?"

"Well, so many questions, even from the short time we've been here, but I would like to, should really, answer your question first," Asant said, then pursed his lips and repeated few short nods. "To be honest, I...I came all the way here, from my home, to redeem myself," Asant said, then regarded the man. Both looked at each other, each waited for something – Asant for a reaction; the man for continuation. The man brought his two hands together, continued his blank stare at Asant, perhaps disappointing Asant and forcing him to continue and reveal more information.

Asant felt his heart beginning to race. In his mind, he revisited his actions, then considered the moment and the options it provided. He concluded it was more important to be open and trusting and that perhaps divulging information could play a role in his redemption. "I did something I should not have," he said. "I attempted to steal even though I knew better. I desired money and comfort." He turned his head, averted the man's eyes, and found some comfort in the blueness of the water. He then turned back to their table. "My teacher taught me about all that, about what money is. I did not want to go to jail. But of course, I had to receive and accept what was coming to me. After fighting with it, after crying, after begging, I understood from my teacher, my guide, spiritual guide, that it was either jail or helping a people. He said the people of Siljap in particular." Asant stopped there, lips pursed and head moving in short nods, now himself observing the man.

"I see," the man said as he looked away. "The country and its people, can use all the help offered." He stopped for a moment, raised his head and stared at the plastic ceiling, appeared lost in a thought. "But," he started, bringing his left hand to his chin and cheek. "How do you suppose you will help?"

"I have no idea. Certainly not with weapons, or any sort of violence for that matter. I don't carry weapons, guns. As far as I know," Asant turned to his left, "Ismael doesn't either." He turned back to the man, cleared his throat. "How about you, you said you're visiting, but have been here for a while. What's the purpose of your visit?"

"I would say I'm not visiting. If I am to be honest with myself, and with you, I would have to say I'm avoiding responsibility. At least that's what I think."

"If you think it then you are probably right," Ismael declared.

Both the man and Asant gawked at Ismael.

"Yes, I agree. I'm avoiding it because what I think I need to do is more than I have the courage for."

The restaurateur swung the clear plastic doors and entered the porch with a large round tray in one hand and a collapsed stand in another. The three patrons watched him in silence as he set the tray and placed a multitude of bowls and plates on their table. Lettuce and cucumber salad sparkled with oil and minced mint; a light brown dip decorated with whole green mint leaves, and another with chopped almonds. The man smiled. "It is incredible food, and presentation, simple but just right. These people know color, I love it here, in this place," he smiled, at the food, talking to it, then motioned to Asant and Ismael, "Please."

Minutes passed, each busy savoring something.

Asant finished what he had put on his plate. His mind now unoccupied, thoughts and questions gradually moving in. His eyes became hazy as he debated something with himself. "Can I ask you what you're avoiding, if you're willing to elaborate?"

The man was finishing what was on his plate as well. He grabbed a couple of spoons and added more of the salad and dips to each of Asant's and Ismael's plates, then to his. "It's a long story, the way I go about it in my head."

Ismael's head snapped upward as if by reflex, curiosity ahead of him. He asked without a pause, "Is it something you can tell us?"

"What about your friend, the person you're expecting to meet?" asked the man.

"Well, I think we're a little early. It doesn't look he's arrived yet," Asant said while looking to his right through the clear plastic into the restaurant's main room.

"I can tell you a bit, at least I can start." He cleared his throat, looked down, took a long breath, then seemed to go deep into a thought, forgetting the salad he was going for. He took another breath, re-positioned himself in his chair, leaned back, brought his hands together. Meanwhile, Asant and Ismael watched, observed, both debated silently if they should say something.

The man seemed to begin another long breath, then, "I like this country very much, this land, and Siljap in particular," he said. "Siljap is my birth country. I used to think that explained it, but now I think there is more. Something draws me to it."

Ismael took in a quick breath. Asant touched his right arm, sensing that with the breath, Ismael was about to ask a question.

"In the span of five to six years," the man continued, "I visited as much as I could, almost every year. Trips there, to Siljap, always felt laborious at first, in part because I felt the country's political landscape was unstable and precarious for decades. Some used to tell me that it was more secure than many other parts of the world. I disagreed. To me, it all felt volatile. Still I wanted to come, to see all that I could see, all that it has, and it has much."

"It is a beautiful country, from what I've seen in our recent exposure," Asant said.

Ismael nodded in agreement.

"But can I ask what drew you, especially considering the volatility you felt?" Asant asked.

"Hmm. Tough question. The country has ruins, history, civilizations that go back centuries, millennia. I loved going to and walking through the old cities, seeing the old walls and gates." The man took a deep breath, looked down at the table, in the direction of the remaining food. "But, it wasn't the ruins, per se, that pulled me, I think it was my roots, my roots are in that country, with that people."

"You mean you were born there? Or did you spend a better part of your life there?" asked Ismael.

"Yes, I was born there. More than that, if you believe in past lives, I probably lived in the region before, or this soul did. This soul has memories of this region."

"Something like nostalgia? Do you think the soul can feel nostalgia?" Ismael asked.

"Another good question. I don't know, don't know about nostalgia. I think the soul has goals, work to do. It desires to be where it needs to do its work. Perhaps work incomplete from another life. And thus, a person feels a pull."

"You had a purpose in Siljap?" Ismael followed.

"Maybe. I'm not sure. It is what I think."

"If you think there is a purpose, then you must think about what the purpose is," Ismael stated, while Asant observed and looked between the two.

"Perhaps," said the man. "Perhaps, perhaps. I have thought about it many a time. In fact, for a while, I felt that my last visit brought me close to that purpose."

"Was that recent?" asked Ismael.

"A few years ago."

"Oh, then before the current conflict?"

"Yes. Before the conflict," the man said, nodding. His eyes moved and became unfocused and glossy. His mind took him to another place.

Again, sensing there was more, Ismael felt anxious. His eyes blinked several times while staring at the man, wanting to ask but undecided what words to use and what exactly to ask. He moved in his chair, then cleared his throat. "Was it a while before the conflict started?" His words and question coming fast. "I mean when you arrived, did you sense a difference from your previous visits? Did you somehow sense chaos or even an uprising was coming?"

The man observed Ismael for a short moment, considering a reply. "Funny question, really," he said, not laughing or smiling. "Who knows what brought what, what caused what, whether there would have been a conflict at all, had the slightest, most innocuous and innocent creature, seemingly all separate from all human activity, decided to be in a different place at a given moment." He stopped. "I am blabbering. To answer your question with direct words, I arrived approximately a month, maybe two, before I think events linked to the conflict began." He stopped again, breathed in for a long moment and sighed. "As to your other question, no, I did not sense a difference from my prior visits, and did not somehow feel an uprising was coming; however, I did feel more anxious, much more anxious, but also, I decided I was ready to face what was to come."

"What do you mean?" asked Ismael.

"I don't understand," the man said.

"That you were ready to face what was to come...were you aware of something beforehand, before it was to happen?"

"No. No, for sure not. I felt that something was going to happen, to me. I did not know what it was but decided I wanted to face it. A part of me did; I think that part of me was either brave enough or desperate enough. Either way, I was for sure tired of the quiet life I was having."

The man was quiet again. Asant and Ismael both gazed at him, entranced by his vague lines, questions in their minds about what he was referring to.

Curiosity got the better of Ismael again. He moved in his chair with restlessness in his psyche, his eyes again blinking too frequently. He shook his head in an attempt to clear his mind, wanting to assert some clarity, to simplify the man's perspective. "So, you decided to visit Siljap. You felt more anxious than in prior visits, but persisted with your choice to visit. I think I understand as much. Did your anxiety prove to be warranted?"

"Yes, you can say that. At the airport's customs, an official asked me to follow him, took me to a room full of rows of shelves, full of files. The official looked through some, took one out, sat at a desk, wrote on a small piece of paper, and handed it to me. He said, 'report to the office in Lamani.'"

"That was all?" Ismael asked.

"Yes, that was all." The man chuckled. "A part of me did not think much of it, another part did not accept that thought – that it was nothing. Regardless, the former part of me prevailed, and by then I was resigned to face whatever it was. You see, my idea of Siljap was, and still is, that a piece of paper such as that, at the border, cannot be good news. Nevertheless, I allowed a flicker, a thought, that this could be simpler than my anxiety was leading me to believe; after all, that official was nonchalant about whatever he saw in the file."

"What was in the paper?" asked Ismael.

"A number, just a number. The man told me to visit the police center in Lamania and give them the paper."

"That was it?"

"That was it. But this police center, mind you, was an intelligence office, not simply a police center."

"So, you went?"

"I went."

"And?" Ismael asked, head moving forward, eyebrows raised, displaying a tinge of impatience.

"It was a wide building, easy enough to find, appearing to be common even with a black metal gate. If I recall correctly it is four levels above the ground. It was surrounding by a high concrete wall, fifteen to twenty feet. Metal gates connected two columns at the ends of the wall. The gates were open, as if there was nothing to hide, leading into a desolate large open space, all concrete, no greenery, the building itself on the left." The man stopped for a deep breath, moved in his chair, brushed his right cheek. A breeze from the sea moved the hangings against each other, making a muffling sound.

"Once inside, a civilian-looking man led me to an office on the second level and gave my piece of paper to a man behind a desk. I sat in that office, on a black leather couch facing him. He looked through files in his drawers, did not even look at me, did not say anything. Then, he stood up, told me to follow him, and led me from that office through a hallway and down a marble staircase to the first level. Then it was another staircase, except this was exposed concrete, and wide. It was a winding staircase. It led into a basement. Going through this staircase, into the basement, I thought – this is not going to be pleasant. Then, the first locked gate. Metal bars. The man from the office rang a bell. Someone from the other side came up to the gate, the two exchanged some words, and, I was inside." The man turned his head and eyes toward his lap, nodded. "I was inside."

"Did you know what this was about? I mean you had traveled to Siljap before but didn't encounter this office...did you have any idea why this trip was different, why you were called to this center?"

"Yes, I had an idea. I suspected it was about religious letters I took part in disseminating during my previous trip."

"Religious letters?"

"Religious letters," the man said, nodding.

"What kind of letters, recent? Were they inciting a coup?"

"They were letters interpreting ancient text. What I had with me were copies. Copies of millennia-old letters. Not inciting anything, not even some religion. Simply interpretation."

"But then, why would the intelligence personnel care? Or for that matter, the government?" asked Ismael. "They must've been threatening in some way."

"I doubt the letters alone were threatening. Where the government thought they came from was threatening. In truth, I knew the letters were black-listed, not allowed in the country. As it was, this government feared religion; but more so, they suspected enemy spies were associated with the letters."

"You mean secret code was being exchanged through the letters?"

"No...however, I suppose this was possible. Maybe there was something I did not know, but I doubt it, I doubt there was any direct connection to the letters, rather, it was about where the letters came from. The country from which they originate was at war with Siljap."

"You mean before the conflict?"

"Yes. That country and Siljap were not friends, still aren't. Something of a cold war, no actual violence."

Asant cleared his throat. "What happened once you were in the basement, on the other side of the barred gate as you said, inside?"

"I was led to another office. This one felt almost innocuous, normal, or perhaps, I was, by then too anxious and preoccupied. I was led to a smaller room, an office in an office. There was a desk and a cushioned chair on one side of the desk, for me. No one was there. Few minutes passed, then a pudgy man walked in and around to the other side of the desk and asked questions. It was an interview, an interrogation."

The man looked away, at the water, into the distance. "*No one is coming. No one will speak on your behalf,*" he thought back to the interrogator's first words.

"Did he ask about the letters?" asked Ismael.

The man's eyes remained distant for another moment, then he breathed and refocused on Ismael. "Yes," the man replied. "Yes, he asked. First about me, my name, my work. Then about the letters. I denied any knowledge. I denied I knew anything about any letters. He had a name for them, of which I knew, but again denied knowing any such name."

"Why?" Ismael asked.

The man re-positioned himself in his chair, raised and straightened his back. "Why what?"

"Why deny knowing of the letters?"

"Because they were black-listed."

Ismael watched the man and stayed quiet, expecting more of an explanation.

"People can be afraid for no good reason," the man said. "Fear of religious letters seemed stupid to me, outlawing them also stupid. Regardless, that was the law – not really law – more of an unspoken intelligence policy, but no matter. Fear complicates matters. There was no point in adding to the complication." The man paused. "Actually, now that I am thinking about it, I had met with a friend the night before I went to this office. An attorney friend. A local. It was him who told me that the letters were black-listed, a while before. And that night, he warned me not to say anything about the letters."

"How did the interrogator, the interviewer, respond?" asked Asant.

"He repeated a few times that no assistance, and no attorney would be coming. But, in retrospect, I think he mostly believed me. He believed that I did not know much."

"But they kept you? I mean, well, they kept you there, right?" Ismael said, continuing the inquiry.

The man looked down toward the table. "Yes. They kept me." He paused and considered his thoughts. "Their behavior two days later was an indication that he, they, believed me. They asked me where I lived, they asked for a local address. In other words, they were completing documents for my release."

"So, they released you? But, I'm not sure that makes sense. I guess I was getting a different impression." Ismael was engaged, his questioning thoughts faster than his analysis, allowing his curiosity the haste it demanded.

"Yes. I gave you a different impression. It was at night, I believe it was the third night when they asked about where I lived, about a local address. And in that moment, something overcame me, perhaps fate, perhaps forces stronger than my mind, perhaps my guard was down. An address evaded me. For one, I had been away from the country for too long, such that recalling an exact address necessitated some thought. I could have, but I didn't. I became confused, like a child who did not know such information. I blurted a city. Then a different city. Then a street name. All without conviction." The man shook his head, pursed his lips. "Life, its energies, its effects, can be strange." He stopped and eyed the white cloth dangling on the sides, an ever-so slight movement with the breeze.

"The inquiring guard chuckled," he continued. "My companions, cell mates if you will, chuckled. The guard then asked if I had any family in the area. I said yes, an uncle. He told me to wait, took me out a few minutes later, handcuffed me, and walked me over to a room where another person was working on the insides of a phone, bugging the phone. My phone. They asked me for my uncle's phone number. I answered. The same first guard then took me and sat me in a different room, and started to un-cuff me. In that instant, he noticed something on my left index finger, a short green string. He knew what it was, its significance, its intended purpose, or at least knew enough to raise alarms. He asked me about it. I said simply that it reminded me of my mother, that she was no longer with the living, that green was her favored color. He did not believe me. And the next day, I was taken out of the shared space to a solitary thirty-square foot, blank, empty, tiled space. No blankets. No foam to sit or sleep on. It was just me and the white tiles, the black and metal door, and the light-less air in between."

The man stopped, took another deep breath.

Ismael reflexively opened his mouth and stared. His thoughts raced to comprehend the escalation in the man's circumstances. Images of the cell and its darkness crisscrossed in his mind, attempting to make sense of solitary confinement. He found himself without words, and watched the man draw that breath.

Asant, with emotions of his own, turned his head to avert the man's face, wanting to avoid imagining such a space altogether. He then looked up in Ismael's direction.

Ismael shook his head to regain focus. Another thought crossed his mind, helping him connect stories he and Asant have heard, particularly from Kadir and Fareez. He looked at Asant, managed eye contact. Asant did not say anything, so Ismael turned back to the man. "Are you Yeshu?"

"Yes. Was it not obvious, considering your inquiries, and the restaurant having been agreed to? My friends, I was the only person here when you walked in."

"Right."

Ismael cleared his throat and shook his head again to come out of that brief stupor. "Sorry. Sorry," he began. "To be honest, I am not sure I understand, about the string. Can you tell us more about it...about the green string?"

"It is strange. I agree. Even more so is how the – how can I say this – let's say the universe or the divine force, how this force can work to help us, to guide us, to warn us with a subtle thought of what is to come, of an action to take. You see, it occurred to me to remove this string from my finger after the first door closed behind me. I heard that subtle voice, but debated and concluded to retain the string, to retain it because of its purpose."

"What purpose is that?" Ismael asked/

"To fend off negative forces. To protect the wearer. It is powerful. For one, no one noticed it until that guard did. That in and of itself, it is something. It is said that it evades the sight of the uninitiated – and it did – but only for so long. Then again, perhaps they knew nothing about it and simply saw some innocuous decoration. Regardless, more powerful is that benevolent guiding force, the force, the voice that guides us. The voice I ignored, the voice I chose to ignore over the benefits from a string."

"You realize this is confusing?" Ismael stated more than asking. "I simply do not connect the string to anything that was happening. Can you understand?"

"The letters spoke of tools, tools to help us, spiritual tools. The string was one such tool. In short, the string connected me to the letters, those same letters of which I denied any knowledge."

"Forgive me, it's still confusing," Ismael shook his head.

"You see, those letters were not something new. They were written centuries ago, and they were associated with a way of practice, including tools such as the green string."

"And this one man was aware of that string, but no one else in that space?"

"Yes, something like that."

"And then?"

"And then the white tiles."

"Solitary?"

"Solitary."

"For how long?"

"Not long really. But long enough for me to change my mind."

"About what?"

"About my admission. My allegiance."

"Allegiance? To what?"

"To my practice. To the worth I put on those letters."

"So... you told them you knew of the letters?"

"Yes."

"What did they do?"

"A higher official became involved. A lieutenant. I recounted that the letters were spiritual and nothing more. I explained their purpose – that the letters interpreted ancient texts and explained our universe. I'm not sure he trusted me. They recorded that interview, but tried to hide that fact. It was too obvious."

"Then?"

"Then back to the first black door."

A group, a family, maybe two, passed through the restaurant's doors. The restaurateur, Laten, was first, followed by three children and then four adults. Ismael watched them as they split into two rows and sat one by one on opposite sides of their assigned table. He then turned his attention back to where he was sitting and Yeshu, then to Asant. Both men were quiet and looking with neutral faces at Ismael, perhaps anticipating another question from him. "Sorry. First black door. The first cell, with others?"

"Yes."

"Was it the same people you met before they moved you?"

"Yes... plus two additional men, Jared was new... I actually never picked up on the other man's name.

"So how many of you were in there?"

"By then, it was five plus me. The next day they released two men, then it was just me, Jared, and Kadir."

Ismael moved up in his seat and closer to the table. "Kadir?"

"Yes." The man breathed a long breath. "I was happy to be with Kadir. He was there at the beginning. His presence was comforting, helpful."

"And the others?" asked Ismael.

"The others. One man they released the following day. He seemed to be very funny, to everyone except me. It was his dialect. Too difficult for me to understand. Another was released that night. By noon the next day it was Kadir, Jared, and me." The man stopped, seemed to consider a thought, or a memory.

Ismael observed Yeshu, imagined him inside with Kadir. "How long were you there? And, if you don't mind, what was Kadir like? Did you get along? I'm assuming you got along. It seemed you did...from our conversations with Kadir. I guess that leaves Jared."

The man considered the string of questions, and waited a few seconds before deciding how to address Ismael's thoughts. He pursed his lips, breathed in. "The three of us were together for a week. Jared cried often and made good jokes the rest of the time. He exercised, or pretended to...funny actually, I distinctly remember him doing two pull-ups off of a pipe, then announcing that that was enough, that he was done for the day.

"Kadir laughed with Jared. They laughed together just about anytime Jared was not crying. The rest of the time Kadir cleaned the space, lamented. I gathered that they knew each other well, but were being held for different, independent reasons. Kadir is a tremendous person. Kind, spiritual, intuitive, helpful, generally quiet. He spoke about being inside infrequently. When he did, it was his way of dealing with it, as opposed to Jared's crying. Kadir taught me how to survive inside. I don't know how he learned himself; regardless, I became a different person, learned how to survive inside from him.

"At one point, they took me out for questioning. They wanted my electronic mailing address. I had four. Gave them one. There was not much in it. They took me out another time, more questioning. There was not any more I would give them. To me, the letters were spiritual. To them, they were camouflage, hiding secrets and agendas. I sensed they were becoming frustrated with me, and later found out that people from outside were asking about me. That higher official saw me again. By then, I did not care as much, was no longer afraid. The official was not happy. The next day, a guard knocked hard on our door, told us to stand and line up. Seconds later, that same official came in, went through the space, the toilet area, lit a flashlight, looked around. He was inspecting the space, for his sake, not ours, in case some foreign official came in. Before stepping out, he looked at us and spoke. Said that he would keep us as long as he wanted – a week, two weeks, regardless of flights or tickets. He was speaking to me, threatening to keep me past my flight date."

"Did he?"

"Yes. My flight date passed. I knew it; I was counting. Another few days and Kadir and Jared were freed. That part was hard. Then I felt alone. Kadir was so kind and supportive that I had become dependent on him, like a child dependent on a parent. Alone that day, after they left, I cried most of the afternoon. Then, something came over me.

"I picked myself up, cleaned the space, washed my clothes, for the first time, mind you, showered, also for the first time. Kadir and Jared used to shower. I refused to do so because I refused to accept that was my reality, until then when I was by myself again. I went under the shower head and turned that rusted knob. It trickled a handful of water drops, cold water drops. When I was done, I moved my sleeping space, and exercised. On this day I accepted being inside, and decided to take care of myself."

Yeshu turned his head a bit and looked into the distance at the water. Asant and Ismael watched, not having anything to say. Silence from around their table highlighted the sounds from the group nearby.

"I think it was then that I began to pray, and meditate," Yeshu said, his gaze still focused at something in the distant, expansive water. He returned his focus to Asant and Ismael. "At first it seemed a logical step after showering and washing my clothes. I think I was reminded of the tools I had learned over the years, was reminded to use them. Exercising, praying, meditating. Sleep was manageable that night. It was good. Funny really, a three-inch sponge, laid on tiles, brown itchy blankets on top, and nowhere to go except with the mind. Then, it was suddenly morning, jam, butter, olives, and bread. An hour later Fareez arrived. In a way, he was an answer to my requests. I did not specifically ask that I have company, but I did not want to be alone."

"Fareez is also a great person – funny, older than me, maybe in his fifties or sixties, I thought. Never talked about why he was there, instead we talked about life, religion. We played games with olive seeds. We kept score. It was fun, to be honest." Yeshu smiled, his eyes became hazy, as if taking him to that moment.

"It was good having his company," he continued. "It seemed they, the guards, were light on him, allowing him to have things they would not allow with others. For one, he had cigarettes. He didn't smoke them, no matches, that they didn't allow. But we used those cigarette boxes and the olive seeds to play something of a basketball game." Yeshu paused again. "Anyways, I continued to pray, meditate, and exercise. Exercising was really just pacing in the space we had. Kadir got us going on that, and I continued it with Fareez. Walking to nowhere for an hour, then again later in the day, then again, and again. In those walks, I prayed. I prayed for every individual I remembered encountering. Beginning from as back as I could. Parents, family, classmates, work. It took me a while to finish. In a way, this was also out of desperation. Also, I think around the second day after Fareez arrived, I began to take meditation in a different direction. I was mad at them. They were trying to control me.

"So, I decided to fight back. I began to build an army..."

"Sorry, build what?" interjected Ismael.

"An army."

"From inside?"

"Yes. From inside. An army of souls."

Ismael stared, mouth open, eyebrows raised in a triangle, flabbergasted. Asant did not react.

"I began with individuals close to me," continued Yeshu. "Individuals I knew for a long time, family, close friends. I made them generals."

"This was an army?" asked Ismael, feeling unclear, disconnected from what he was hearing.

"I recruited maybe ten to fifteen souls."

Ismael continued to feel confused. "Forgive me, Yeshu. Please. I don't understand."

Yeshu looked at him. "Why is that?"

"Well, how does one recruit a soul?"

"Simple really. You call him or her. You think of him. And then think about what you want to do. Tell him what you want to do and what you want from him."

"Thinking? That's all?"

"Yes. Simple. But it is a process."

"It simply does not make sense to me."

"You are thinking too hard. Consider how we do things in this realm. We talk. Communicate. Make requests. We plan. It is no different in other realms, except that one has to work in that realm's methods."

"It is difficult to follow, Yeshu."

"Granted. But try to think of it through different logic. We have flesh, we are physical beings, so we work in the physical realm. Souls are energy. They work in the energy realm, using flow of energy. Thoughts are energy."

Yeshu paused, continued when Ismael did not offer another question. "I worked with individuals I was familiar with. I trained them..."

"Trained them in what?"

"In combat."

"In combat? How do you train energy in combat?"

"It becomes interesting, and engaging. You would train the souls to work in unison. With that, their resistance to chaos grows. It's what you and I in the physical would call confidence and strength. And, confidence can change conditions."

Yeshu gazed toward the water, again appeared to drift into another space. He turned back to the table, and to the men in front of him. "Then I requested that each one recruit ten souls."

"Why ten?"

"Just a number I chose." He nodded. "Easy to multiply."

"To multiply... to make it bigger?"

"Yes. At some point, I decided it had to be a big army, so I requested of each general to train their recruits, then, after another night, I wanted each general to request from their recruits that each soldier soul recruit ten; I repeated this the following night. I wanted an army."

"But, didn't you...they need more time to train? I mean training takes months."

"Months can pass in a mind's second."

Ismael, still unconvinced, watched Yeshu. "Did you tell Fareez?"

"No. These...meditations, I was doing at night, when it was quiet, when I thought everyone including Fareez was asleep. Around two or three in the morning, I would sit up on the sponge, lean back on the wall, cross my legs, and go to work.

"It turned out though that, of course, the guards stayed up. One night, possibly four days after Fareez' arrival, I felt someone, a guard look through the slit in our otherwise solid black door. He saw me up, at that strange hour. The following morning, they took Fareez out. When he came back, he was happy. He told me that they let him sit on a couch, that they treated him with respect, told him he would be freed in no time, just formalities. Then, later that night, he asked me whether I was okay, whether I was able to sleep. It occurred to me that they were trying to use him to spy on me or that they were worried about my mental health. Maybe they thought I was losing it. I don't know. I mattered to them. But to me, we were beyond that point, the deed, the damage was done, and the work had already begun. No stopping it then.

"I was on a mission. From my perspective, they began a war against me, although I doubt they knew what they were getting into."

Ismael was still staring, lost for words. Yeshu went quiet for longer than a moment. It gave Ismael time to refocus; he shook his head and brushed his face with his hands. "You realize, sir, this is hard, umm, hard to understand."

Yeshu looked at the expanse of the water.

Ismael continued, "I'm not sure what to ask exactly, but if I may, I still would like to ask something, if only to help me understand."

Yeshu now looked at Ismael and nodded gently in response, providing Ismael with the space to ask what was on his mind.

"Well, you said, 'they,' that 'they' began a war against you, but it is not clear...I don't understand what you mean, I don't understand who 'they' would be. Is it those doing the questioning, or those who locked the door, or perhaps others unseen by the rest, or are they unseen and from another plane?"

"They would be the government. Those ruling the country." Yeshu's eyes, face, were blank, relaxed, unmoving, unwavering.

"Is it, possibly, unfair, then? Did the government order – I'm not sure what word to use – difficulties to be imposed on you, or order your confinement?"

"Of course. The individuals around me, the ones I encountered, at the airport, and in that building, the ones with weapons and files and questions, were all agents of the government. They were extensions of its impositions and authority, executing its policies, protecting it."

"So then, your, I suppose, your war, was against the government?"

"Of course."

"Did you want that government removed?"

"Yes." Yeshu's eyes moved down to their table and the empty plates on it. "I wanted it removed."

"But isn't that unfair, extreme, considering you had at that time been confined for only a few days, a couple of weeks, when others suffer for lifetimes?"

"I believed it was fitting. In reality, truly there is no fair or unfair. We do, we respond. They attempted to limit my choice, my life. That is not for them to do. I responded."

"But you broke their laws!"

"Yes, I went against that government's policies."

"And still you felt justified?"

"Laws that limited people's choices, hindered growth, laws that attempted to control knowledge and practice. No sense. No sense in them. That government was corrupt. And they declared war against me."

"They didn't declare. They couldn't. Yes, they confined you, and perhaps treated you badly."

"Same thing."

"I am still at a loss. I hope you can forgive me for not quite understanding, maybe I see it differently...but if truly what you did had any connection to the current conflict, then you had a hand in killing thousands, orphaning children, destroying whole cities."

Yeshu pulled in a long breath. "That's true. I did not foresee this conflict. And I did not have the strength, nor the intelligence, to understand, to consider possible consequences."

"Did you think about the consequences?"

"Yes. I thought it would be good." Yeshu paused. "I thought it would be for the people. That they would have a better government, one that cares about them."

"But how? How could that have happened? For one, I'm sure you are aware that suddenly removing a legal structure only creates a vacuum, leaving a country, its people, prey to chaos and likely violence."

Asant turned to look at Ismael, surprised at his words and conclusion. The two of them had yet to talk government and politics, in spite of having spent months together.

"I did not know. It is a fault in me. I was angry, and decided on a course of action. Decided it was time for the government to be removed. In fact, it *was time* for it to be removed, that needed to happen, still does. Or it needs to change its attitude and treatment of its people. Regardless, the vacuum you speak of could have been filled."

"How?" Ismael asked bluntly. His eyes were wide open, right arm in the air, expressing exasperation. It was clear he was flabbergasted.

"Ismael," Asant intervened. "You are being unfair."

"No, Asant. Wars do no one any good. I lost my family, my parents, my sibling, my life because of people resorting to arms. I do not understand how one person could decide to start one."

"I did not start the war. People could have chosen differently. The government, its backers, if they were with conscience...those governing could have reacted differently. The blame cannot be squarely on me."

"I agree," Asant said, still looking at Ismael.

"Nonetheless, Ismael, I could have helped in preventing the war, the conflict, from growing to what it is today. I needed to have a role in filling that vacuum you spoke of a moment ago."

Ismael was lost. He shook his head and did not know what to think, now wanting to heed Asant's objections.

"A role when?" Asant asked, considering Yeshu's words.

"A role after they released me."

Asant thought for a moment. "A role in helping the country form a new government?"

"Yes."

"I must admit, I am now a bit confused," said Asant. "The timing of all this is unclear. Can you elaborate a bit on when the conflict began? Or perhaps give us a timeline...of when you were first in and when you began your work, relative to when the conflict began?"

"Of course." Yeshu cleared his throat. "I began my effort about a week after they locked that first door. A month later, conflicts began to sprout in other parts of the region. A few weeks after, various local incidents began to occur in this country, and the government responded viciously. The authorities made the choice to retaliate with a heavy hammer. Another month turned those local incidents into protests. Again, the government did what it always does. Suppress. Torture. Imprison. Kill. It worked to not only thwart but also annihilate any voice against it. It did not listen to its people; it did not observe what was happening.

"In between, they transferred me to a different location, to the capital. By then the army was active, clearing every city in the nation. I tried to continue my work, but could not in the new location. That place where they had me, in the capital, was full of trauma. There was torture. Against me. Against others. I heard screams. Saw inflamed blue faces, feet, hands.

After about three months, they finished with me. They finished their interrogation. A corporal wrote a report, then transferred me yet again. In this third location, we heard of the uprising. It had begun. My efforts manifested into an uprising. But by then I could not stop it even if I wanted to. By then my army was no longer intact. Without a leader, it had no purpose, it dispersed, leaving the chaos to its will. I did not see it then, only saw that I wanted to be free.

"First, rebels took control of two cities, I think Tannis was one of them. This I learned after my release. When I was in fact released, I met with a friend who did have a hand in the uprising. This friend, somehow, came to suspect my role.

He believed in me. He began to introduce me to some rebels, some leaders in the movement. In short, I was being given the option to be more involved, to lead. This also I did not see. It was an opportunity to make everything right. But, it was a role I did not have the courage to accept."

"Wait. Did not have the courage to take up arms?" asked Ismael.

"Did not have the courage to lead. Arms are different. We make them for the sole purpose of killing humans. I never wished to, and will not, carry arms."

An hour and a half had already passed. The patio was not completely full, but certainly crowded. The restaurateur stopped at their table and asked if they would like coffee.

"That would be all, Laten, thank you, you've been patient with us." Yeshu responded, then turned to Asant and Ismael.

"Yeshu, I thank you for talking with us, for answering our questions. I was wondering, if you would be willing to spend more time with us, I would like to talk more?" Asant asked.

"Sure. No good reason not to. We can walk to a nearby cafe. But I will need to know more from you as well."

With Yeshu leading, they walked out of the restaurant, into the parking space, then along the shore on a paved sidewalk. The road was to their left, sand and water to their right. All three remained quiet. Yeshu walked small steps, at a leisurely pace, two to three yards in front, looking straight ahead. Asant and Ismael were side by side, looking at their surroundings. Only a couple of small one-story buildings stood near them, but a few lurked along the shoreline, a short walking distance away.

Asant moved a step closer to Yeshu. "Is this where you're now living, Yeshu?"

"Difficult question."

Asant thought it was a simple question and did not understand how it could be difficult. Puzzled, he looked at Yeshu's back, waited for him to elaborate.

"I've been moving often, it's hard to know where I'm living."

"I see. How long have you been here?"

"Off and on... about three years."

"That's a while, don't you think?" Ismael called out, from behind Asant.

"Perhaps. Not continuous three years, though."

"I think I understand," said Asant, having reached a widened sidewalk. He moved closer to Yeshu's right side.

Ismael picked up his pace and moved closer to walk along with them. "Is there a place you would like to live in? Or a place you'd like to call home?" he asked.

"Also a difficult question. I like to think that home is wherever one happens to be, but I find it a difficult mindset to reach." Yeshu looked down toward the pavement ahead of him. "As for where I'd like to be...Siljap. It is in part where I think I should be, or need to be."

"Why would you need to be there?" asked Ismael.

"It is where I was born, and sometimes I feel it is where my work lies."

"Work? You have a company or a business there?" Ismael asked.

"No. I don't mean in that sense...although in the scheme of life, it is the same idea. Rather, I am referring to our service, my service. Each of us has work to do in this life. We come into existence to do work, for ourselves and for others around us. I often feel that my work is related to where I was born."

"That would make sense...can you tell us more? If you are comfortable doing so, that is. What do you think your work is?"

Asant, himself having similar thoughts, admired Ismael's directness.

"Here we are," Yeshu announced.

The three stood by an imaginary line, dotted by scratched wooden tables and numerous sporadic chairs, some occupied, some not, all shaded under several giant eucalyptuses. Leaves moved just enough to signal a breeze. A four-story building, painted predominantly white, with small windows, occupied the entire up-coming block in an austere government style. Another, much taller than its white neighbor, showing more glass than anything else, reflected back images of its surroundings, and held a sign near its top, "City Center".

"Let's take this corner table." Yeshu walked to a rather secluded spot by the imaginary line. He grabbed a chair to make it three.

Asant looked around him. The nearest patrons were a man and a woman. They were three tables away, one sipping tea from a clear, curved glass, the other holding a small porcelain coffee cup with one hand and a saucer in the other. A pastry was half-way between them. Asant stared at them, in particular at the pastry, recalling how much he yearned for such simple things only a few months prior. He pursed his lips, then turned to observe another pair on the opposite end. It was two men with dice and some pieces of a game between them.

"Please," Yeshu said. He looked at Ismael, then at Asant, and motioned with his right hand for them to sit. Asant heard Yeshu's voice, it brought him back to the present. "They have good coffee here, and tea."

Ismael sat, keeping his gaze on Yehsu. "Can you tell us what you think your work is, Yeshu?"

Yeshu smiled. "In good time my friend. Let us get our drinks first."

Silver tray on hand, a man approached them, and asked for their orders. After that, Yeshu was quiet, contemplative, looking at nothing in particular. "This is a great city. Absolutely beautiful, especially from a bird's eye, from a plane. Its green hills, so close to the blue water, makes for a tremendous sight. Brings a smile just thinking about it. Yet, it is not where I was born. It is not where my work is."

"You believe one's work is where he, or she, is born?" asked Ismael.

"Not necessarily. For me it is."

"And you were born in Siljap," Ismael said.

"Let's turn to you for a bit. Did you two start your journey here together?" Yeshu asked.

"No," began Asant. "Actually, we met a few weeks after I was on my way. Ismael wanted to help, and I thank the heavens for the gift of his presence and company."

"Why Siljap?"

"Your story and mine have an interesting intersection. You see, I attempted what my country, my people, consider a crime, and would have probably been imprisoned had I remained there. I simply could not fathom being confined in my country's prisons."

"Lahab. Excellent Lahab," a young man was announcing, pushing a stainless-steel cart on the sidewalk.

Yeshu turned around to look at him. "This is fortuitous. You have to try this dessert."

"Dessert?"

"Yes. It's sweet cheese. I must say it's much better in Siljap, but this will do. It's great with tea." Yeshu went to the young man, came back with two small forks and plates, each with the square dessert.

It was orange-pink flakes over the white cheese; clear syrup spread and dripped from its center down each side.

Ismael and Asant looked at the plates in front of them, then at Yeshu, and back at the plates, inspecting the contents. Asant tried it first.

"So? What do you think?" Yeshu asked, smiling, waiting for a reaction.

"It is excellent, I must say. Cannot imaging it being better," replied Ismael.

"Food can be a tremendous reprieve. Regardless of the circumstances. Don't you think?"

"It can. I agree," replied Asant, taking his third and last bite.

Yeshu smiled. "Back to you Asant. Tell me. What did you attempt?"

Asant cleared his throat. "It is a bit of a quick jump. Allow me a moment." He drew a long breath. "Simply, to steal money, for food," he said, looking at the empty small plate. "I wanted to taste something unavailable to my class. And I wanted comforts." He looked up at Yeshu. "I was wrong. For two days, my desires had a grasp on me, even if those foods and comforts would have been temporary. But, in spite of a wrong, in spite of my attempt, I believe my country's system punishes to an inhumane level, plus other inmates project their despair on each other and extend the torture. What happens behind those walls is unspeakable."

"I see," said Yeshu. "Nonetheless, I get the sense that you did not run away."

"I'm not sure. I suppose that's for the universe to judge. I did not want to be imprisoned. I begged my teacher, my guide in this life, for another way. Eventually he suggested that I may pay my dues by helping Siljap's people."

"Your teacher?" asked Yeshu.

"My guide. Spiritual guide."

"I'm not sure I understand. To be clear, I have an idea, but please, would you kindly say more?"

"On how a spiritual guide can help with crime and punishment?"

Yeshu smiled. "Yes, and also what about your country's system that you think is inhumane."

"Imprisonment is inhumane, anywhere. Taking another's freedom..."

"But so is taking another's earnings, don't you think?"

"Yes. Today though it's not simply about taking another's earnings. There are those of us who take advantage of others, and abuse our resources. There are people in the name of commerce who lead others to work for minuscule pay, while the business owners reap disproportionate rewards. That's also stealing. It's stealing another's time and livelihood."

"Wait, what about the choice people make, the choice to work?"

"It's not much of a choice. Not working means starvation, or begging, or in some cases resorting to theft."

"I don't know, Asant. I see your point, But the choice remains with us. I don't believe anybody forced you to attempt stealing another's earnings."

"True. Nobody forced me. I succumbed to my desires, my desperation for some comfort, to once taste food others are bored of. It was my choice, and I am paying a price, but others had a hand in that choice as well. Those who are unkind and greedy."

"You'll have to forgive me. I still disagree. The choice was yours. Plus, you should not allot any power to others over you. Nobody had the power to take your choice from you," Yeshu said, eyes focused on Asant.

"Point taken," Asant replied, looking back at Yeshu. "Regardless, imprisonment is inhumane punishment for such desperation."

"Maybe, but what would you propose? No retribution? No punishment? We need a system. We need rules to follow. That has been the case for millennia, likely for our entire existence."

"A system, yes, but punishment only as a last resort. It is counterproductive. Instead, perhaps service; plus, I don't know, something from those you might call owners."

"Owners? You want the owners to give something to the thief?"

"Yes. I believe those stealing should be given something, the items they wished for. Generosity and sharing would go much further than any punishment. And perhaps training to help them decide how to attain what they wish for. At the minimum, there should be a meeting. Those who own – as my country's legal system defines ownership – need to understand that we humans in fact do not own anything. Ownership is a construct, granted to maintain some order, certainly control, but that it also deprives others less fortunate, and sometimes leads to this thing we call theft."

"I understand the point you're arguing, but it is a stretch. For one it could lead to repeated offenses. It might simply encourage more theft if only to gain."

"Second or third incidents could then be punishable in some way. Perhaps it is a stretch, to some, to most. I stand by my position, however. Punishment is a method to subdue. It is a form of mind-control to conform." Asant stopped.

Ismael cleared his throat, drawing attention. "I must point out a contradiction, or possibly highlight my lack of understanding. But, Yeshu, from your point about a system, and rules, wouldn't you say that Siljap's authorities were justified in confining you?"

"No," Yeshu said. "Not from my perspective. These were papers, documents for humanity, meant to help humanity. Guidance. Ancient texts explaining life. There was a positive intent behind spreading those documents. Yet, Siljap's government feared them, meaning they feared losing control. I still do not understand how it is that anyone one person, let alone a whole government, thinks it is acceptable to keep positive knowledge a secret."

"But you said they thought you were a spy," responded Ismael.

"Yes. They did. They were in the dark, in large part. The documents were blacklisted for several reasons. At one point, I inferred from their interrogations that the same smugglers were being hired to bring into the country not only similar documents, but also weapons. In turn, I am guessing, the government associated such documents with its regional adversaries."

"So, they wanted to know the sources, and they thought you were connected to those sources?" Ismael asked.

"Yes."

"Were you?" Ismael continued.

"No, not for any weapons," Yeshu answered, then stopped. His eyes drifted, and he seemed to have taken himself elsewhere. While still looking into the distance, at a distant tree, between the people sitting at the other tables, he continued, "I do see some contradiction; however, I was angry. I believe I understand your position about confinement, Asant. I resented it, but did not abhor those moments. It was strange. Hating the situation, my situation, would have meant I did not have control over my mind, over my life. That was not the case. Rather, it was anger." He moved in his chair, cleared his throat, turned his eyes back to their table, then to Ismael and Asant. "Let's return to you, Asant, and your guide's instructions."

Asant looked on and waited, outwardly showing no objection.

"What is your understanding of your guide's instructions?"

It was an inquisitive question, driving into Asant's insecurities that were embedded through years of poverty, hunger, abandonment, and fear of authorities. The question on its own may have been simple, until it taps into the web strung by memories.

Asant's looked away, wanting a bit of space, a moment's time to re-collect his thoughts and to re-focus on Siljap and his task. He cleared his throat.

"It's a difficult question," he said, now looking down at random, at brown-black sparrows walking between tables. "I had heard of news of the conflict here. I had heard that it was spiraling from bad to worse, that it was already worse than just about every other current conflict. Since then, I believe one other conflict had arisen and had become even worse." He straightened, cleared his throat. "My teacher, my guide, is aware of many things, much more than I ever found myself to be. He knew of the difficulties Siljap's people were experiencing. I saw in his face, when he was speaking to me, the same pain I saw after I, we, arrived into the country, in particular Lamania. My understanding, back then, was to help people, to help alleviate pain. Perhaps to work at a hospital, or to help rebuild. But he said I was to end the war. Simple as that. He did not say attend to people, or work to relieve suffering. End the war."

"What did you think of that?" asked Yeshu.

Asant fell silent again. He breathed a long breath. "I thought...I thought that was too much. I told my teacher it was impossible. But truly, I rather thought it was not something I could do. He then reminded me that anything is possible. I thought that, of course, but it was not ingrained in me; rather, impossibility was."

"But you are here."

"Yes. It was either this or prison. Either I find a way, make the effort, or, well you know. Anyway, he said to go to the city of Kamur, and let its people send me in the right direction."

"And?" asked Yeshu.

"They sent me in your direction." Asant was now looking into Yeshu's eyes.

"Are you sure of that?" asked Yeshu.

"Of whether they were referring to you? If I left it to logic. Physical logic? No, I would not be sure; but when I think bigger and beyond myself as an individual, when I think of how the world is interconnected, how the world is energy, how we humans have the ability to work with that energy, then, then I know. Yes, I am sure they were referring to you. You see, over these past few months, through this journey, with Ismael as my companion, I have come to see more how we all are but co-stars in this physical existence."

"Co-stars," Yeshu said, smiling.

"Right. Co-stars in the play, in this theatre. As importantly, we choose our role. Albeit often with guidance and support from others..." now Asant smiled, "from other co-stars."

"Let's say I am to go along. Mind you, I had a hand in this conflict, but let's say I go along with your thought that I have a hand in ending it, what do you suppose your role will be, and Ismael's?"

"My role, I now believe, is to support you, to work alongside you. Ismael's," Asant turned to Ismael, "that is for him to choose, to decide."

"To support me with what?"

"Yeshu, if you started this, as you say, then it is you who must end it. In time, I have no doubt it will end. Whether it takes days, or years, or decades is likely up to those involved, perhaps up to us. I now believe that you must stop what you started. Else, it takes its course, spreading pain and death, lasting at least a generation."

"I cannot. That is simple."

"You can. If you knew how to bring this about, then you must know how end it, and be a part of a new age."

"No. It does not work like that."

"Then make it work."

"No. You see. It is like a storm. Once it begins, it must live its course."

"We disagree, then," Asant said. "But even if you were right, you cannot simply watch the horror from a distance, from the comforts of a peaceful mountain in a neighboring country. Even if it were not you who made it become a catastrophic conflict, as you claim, you would still have the responsibility to do something. It is your country. You were born there. Moreover, you said your role, your purpose lies there, in Siljap."

"I am not obligated."

"It is not about obligation." Asant declared.

"I agree," Ismael interjected. "I believe you are avoiding or evading something."

"Yes. That's true, Ismael, thank you." Asant turned back to Yeshu. "Yeshu, if I understood you correctly, and I agree, that we are usually born where we need to do work. You have work to do in Siljap. Work that is beyond obligation. As you said, it is your life's mission, in addition to your obligation to help the people who nurtured you and educated you."

"Nothing can be done."

"Please, tell us what you have tried to do already," Ismael suggested.

"Tried? No. I do not carry arms. I will not become involved in a war," Yeshu responded with gravity in his voice. His words carried weight, they were quick; and his eyes were focused on Ismael.

Ismael spoke, "You said you started this whole thing while you were behind walls, with your eyes closed. Have you even asked for guidance about what to do after you learned a conflict had started?"

"I have."

"And?" asked Asant.

"And nothing."

"What do you mean nothing?" Asant pressed.

"I know. I know what he means," Ismael said to Asant, then turned to look at Yeshu. "I bet he already knows. He already knows what he should be doing, but avoiding it."

"You are talking crazy talk. I am avoiding nothing."

"You are becoming defensive," Ismael observed. "For me, that is confirmation enough."

"Hold it. Although I agreed to see you and to speak with you, please recall that I do not owe you any time or any explanation, for anything."

Yeshu's words surprised both Asant and Ismael.

Asant, for his part, considered his purpose, and thought about his teacher's words. He recognized the direction the meeting was beginning to head. "Yeshu," he said as he repositioned himself. "You are correct. I, we, sought you out, not the other way around. And, I am the one with a mission. I am indebted to you for agreeing to meet, and for talking about your experience. As importantly, from your recollections to us, I have the impression that it was not violence that you intended, is that safe to say?"

"Of course. I wanted a change, for the better, through benevolence."

"Right. Granted. You also said that you were angry at the government. Is it also safe to say at its entire franchise?"

Yeshu considered Asant, and the implications of the question. "Yes, I was angry."

"Right. Please understand I do not mean any offense, but, kindly allow me this question. Would you also agree that anger does not beget peace?"

Yeshu looked on, while Asant waited for a response.

"My question, really, is about our roles. Each person has a role in this existence, a role in each given moment that collectively amount to that person's purpose."

"Your point please," Yeshu interjected.

"If, as you say, you had a hand in Siljap's...current process of change, then wouldn't you say that you have a role in its ultimate transformation for the better?"

"I cannot say that I understand your point."

"Is it possible that you are avoiding my point?"

To Asant, Yeshu's face was blank. It was not discernible whether Yeshu was indifferent, dealing with anger, or ready to interrupt their meeting. To avoid the latter, Asant said, "Forgive me, again, Yeshu. I hope you understand my purpose here, and the commitment I have made." He smiled, and again inadvertently recalled the desires and the deed that led him to meet Yeshu in the first place. He looked away in attempt to retain his focus and shake off the memory. "Kindly allow me to shift our conversation...to Siljap's current circumstances."

"What are you asking?" Yeshu responded immediately.

"Well, I have committed to...somehow assisting Siljap and its people, yet I have only simple knowledge of what is in fact happening and why. Can you help me understand what groups are involved in the fighting and their motivation?"

"I would not be the best person to do so," replied Yeshu.

"You are the best person for me, Yeshu. I know no one in the country, aside from the few I encountered along my way here, and those I know no better than I know you now." Asant stopped and observed Yeshu, while searching for the right words. "And, Yeshu, dare I say, I have no doubt that you care about the country, and probably feel it is your home." He stopped again, but this time decided to allow Yeshu the time to consider the implications.

"Either way," Yeshu said finally, "I can provide only basics. My knowledge is likely only a bit deeper than yours."

"Thank you, Yeshu! As I expect you understand from my reasons for being here, I will be indebted to you; and, while I do hope that we will work together to help this nation, I recognize that you will, of course, only do what you think is right for you...even talking with me is more than I had hoped for. Please accept my gratitude."

"You are right, more so than perhaps I generally admit. I care for this land, for its people, for its history," Yeshu said. He straightened himself in his chair, drew in a long breath.

"There are five primary groups fighting against the government, and in some ways against each other. Some weak alliances exist between two or three of these groups against the remaining groups. These alliances extend only to limited communication and perhaps an occasional cohesion in attacking a government stronghold. Aside from such cooperation, not one side has come to acknowledge any benefit from compromising."

"Have these groups been in existence for long, or have they formed more recently perhaps when the conflict began?" asked Asant.

"They have existed for a long time, awaiting their moment, carrying out random acts. There are other groups, but it is these five that matter. It is these five that have had a role in manifesting the current conflict."

"They must be established then...each with a mission and an ordained motto and name," Ismael noted.

"Yes. These five have become entities, movements, with goals and motivations."

"Did one in particular ignite the conflict, or did any two or more work together?" Ismael asked.

"My work gave them the energy, unbeknownst to me, and unbeknownst to them. Although these groups have existed and have been collecting weapons for years, it was the energy I mounted and allowed into our realm that provided them with the underlying means."

"I think I understand, Yeshu. Do you know the name of each group?" asked Asant.

"I did not before. I did not even know they existed, when, as you say, I was confronted with my anger." Yeshu stopped, cleared his throat. "You are right. Anger never begets peace." He looked away for a distraction, noticed the other patrons again, those immersed in a game of dice. His line of sight was in their direction but he looked past them into the distance. "To answer your question...yes, I now know their names."

"You implied earlier that you are also aware of their goals and motivations?" asked Asant.

"Yes, but superficially. I met only a few individuals, and even then, for short encounters, general introductions and discussions, devoid of any detail."

"How did you come to meet them?" asked Ismael.

"A friend made the arrangements. One I mentioned earlier. I did not understand it, did not understand his position or thinking. Now, I believe he was acting for the benefit of the country. He believed in me. He believed I was a servant of the Higher Light. As I said, I believe he made these arrangements to guide me into a leadership role."

"Do you think you did not understand him, or is it that you did not want the role?" Ismael asked.

"I must say, Ismael...you are direct and astute." Yeshu pursed his lips. "I will be honest, with myself and with you." He drew another long breath. "Internally, I rejected the role. From fear, lack of confidence, lack of faith." Yeshu turned again, almost looking at the patrons in the opposite corner. "Such a role would have been new to me. I did not have the courage, never did, even though I always aspired to such a role. Plus, at the time, I decided I wanted to go back to what I knew, to the relative comforts of familiarity; and, to seek the person, the woman, I wanted to be with."

"Did you find her?" Ismael asked.

"I knew where she was. I tried, just not hard enough. Lost the connection due to doubt. Really, another example of lack of faith. And, here I am.

"Again... Being honest with myself, I knew. I knew what that friend wanted. I was told that those comforts I sought did not matter. I knew I would gain new comforts, that she and I would be together, albeit later. I chose not to believe, and did not listen. Chose not to lead."

"Thank you for being open, Yeshu. I am already indebted to you. I can even say I owe you my freedom," Asant said, smiling.

Yeshu continued to gaze into the distance past the patrons by the opposite corner. "So, how do you think these five groups are relevant to this discussion?"

"Perhaps time will tell us, as long as we make the effort," Asant responded.

"Well, do you propose meetings?" asked Yeshu.

"I'm not sure. I think we should go by what you think is best," answered Asant.

"Meetings would be dangerous, considering the current circumstances in Siljap," Yeshu said.

"I think it's better to consider options, and not yet rule anything out," Ismael said.

"It's too dangerous. For one, I don't know how the government – its forces that is – will react to me entering the country. My name might still be on some list with border agents and their files."

"We're getting too far ahead for my mind," Asant said. "Yeshu, can I ask you instead to help us better understand the conflict, from a practical and current perspective. I'm not sure about Ismael, I know I don't have a reasonable understanding of it."

"I suppose. There is of course the government, working to regain complete control. It simply cannot get there without alliances, although it has regained power over ports and the economic centers. Its interests lie in security for its supporters; and, second to that, in having access to all the country's land, rather than allowing the country to be divided. Its supporters, I think, would want security but also stability and economic opportunities. This is the minimum anyone should expect from a government.

"The groups have been distinct according to their interests and geographic lines. Each wants some autonomy. One wants to be religious, another wants freedom from religion, another wants to be free from what it considers occupation and oppression, and yet another cares only about safety and security."

"Can I ask which group you met with?" asked Asant.

"I met with members of the religious group, although I didn't know it at the time. I didn't understand there were distinct and organized groups."

"What did you think of the meeting?" asked Ismael.

"Disheartening. One spoke of being ready to use the weapons they had. He said they had the ability. It was disheartening because I did not want to see violence, because I did not want civil war in the country. It seemed to be an all-around bad idea. Later on, I spoke with my friend, privately, and recommended that they not use arms. I predicted that the country would become ruins."

"How did he respond?" asked Ismael.

"His response was unclear – and I didn't push for a clearer answer. He and I have found each other since then, not in person though. He is now in a different country. Siljap is no longer safe for him. He has told me of the current situation – the chaos, the ruined cities – it is not what they wanted. Alas, it is too late for these sentiments."

"Do you still speak?" asked Asant.

"We do. Once in a while."

"Do you think he still has contacts with people in Siljap?" asked Asant.

"Likely, yes."

"Assuming he does, what do you think of asking him to arrange a meeting?"

"You mean with me?"

"Right."

"Too dangerous."

"What is? Asking or meeting?"

"For sure, the meeting. I don't know about the asking part; that might be dangerous for him."

"Yeshu, it is clear you and him care for the country, and its people. Don't you think it's worth the risk?"

"I'm not convinced losing a life is worth it. For one, he has a family, five children. It would not do for them to lose their father."

Yeshu stopped. His expression changed. Asant watched his face, saw a memory go through his mind, and pain through his eyes.

Yeshu's gaze returned to Asant. "Regardless, it is too risky to enter the country. Any of the groups, or the government, could see me as hostile to them, or they might think there is something to gain from taking us."

"How about meeting outside the country? How about here, in Vant, in Arapali?" asked Asant.

"Why? What would be our goal?"

"To be honest, I'm not sure. But we have to do something. I know I have to do something. I am proposing that you have to do something as well, Yeshu, granted for different reasons." Asant pleaded.

Yeshu did not respond.

"I think he's right," said Ismael, looking at Yeshu.

"The ultimate goal is simple," said Asant. "Peace and order for Siljap and its people. For certain, it is complex around the immediate goal, around what and how we talk with any group. Some of that we can think about and plan for before a meeting; for the most part we will have make decisions as we proceed. But it can be done, we can do it, Yeshu, as long as we remain focused on the ultimate goal."

"You sound unrealistic, unpragmatic," Yeshu replied.

"You know we're right," Asant said, looking into Yeshu's eyes. "It doesn't sound like you thought you were unrealistic when you met with your friend and members from one of the groups...or when you made the recommendation to your friend."

"I didn't know whom I was meeting. I trusted my friend."

Asant continued to plead. "And he trusted you, for a reason. Not only that, but you also considered it an idea, and your role, albeit distantly in the back of your mind. You even revisited it and wondered if you had made the right decision. Lack of faith. That's what you said."

"It is different now. We would be risking our lives. Mine. Yours. I'm not prepared to do so."

"Not necessarily. Not if we meet outside Siljap," replied Asant.

"In Siljap or outside Siljap – it doesn't matter all that much. There is too much risk. They can kill us, kidnap us, harm us, torture, threaten families..."

"I don't have any family. And it sounds like you're alone here." Asant stopped, waited. "Yeshu, I know you know that a higher cause warrants the effort no matter the risk. Trying is the minimum we must do. We must make the effort. Me. You." Asant turned to Ismael, "Ismael, if so he chooses."

"Of course. I'm with you all the way," Ismael said. "Asant is right. Risk or no risk, we must do our work. We were brought together for a reason. This meeting would not have happened if it were not right."

"Yeshu," Asant said. "You are getting a second chance!"

Yeshu looked away and did not respond. Asant dropped his head. He recalled his goal, the task he had accepted, but now felt unsure of what he could add, as if he had hit a wall.

"Alright." said Yeshu.

"Alright?" asked Asant.

"I will ask my friend what he thinks of a meeting. For now, that's all."

"And you will let us know?"

"I will let you know," replied Yeshu.

"You will be honest and forthcoming about the results of your discussion?"

Yeshu smiled. "That might just be an insult, but I suppose it's fair. Yes. Yes. I will be open and forthcoming. Meanwhile, what will you do? Do you have a place to stay?"

"Now that you mention it, we have not thought about that," Asant said, looking at Ismael. "It has worked out well since we...ventured out of our country. Without a doubt, what is needed has been provided. It is helpful to believe that this is what happens if one's goal is noble..." Asant paused. "I have learned," he muttered, then stopped himself, and decided to avoid a comparison to his attempted robbery.

Yeshu moved himself away from the table and stood up. "I am staying with my aunt in the city. She is a kind person. I would ask that you stay with us, but I feel I may be burdening her too much. But, I think neighbors in the same building have a room we could rent for a week or two. Of course, I will take care of it all, if you allow me."

"That is kind of you, Yeshu."

Part VII – The Decision

"ASANT, ISMAEL, THIS IS STORI. A dear friend, and attorney. Stori, Asant and Ismael came a long way in attempt to help Siljap. They have their reasons, as we all do, suffice it to say their intentions are good."

"Of course," Stori began, standing short and plumb, belly tight behind a pink shirt and a gray jacket. Both his eyes sparkled, leaving one to smile. A constant sparkle like that of a star, earning him his name.

Ismael interrupted. "Attorney? Are you the attorney who spoke with Yeshu before his incident?"

"Yes. Yeshu and I have worked together for years. It is good to meet you both. You know, Yeshu surprised me when he called me last week. We speak often enough, but this time the reason for his call was different."

"It is good to meet you as well, Stori," Asant said. "Your surprise is natural and understandable. But, I suspect you also came a long way from your current residence; as such I trust you are motivated to work with us."

"Yes, I am. I want to be in my country. I want the country I grew up in to be the country of my children. Siljap must return to normalcy. I will use every opportunity to make it happen, however desperate or far-fetched, except for endangering my family, my children."

"Thank you, Stori," Yeshu said. "We do want a plan that has a good chance of working."

Stori smiled. "I have faith in your strength and leadership, Yeshu."

Yeshu continued to look at Stori for another brief moment and attempted a smile. Stori's words reminded Yeshu of their relationship, the long discussions they had had, about Siljap, and about personal experiences. But at the forefront of his mind was the one discussion they had before Yeshu reported to the intelligence office, and the warnings Stori exclaimed. The seconds passed. He looked down, breathed in, and out a prolonged exhale.

"Yeshu, we will make it happen as long as we remain true to our goal and we maintain our faith." Stori patted Yeshu on the right shoulder and continued to smile. "I am here because I have faith."

"I know. And I know your faith is strong, stronger than mine. I look up to you in that regard."

"Only in that regard?" Stori smiled

"It's the only one I'm willing to admit to you," Yeshu replied, then his smile disappeared. "Stori, you came to mind, and I called you about this because, you may recall, you introduced me to a few men in your circle."

"Yes, yes, I remember."

"I want to make a point before starting, that I want us to maintain our focus on the goal, on Siljap's stability. That we must refrain from seeking power or gains."

"I understand, Yeshu. There was a time when I thought about being the country's leader, when I thought that I would be a good fit. If you wish me to refrain from such aspirations, then I will do my best to do so. Our people, our kin, Siljap, is our first priority."

"Yes. Priority. So, there cannot be wavering in this regard. In other words, we take any leadership consideration off the table altogether, even if perchance the opportunity presents itself to you. Are you okay with that?"

Stori turned his head and looked into the air in front of him.

"Stori, having such an aspiration is at odds with that of achieving stability. One is personal; the other is objective. They cannot co-exist. Each of us must commit wholeheartedly to only one goal."

Stori remained silent.

"We must choose, Stori. We must choose our goal, and pledge allegiance to it, if we are to continue this..." Yeshu moved his arm around the table between the four of them, palm facing the sky. "...this, discussion."

"I worry, Yeshu. I am not confident there is a person fit to lead the people and the country."

"He, or she for that matter, will be revealed in due time. This cannot be our concern at this moment."

Neither man said anything. Yeshu continued to observe Stori, waiting, while Stori looked through the air in front of him. Asant and Ismael, both sensed the significance of the moment, Yeshu's demand, his requirement, and how it collided with the thoughts in Stori's mind.

"You know, Yeshu, I want the best for our people."

"Of course. I have no doubt."

"But you appear to be questioning my motives."

"Absolutely not. Only our nature. An aspiration in this regard is a personal agenda; and, a personal agenda will always conflict with the people's needs."

"If I did not know you better, I would be offended."

"Please do not be, Stori. You are my brother above all, and I trust you with my life. The process of achieving peace, however, requires that we not allow even the smallest of possibilities for a conflict of interest to exist."

Stori sighed and nodded. "I trust you as well, Yeshu." He paused. "I am with you."

"Our only goal is Siljap's normalcy. No one here can have thoughts of leadership," Yeshu reiterated.

"Yes. No thoughts of a leadership role."

"Do you agree with me on why this must be so, Stori?"

"I do. I know you are right my friend. As I stated earlier, I trust you; I trust your judgment."

"Thank you, Stori." Yeshu turned in his chair and put his right hand on Stori's right arm. He then re-positioned himself, cleared his throat. "I think we need to bring a representative from each group to a high-level meeting."

"I agree. But we first need to set the agenda. We cannot allow any one of them to go off with their demands and interests."

"Right, which means we must meet with each group beforehand. We need to prepare and convince each group, and the government, in what we want and how we expect to achieve it."

"I think we should set a date, six to eight months from now. A date to bring the leaders of all the groups together for this high-level meeting. It is tight, but it might be enough. What do you think, Yeshu?"

"It is tight, but it is a good idea. It also gives us a mark towards our goal." Yeshu stopped. "Asant, Ismael, any thoughts?".

"Uhh, no, no," replied Asant.

"I think It's good," Ismael said, looking at Asant, then Yeshu and Stori.

"Excellent. Stori, then please start planning, and decide how and whom we must reach out among your closest friends."

"Absolutely."

"Do you think we can make it happen within a week or two?" asked Yeshu.

"I will make it happen within a few days. I want us to move fast," replied Stori.

"Here?" asked Yeshu.

"Here, in Arapali. It would not be safe to meet in Siljap just yet. Probably not until all sides agree and commit. Arapali is convenient and safe enough, at least relative to Siljap," said Stori.

"Relative to Siljap... so you don't think Arapali is safe?" asked Ismael.

"No. There are spies everywhere. But it is safe enough. And it is accessible to all groups, so it's better than places farther away.

"Good. Good. Stori, do your work, tonight and tomorrow. Let's gather tomorrow evening to plan."

"Excellent," responded Stori. "Where are you staying, Asant and Ismael?"

"At my aunt's building."

"It's set. Hais and a comrade will be coming in two days to meet us," Stori said to Yeshu several evenings thereafter.

"Hais? The man you introduced me to three years ago?"

"Yes."

"Does he have a leadership role?"

"Yes, and no. Yes in that people listen to him. No in that only some people listen to him. Ultimately, he can direct us to those we need to speak with, if we manage to convince him of our goal."

"Right...it will be a good start."

"I agree."

Asant was elated. He displayed a wide smile as he looked at Ismael, both nodding.

"Then let's start talking about what we want," said Yeshu. He moved toward the table in front of him, rested his elbows on it and held his hands together. "Siljap and Vant need to be under the same legal umbrella again."

"What?" asked Stori quickly, undeterred in showing his surprise.

"You know it's necessary, Stori," replied Yeshu.

"Yeshu, it's impossible. They are two countries, and they became two countries for good reason."

"They can remain two countries, but they need to be federated. They need to recognize they have the same interests, and that it's to their benefit to cooperate with each other."

"When did you come to this conclusion?"

"I've been considering it for some weeks now." Yeshu stopped and considered Stori. "Think about it my friend. They have almost identical cultures. They share a lineage and history ties them. They would only benefit from working together, as opposed to now where one is contriving against the other, smuggling weapons and spying. You know how it's been."

"Of course, I know. And I know the history, recent and ancient. But nobody, no one in either country will consider creating a relationship with the other. I don't know of anyone who would be open to that idea, never mind the two governments."

"We have to convince them, Stori. This is the only way for peace."

"It's impossible."

"It is, yes, if we don't work on it." Yeshu watched Stori for a moment with discernment, wanting to decipher his thought process. "Stori, these two countries have intertwined interests. Their economies are tied, and the people of both nations would do much better if there was cooperation between the two governments. Instead, now, they are at each other's throats, sending spies, attempting to undermine systems, cooperating with regional allies to weaken each other. Siljap's president will for sure undermine Vant's government if he ever manages to stabilize Siljap. We have to prevent this, otherwise it will be a vicious cycle."

"That may all be true. But having them consider cooperation, now, is another question."

"With consistent effort, it's really not that hard. One person at time, through the leadership ladders of the rebels and the governments. All we have to do is bring them into the same room."

"Much much easier said than done."

"Of course. It will take effort." Yeshu stopped. "Stori, think about it. Nothing else has worked yet. Siljap's turmoil is only worsening, even with the government gaining ground over the rebels. The country has had to ally with some regional neighbors against other neighbors, so the problem is spreading and it is only a matter of time until Siljap and its allies bring the conflict into Vant. Everybody will lose, more so Siljap and Vant because the fighting will be here, within their borders."

"I don't know, Yeshu."

"There is no way around it. The one way for us to quell the conflict is for Siljap and Vant to unite."

"Why? Why would that accomplish anything? Forgive me for asking, but why do you think that now?"

Asant and Ismael continued to observe and listen to the discussion, turning their eyes from one to the other.

Yeshu sighed. "Why," he said, then inhaled a long breath. "I know, Stori. I know it's hard to see, never mind agreeing with it." He looked at the center of the table in between the four of them, its innocuousness giving him the space to articulate his thoughts. He then turned back to Stori. "The first why is easy. What we have today is pinning Siljap and Vant against one another, in addition to the competing forces inside each country. It is the reason why good leaders in both countries have failed and weak leaders have resorted to tyranny. And it will only become worse. The arrangement we have today was a fermentation period for disaster. It was a monster waiting for the right moment to show its capability." He stopped, looked at the table again. "Unfortunately," he stopped again. "History has shown that it was granted that moment."

Stori, not convinced, shook his head. "That does not explain how uniting them would change anything."

"Uniting them would eliminate their need to fight each other; and it would eliminate at least one of their big excuses for tyranny. It would help them be stronger in handling the self-serving interests of their neighbors. Their economies would have better opportunities to grow, and compete." Yeshu decided these were overwhelming reasons, and stopped.

"It will not happen."

"Not overnight. Over time, yes, it will. We have to bring them together, plant the seed, guide them into a long-term plan. Ten years, maybe twenty or thirty. As long as they commit to the idea and draw the steps for it."

Stori remained quiet, hands cupped together on his lap.

"You have trusted me before, Stori. Trust me on this." He looked at Stori who in turn averted Yeshu's eyes. Yeshu continued when no response came. "As to the second why, well, you know I care about the country. I've been thinking about Siljap a lot. I have wanted to do something for the country, to help." Yeshu said, and paused to contemplate the thought. "It hit me one night, the idea. I thought about it after, thought about its impossibility, but then concluded that it is the only way. Instability, conflict, war, will continue, unless we change the nature of the relationship between these two countries."

Yeshu observed Stori and smiled. The two looked at each other for a long moment.

"As you said, Yeshu, I trust you. I trust your instincts, and your intentions."

"Thank you, my friend." He cleared his throat. "We will need to understand the interests of each group and both governments, consider and plan how each interest can be addressed, and where there must be compromise. Then we reach all the leaders, discuss the goal, and the reasons. Each will have to commit to meeting as one big group."

Stori's mouth was agape as he stared at Yeshu.

"I know." Yeshu said while nodding in affirmation. "And, as we decided earlier, that inclusive meeting needs to be eight or so months from now."

Stori could not muster any words. Yeshu looked at him and waited for something.

"We better get to work then," Ismael extorted. Asant, Yeshu, and Stori turned and looked at him, all with raised eyebrows, surprised at the interjection, and more so at him having been quiet for a while.

"Yes, we better get to work," Yeshu said.

"Forgive me, this is overwhelming my mind," Stori replied, then cleared his throat. "Yeshu, again, I trust you and believe in your intentions and vision. I need time, however, to organize my thoughts such that I am on the same page as you are, in regards to execution."

"Stori," Asant began with excitement, his tone raised. "How about discussing this with another person you know well and trust, someone with whom you can have a dialogue? Perhaps Hais? Then it would be an opportunity for you to further consider and analyze the motivation, and a plan."

"I agree," Yeshu added. "Stori, do what you need to do."

"Fair enough," Stori replied. "I only need a bit of time to process our conversation. It will help me speak with conviction once we reach members less familiar to me and the other groups."

"Excellent. Meanwhile, is it acceptable for you to arrange for Hais to meet us here?"

Stori cleared his throat. "Yes, yes. It's a good start. I will get on it today."

"Perhaps the next step, when you feel ready, would be to reach other trusted contacts and lieutenants in other groups and arrange for meetings, also here, in Arapali? And, as a preliminary goal, within the next two months, meet with representatives from all the groups as well as the government?" asked Yeshu.

"I think so...low level representatives, but yes, I think so," replied Stori, adjusting his position in his chair. "Yeshu, you know there is a risk at every step we would take?"

"Yes. Of course," replied Yeshu.

"You know at least one group, or even some individual, at least one, if not most, may pretend to be going along with the idea when in reality harbor reservations, and then turn against us."

Yeshu nodded. "I know, I know, Stori."

"That includes government officials in particular. In other words, someone, at some point may decide we're worth more as hostages. The government may fear we're spies trying to topple them. They may consider detaining us in intelligence prisons. Yeshu...they will torture us."

Asant moved in his chair and sat up. His face tensed; his heart began to beat a tad faster.

"You know I'm not a stranger to such circumstances. I've been exposed to their fears. I've been a victim of this instability and all the risks that surround it." Stori continued.

"Chances are we will be detained at some point. As it is the government who has me blacklisted."

"I know, Stori. You are right, and wise. For me, it is work we must do. We must save this region and its people from these horrors." Yeshu drew a long breath, looked at Asant for an instant. "For sure, I must." He then looked down at his gripped hands on his lap.

The other three looked at him. With plenty to digest and accept, each face expressed doubts and hesitation in a unique way, each mind trapped between his own thoughts and Yeshu's words.

"So," Yeshu said, his eyes still connected to his hands and lap. "Each of us, here, today, must decide what is right for him. As you implied, Stori, each of us must decide whether to commit to this, to the end, whatever that end may be, or to reach for a different cause." He looked up at Asant and waited.

Asant turned to Ismael, then Stori, as if pleading. At first, he avoided Yeshu's gaze. Then, his eyes locked with Yeshu's.

Yeshu's lips squeezed together; his eyes expressed kindness and sympathy, acknowledging the pressure Asant was feeling. Neither said anything.

Then, "prison?" Asant whispered. He looked away into the distance. "Perhaps there is no way around it," he muttered rather to himself.

He cleared his throat and returned his attention to Yeshu. "I came all the way, here, to meet you Yeshu. My teacher mentioned you. I am behind you, with you," he concluded while nodding, wanting to show that he is determined and committed, his lips pursed.

"I am with you both," Ismael declared, barely a fraction of a second after Asant.

The three turned to look at Stori.

"Stori, my dear friend," Yeshu said. "You have a family to worry about. Five children. Five children who need their father. I cannot imagine what you're going through. Forgive me for putting you in this position."

"We must decide, Yeshu, I want my children to grow up and know their land – their family's land. And I have a hand in what is happening today." Stori's words were slow and soft. Redness had overcome his eyes. "I may need a bit of time to consider the plan, but I am committed to the cause. I am committed to Siljap. And I agree with you. Looking through the years and decades ahead, you are likely right in that...there is no other way."

Part VIII – An Attempt at Redemption

THEY MET WITH HAIS, then with a superior; then with yet another superior. These meetings went well in large part due to Stori's relationships and familiarity with the situation. Hais, for his part, came to believe in the idea; and, decided to assist because he saw no better solution, having become disillusioned at the direction of the conflict that seemed to be without end.

"Far-fetched, but more deserving of the effort than continued bombing and killing." Hais had said. He eventually convinced enough of his group's leaders to agree in principle, and to allow for the negotiations to take place over the full eight months.

They were willing to meet with government representatives on the condition that the government guarantees safety. More specifically, that everyone from the group present at any meeting would not be pursued by the government, would not be blacklisted, and would not be imprisoned at any time during the eight-month period.

From the onset, both Stori and Hais began to build new connections and arrange meetings with members of the other groups. They both worked to highlight the potential benefits of Yeshu's preached goals; nonetheless, two groups held out, one outright distrustful of the government and the other demanding that the country be "cleansed" of the existing ruling family. The former of these refused to meet in person, insisting that the government was committed to its rule, fixed on wiping all rebelling groups, and that its spies were in Vant.

Guarantees from the government were going to be difficult to obtain. Yeshu, usually accompanied by Asant and Ismael, attempted to engage Vant officials in connecting him with Siljap officials, and for Vant to act as a host nation for such meetings. Whether Siljap's leadership was genuinely interested or simply playing along to maintain awareness of their movements was unclear. Regardless, Yeshu was undeterred at this point, in spite of his estimation that by then he was under surveillance. As a precaution, he did not speak of his connections with any of the opposition groups or rebelling individuals, including Stori or Hais.

The first meeting was with an officer from a Siljap diplomatic office in Vant, a low-level meeting with an official at a low-level office to discern Yeshu's intentions and connections. Given that a low-ranking official would be more effective in raising flags against Yeshu than in arranging a meeting with a government diplomat of import, the risk was much greater than the possible benefits. Moreover, Yeshu expected that the officer or the ensuing diplomat would recognize Yeshu's name, and would at least be curious about the purpose of the request.

An administrator led them to the officer's office door. He knocked. "Sir, your appointment," he said in the local language, and stood close to the door with his hand on the handle. The door itself was a thin layer of compressed wood. The administrator waited for a moment, then opened it.

In the office sat a man in camouflaged garb. He appeared to be on the latter end of middle age, head covered by full stark black hair. Light from the one neon bulb reflected off his hair in strange ways. The man was seated on a chair behind a large metal desk. Both he and the desk seemed to be drowning under papers and files, organized in piles but that all looked identical from where Ismael, Asant, and Yeshu stood.

The officer stood up after a moment. "Please, make yourselves comfortable," he motioned with his left hand. "Would you like tea or coffee?"

Yeshu did not flinch. He knew the local language well, understood the question, and the officer's intention, but remained silent while Asant's and Ismael's faces did not hide their puzzlement.

"Forgive me, forgive me," the officer said, smiling, now speaking in the common language. "How shameful. I should have known better. Please." He motioned again, looking at Ismael then Asant. "Jasey, please bring us tea," he said with a voice loud enough for neighbors to hear which was unnecessary considering the flimsiness of the office door.

The officer sat back into his chair, looked at Yeshu, then moved a pen from one pile to another. He continued to observe Yeshu, then brought his hands together and leaned on some empty space in front of him.

Yeshu, for his turn, maintained a neutral face and simply returned the official's gaze. He again understood the officer's tactic. He cleared his throat. "Sir, first I want to thank you for agreeing to meet with us – with me in particular – given my recent history."

"Of course, Yeshu, of course. You must understand, however, that I am perplexed, given, as you say, your recent history," the officer said, continuing to use the local language.

"Sir, if it does not offend you, may I ask that we speak in the common language?" Yeshu requested.

"It does not offend me," the officer said in the local language while looking at his desk, switched to the common one. "Now, please tell me to what do I owe this visit?"

"I wish to ask for your assistance, in arranging a meeting with," Yeshu motioned to Asant and Ismael, "and with the diplomat to Vant."

"The diplomat?"

"Yes, sir. The diplomat to Vant."

"I assure you, you can speak to me about whatever you wish."

"Ordinarily, I would of course rather speak with you, sir; however, with this matter, I must wait until I meet with your superiors."

"It cannot be done, Yeshu."

"It must, sir. It must. It involves the fate of Siljap. Our country."

"You deserted Siljap a long time ago."

Yeshu looked at and motioned to Asant, then himself moved and took out a box from between thin gray paper. "Forgive me, it almost escaped me," he said almost with a whisper, his words flowing slowly and softly. "We should have been respectful and provided you our gifts as thanks for meeting with us." Yeshu reached over the desk and gently slid the box until it was about a foot from the officer. Asant did the same, mimicking Yeshu's demeanor. "We thought you would appreciate a framed painting of our fearless and kind leader...as well as two esteemed and specially styled pens for you."

The officer picked the framed painting, looked at it with blank eyes, rather gazing into some distance beyond the painting itself. "This is good. Thank you all. Most generous of you. I will for certain hang it behind me the moment we end our meeting. It will look well next to the picture of our leader I already have."

Asant and Ismael looked up and behind the officer, indifferent to the undertones. From how the official pretended to admire the painting, it was clear he did not care for another portrait. The gesture from Yeshu was rather to intimate loyalty to Siljap and respect to its leader; and, they were common enough even in Vant.

The officer put down the painting, and smiled as he moved his hands to the box with the two pens. He opened the box, picked out one of the pens and raised into the space in front of his eyes. "This is excellent, I must say. Thank you, indeed."

He put the pen back into its holder, then moved the holder from the box and found two large bills folded underneath the holder at the base of the box. "The box is beautiful as well, hand-crafted. But, Yeshu, you should not have. I cannot accept this."

"Sir, please. It is the least we can do to show our appreciation."

"Yeshu, my friend, only if it is from your heart. Only!"

Siljap's governing body had its share of bureaucracy and hierarchy. It was akin to a ladder and its rungs. Those at the bottom were area and local officials; they were accessible but did not have a view of the country's well-being and did not make decisions. Rather, their role was to collect information from the locals and the poor while threatening and squeezing bribes. On the other hand, those near the top were unknown to the common person. As for important decisions, only the country's president and his immediate circle made them.

A meeting was arranged. It was with one of Siljap's area diplomats, but not a primary one. And, a similar dialogue ensued, where Yeshu again requested to meet with a superior, another rung to climb. Then it was another and another. It was unclear whether they were being toyed with. Ismael voiced a concern about wasting time. Yeshu, however, insisted on continuing; and, to his credit, the fifth of these meetings was different.

The subsequent superior who was also in camouflage garb did not say much, and asked short questions – why was Yeshu requesting meetings, who was working with Yeshu, how did this initiative start. The diplomat listened more, his face unchanging and blank, revealing nothing. There did not seem to be a need for him to establish his importance – his hair was plain gray; garb clean and unwrinkled. His relative silence and unrevealing expressions created a clout about him, and if not clout, then confidence, perhaps patriotism, loyalty. His tone, demeanor, and lack of need for meeting tactics stated as much. A title plaque on the wooden desk announced him as Lieutenant General Kan.

At this meeting, unlike the preceding ones, Yeshu found himself saying more, explaining, even defending his position and speaking for the better part of a whole hour. He spoke of his theory, that there needs to be a union between the government its opponents, and Vant. "It is for the fate of Siljap, its people," Yeshu said. "Even the region. If we help attain stability around us, we will be that much stronger, we will ensure our stability and our ability to thwart outside interference."

"I agree," the officer said.

"What?" Yeshu was surprised. By then, he had expected to spend more time explaining his reasoning.

"Yes, there needs to be a union. It is obvious. The problem is whether we will agree to the terms."

"Forgive me, sir. Who do you mean by we?" asked Yeshu.

"Our government. Our leadership." He stopped and observed Yeshu, not betraying his initial demeanor, still speaking only a few words and maintaining the neutral face, as expressionless as it was at the moment Yeshu, Asant, and Ismael first entered the office. "We will meet with the opposition, the so-called factions and groups. Myself, our diplomat in Vant, and two officials from the residential palace from our capital. We will allow for three meetings, in Vant, before deciding whether to continue with or to abandon this effort. And we will not guarantee anyone's safety."

"Sir, the rebels, the opposition as you call them, will not meet without such a guarantee. Two of the five groups will not even consider appearing in Vant. They," Yeshu cleared his throat. "They do not trust, forgive me, Siljap officials. I must say such distrust is warranted given the history of imprisonment and torture of all dissenters, including families. They fear your forces will detain them once identified."

"Those are our terms." The officer stood up. "I will send you word regarding time and location. We will stop our current offensive strategy after the third meeting if it occurs and only if we reach an agreement."

Vant officials agreed to and provided a venue and security for the first meeting. Two of Siljap's rebel groups participated, but they sent representatives rather than leaders. Two groups relayed their extensive distrust of all those from Siljap's capital, and that they would not attend even if a guarantee had been offered. The remaining group did not communicate.

Stori, still concerned for his and his family's safety did not participate directly but remained a liaison between the rebel groups and Yeshu – he sent messages imploring each group leader to participate, and received replies himself.

Siljap sent four representatives as the officer had stated. They were in effect the only high-level officials at the meeting; nonetheless, Yeshu, and Asant, both felt the meeting taking place was progress in of itself. That sense of progress was then further supported when the attendees planned a second meeting.

Yeshu's goal was to have leaders from all five groups attend and become personally involved in the planning by the third meeting. For this, he decided to work with General Kan and officials from the capital to make a commitment to the ultimate goal. Short-term goals were to allow aid to civilian areas controlled by the rebels and to make at least temporary security guarantees to leaders of those groups. In turn, Yeshu worked to build a rapport with Siljap's representatives, in particular with the General, by requesting independent meetings with each. Yeshu also sent word to the three rebel groups holding out that he intended to introduce the ultimate goal in the upcoming second meeting and that their participation was imperative if they wanted to take part in any future government. It did not work.

"General, I must meet with the three groups not yet participating," he said at a meeting with General Kan, where Asant and Ismael were also present.

"Yeshu, I am an army officer. My duty is to protect my country's integrity in times of war. And, mind you, my general, my superior, has stationed me in Vant to work with our allies here. I cannot protect you from our intelligence forces if you decide to go into Siljap."

"I understand, sir. You cannot accompany me, and would not be able to provide me with an escort. But, perhaps, you can draft a letter to allow me, Asant and Ismael, safe entry."

"Unlikely to benefit you. Just as I am committed to protecting Siljap, so are our intelligence units along our borders. They will want to know your intent...and will hold you."

"What if I met with them here before attempting to cross the border?"

"They are not interested in sharing the country's power structure with any of the rebel groups. My superior, through our President, has requested that we attend these meetings with you and the representatives from rebel groups. However, the President has not committed to this cause. In other words, the President has not shifted the intelligence forces' mission. Their orders remain as they have been throughout the war."

"Then I must take the risk."

"It is your choice, but please know that it is a certainty – not a risk – that you will be taken, held, interrogated, and more: for names and locations of the rebels and their leaders."

"But I don't have names, or locations. You saw who attended our first meeting."

"That may, or may not be so. What matters is that they will squeeze from you and from whomever is with you any information you have until they are satisfied."

Yeshu whipped his head to look at Asant and Ismael, recalling Asant's story. Looking into Asant's eyes, he thought it was clear that fear of such daunting prospects continued to haunt the young man. He cleared his throat, and turned back to the General.

Later the same day, with Asant and Ismael, Yeshu expressed his concern for them and for Stori. "We cannot any longer even meet with Stori. They're already following us. I doubt they would take any of us at his point, but we have to account for the possibility."

"What is our next step?" asked Ismael.

"I must go into Siljap. I will have to take that chance," declared Yeshu.

Asant observed Yeshu, allowing himself a moment to overcome images of risks and encounters with soldiers.

"Yeshu, do you think it is true what the General said, about the certainty that we would be taken?" Asant asked.

"Yes. They patrol the better part of the border. And, those whom they suspect but allow to cross, it is only because they wish to collect information about their whereabouts and destinations."

Asant took a deep breath. "I must do this with you. I'm coming with you. I must be a part of it," he said.

"It is too risky for you Asant," said Yeshu.

"I understand," Asant replied, then paused while maintaining his focus on Yeshu. He took another deep breath. "I am ready. I made it this far. It is only fitting that I continue with my effort."

"I as well," said Ismael.

"Asant, forgive me for revisiting this. But you left your country to find, well, I'm not sure what the appropriate word is, but let's say an alternative means...to find an alternative journey...bluntly, you came here to avoid jail. And, might I add, it is one thing to speak of a risk, such as being confined in jail; it is quite another to actually live it."

"Granted. But we all can grow and become stronger," Asant replied.

Yeshu gazed at him. "Asant, I'm not convinced you heard me or that you truly understand the risk that..."

"I heard you, Yeshu." Asant interjected. He spoke quickly. "Again, I like to think I've grown stronger or perhaps gained a new perspective. Take you for example, I know you have a new perspective. You were not ready to take such a risk three or two years ago," Asant said.

"Ah. You're turning the table; but, I maintain my point." Yeshu pursed his lips. "Also, we cannot meet with Stori any longer. But we might be able to communicate in other ways. And, still, we must make it into Siljap in spite of the risk." Yeshu appeared to think for a moment. "We would be more effective with free movement as opposed to being detained in some underground jail. Perhaps we can avoid being caught."

"Can we?" asked Ismael.

"I think we can, but it would likely give Siljap's intelligence more reason to suspect us," answered Yeshu.

"What do you mean?"

"When I was held, I heard a lot of talk about smuggling through the border and evading detection."

"You're thinking you would like to be smuggled in?" Ismael asked, ending with a lower inflection at the end and coming across with more of a statement than a question.

"Right." Yeshu nodded once.

"Wouldn't it be more dangerous?" Ismael asked.

"Yes. But worth the risk for our purposes. And since we have committed to those purposes, we must do what is necessary."

"Do you know anyone here in Vant?" It was Ismael again.

"No," smiled Yeshu. "You're a quick thinker, Ismael. I don't know anyone in Vant I can trust. Let me think a moment."

"Wait, what about the driver who brought us into Arapali?" asked Ismael. "He seemed good, and he seemed to have some connection to Fareez."

"Not to Fareez, but maybe to the driver from Tannis whom Fareez found for us," Asant said. "I have his card."

"It is worth a try," began Yeshu. "Asant, please contact him and ask for a tour of the area. When you're with him, broach the subject of how people are traveling between the two countries. Don't mention me or my name. Then, if the two of you feel comfortable enough, ask if he can help transport the three of us into Siljap without detection. If he is an informant or a spy, he will likely not hesitate and would be happy to do so; if not a spy, then he will hesitate considering he does not know who this third person is. Then I can explain that I am Fareez's friend, that I am not armed and that I want to effect peace. This last bit will help if he in fact happens to know Fareez."

"When should we plan for this transport?" asked Ismael.

"Ask for the tour to be within a couple of days and for the one to Siljap within two weeks."

"Do you think they can arrange for it that quickly?" asked Ismael.

"I think so," replied Yeshu.

"How about you, what will you do between now and then?"

"I will arrange for the second meeting with General Kan. It needs to occur within thirty days."

"That's too close, considering all that we have to do to get there," Ismael noted.

"True, it is a tight window, and it assumes we will manage to get back into Vant safely. We will just have to improvise and do what's necessary as we go."

The driver pointed Asant and Ismael to another man, a friend, who sent them yet to another person. It was strange having to go through several individuals to find a safe way across the border; then again, it was a time of war. Those individuals were as distrustful as one might expect, considering they had not met Asant or Ismael before. And it was not about money. They were allies with several rebel groups and were perpetually scheming against Siljap's government from Vant. They smuggled weapons, fighters, and disseminated propaganda. Asking for their help did not seem right, but Asant was open with them about the intent and the goal. He mentioned some of those involved, but not by name, including General Kan and Hais. It seemed they sent word to the rebel groups for input before deciding what to do, before even deciding Asant's and Ismael's fate.

Each of the rebel groups agreed to meet, in secret, alone. In turn, Yeshu, Asant, and Ismael, were led to a restaurant, then a restroom, given directions, later blindfolded, and taken away in a car. They drove a short distance, about fifteen minutes, perhaps ten miles, then seemed to drive off pavement onto a gravel and jolting road. The car moved slowly, jerked up and down until it stopped, and they were let out.

They found themselves at the nearby woods by the mountains. From a distance, from this one mountain's base, it all seemed innocuous, neutral, a mountain standing between other mountains, covered by evergreens just like the others, looking like one high structure. The three sensed the ground's softness and dampness, covered by millions of pointed needles and an occasional crunch of a pine cone. The hike started with one additional person, who removed their folds after they were behind the cover of the woods. An hour later, another appeared from between the trees and joined them, looking ordinary except for the machine gun straddled in his hands. Another half hour and a second 'civilian' joined them along with additional firearms, then another, and another.

Yeshu, Asant, and Ismael had no idea where they were. They knew they were now at the mercy of six heavily armed individuals. The three walked in the middle, following the man from the base and the sixth man to join them. After about two hours of hiking, of turns, frequent stops, and some hunkering down to the floor of the mountain and its forest, they stopped a final time. One of the fighters moved to the front and seemed to stand guard, then a second one followed him, crouched to the floor just behind him and began moving needles, cones, soil, then what seemed to be several brown blankets, and finally a five-by-five square foot wooden crate.

The man moved the crate and exposed empty space, a large hole. Two jumped into the hole, one after the other. One remained still on the mountain's floor motioned to Yeshu to follow, then to Asant, and Ismael.

From there, it was a single file through the mountain's belly for at least an hour, as dark as one can imagine, guided by each other's voices and the walls against their shoulders, until the walls seemed to disappear.

One of the men seemed to be moving away and making some noise whilst the others moved around and spread out. They were in a wider space.

The sound and smell of a match struck a rough surface and turned into a flame, filling the air. In the pitch darkness, its otherwise minute light appeared like a luminous source. From that light, the man lit a torch.

It was a resting point, with food and water. The group remained there for barely ten minutes before everyone stood, and helped Yeshu and the others enter a second tunnel, on the opposite side of the one they exited.

They walked – if it can be called as such – for perhaps another two to three hours, when they seemed to begin on an incline and within a half-hour could smell fresh air. No sooner, a few men helped Yeshu, Ismael, and Asant off a ladder and out into the woods. It was another mountain, covered and surrounded by identical needles, cones, and trees, as if they were in the exact same spot hours earlier, except that now they were in Siljap, on the other side of a border that defined the two countries.

Blindfolded again, they were led down this mountain, and into a car about an hour later. Within another twenty minutes, they could hear sounds of other cars moving around them and blowing their horns. Yeshu decided they were likely in an urban area.

Shortly after, they were led out of the vehicle, finding themselves inside a building, an apartment, where their blindfolds were removed and they were allowed to see their surroundings. There was not much light in the room and their eyes did not take long to adjust. A window to their left told them the day had already passed. The rest of the room was bare concrete walls, floor covered with a few rugs, and cushions where the floor and the walls met.

Hais sat on the other end. A light smile extended from his face. Two other men were sitting on the same side. All three stood up and approached them.

"Yeshu, we have not met, I am Mase. All of us here have heard much about you." The man moved to embrace Yeshu. "I hope you will forgive us for the journey we put you through."

"It is of no import," said Yeshu. "Meet Asant and Ismael. They are both here, as I trust you know, to help us all achieve peace."

"Yes." The man embraced Asant, then Ismael. The third man moved and did the same. Then it was Hais' turn.

"It is good to see you again, Yeshu!"

"It is good to see you as well."

Mase moved back to the center of the room and brought his hands together. "We will have dinner together, here. The three of you will rest, and we will talk in the morning." Mase stopped, looked around the space. "You will have to forgive us. We do not have the luxury of furniture, but we will do our best so that you are comfortable."

"I know what you are trying to do, Yeshu," Mase began the next morning. "I admire your effort. And I want to tell you, we want to take part. Not just us, but the other groups as well. Every single one of them. I must also tell you, however, that it is impossible. It will not work."

Yeshu drew a long breath, expecting such sentiments, misgivings, yet still unprepared. "Mase, my brother, we are brothers after all, we are of the same motherland, of the same age. This is our age; the future is up to us. What we speak of is impossible only if we do not make the effort. You must know, I am sure, that it is the only way."

"Ah, I am not with you on that last part. There is another way," Mase replied with a friendly smile.

"Hmm, I trust you speak of the president stepping down, and his government relinquishing power."

Mase nodded a few times ever so slightly, his eyes maintaining contact with Yeshu's.

"I know that is what you want, what you have wanted for several years now. I do not blame you. I do not blame you for losing faith and trust in the president, and in his followers, considering their ruthlessness. Nonetheless, removing him will only create one more armed group, a likely lawless faction. In the end, this development is bound to create a lawless land."

"I disagree. We will all manage and agree to create boundaries based on where our people are."

"We are one people. One ancestry."

"We were. No longer so."

"We do see matters differently. Even if you are correct, we must repair the damage, rather than extend it. If only for our children, yours, Hais', the children of all the groups. We must acknowledge that we are one people. Otherwise the fighting will continue on for generations. We are fooling ourselves in believing that all the groups would agree to any new boundaries."

"Perhaps. However, the alternative of the president along with his followers agreeing to a united government is even less likely."

"It may seem so today, Mase, but it will not be so after the next two meetings."

"You have not spoken with two of the groups. Moreover, the president has not guaranteed our security. No leader, under these circumstances, will agree to meeting and negotiating. We have tried that in the past, and it cost us heavily."

"For now, all I ask is that you stand with me when we speak with the other groups. Let us agree to the premise – that you will all meet twice – with government officials. Then, we will make plans for the security of each leader."

An entourage of fifteen armed men and women arrived some minutes thereafter, most with scarves covering their faces. Another followed within a half-hour. Some greeted each other, some were restrained and appeared tense. Mase spoke and greeted just about everyone close enough and invited a few to sit, albeit the room was humble, adorned by only the rugs and cushions. The pleasantries were short.

"Let us start," a woman sitting across from Mase said.

"Thank you, Janna," Mase replied. "Thank you for coming. It is a risk, and we are all disillusioned from carrying on further negotiations – yet you are here and I am here. Because, in spite of today's divisions, we love our country and our peoples. What is happening today is not what we wanted at the beginning..."

"We will fight to the end, Mase," one man a few cushions to Mase's left retorted.

"I know you will, Georjus, I know. You have always been brave, dedicated to the cause, and in particular that of your clan's. Your misgivings of our president are no secret..."

"Not my president. He stopped being so when he allowed the killing of our children. Children. Unarmed. Innocent. Nothing to do with our politics."

Georjus had a trimmed white-peppered beard and short hair. He wore a thick dark green jacket. Janna had a black crochet scarf on her head, showing only her hair line. They were the two leaders of the two groups who communicated their refusal to attend a meeting where Siljap officials were present.

"I know, Georjus. We will not forget. None of us will. Nevertheless, I also do not want more of my children to die." Mase stopped. "We are here because of this man," Mase pointed at Yeshu. "I trust you have heard of him. If not before these past few weeks, then from several years prior."

"We have heard of him. We heard that he left," Janna said.

"Yes, I left," Yeshu interjected.

"And now you want us to listen to you?" Janna asked.

"First, I want to say, you are here because of Asant, and not because of me. It is Asant, and Ismael, who had the courage to travel thousands of leagues to our country. It is they who reminded me how much I care for our country..."

"Not your country," Georjus snorted.

"It is my country. My heart never left it. But yes, I was a coward, and I may still be so. That, however, does not change anything. The war must stop. If we, you, are to save the children who are still alive. This war is destroying the country and everyone in it. It is not destroying the government. It is not helping you – or anyone for that matter."

"I will not surrender," Georjus said. His words were quick, tone low, coming across as a matter-of-fact.

"Of course not. No one should. We need each of you to have autonomy, but under one umbrella."

"A confederation." It was Mase.

"The one currently calling himself a president must step away from his position. That is the only issue."

"What if each of you had equal power as him, but each over a separate region?" asked Yeshu.

"Has he agreed to this?" asked Janna.

"No. That is the goal of these two meetings, to agree, and begin planning," replied Yeshu.

Georjus began to laugh, then snorted and shook his head, at once expressing his distrust and disdain of Siljap's current governing body.

"What about our security, Yeshu? They will round us up," Janna exclaimed.

"Vant will host and secure the meeting," Yeshu said.

"You are missing the point. Once they identify us, they will target us. And once they know who we are, and more importantly where we are, we will not stand a chance. They will simply fly their bombers over our heads. They will stop at nothing and will continue to kill and murder us and others until there is no opposition."

"What if we convince the president's allies to guarantee a temporary security?" asked Yeshu.

"That might work," said Mase.

"It did not before. You forget too easily, Mase," replied Georjus.

"That was then. Today is different," said Mase. "They, too, have lost too much since then. If we manage to convince their allies of this as a solution, it might just work. I am with Yeshu, if he manages that part. That much at least I think is worth a try."

"We will not go. We cannot trust him. Period," Georjus declared.

"I speak on behalf of Jey." The voice was from one of the persons standing in the back of the room. "And I believe he would consider the proposal and would listen."

"Thank you, Taylar! We are aware of Jey's efforts, and I for one am happy to hear your position. We must make the effort." Mase smiled and nodded. He turned to Yeshu. "If you get their allies to agree, then we will send a high-level representative along with our conditions. Yeshu, is this something you can manage?"

"I think so," Yeshu said.

"You THINK so?" laughed Georjus.

"I can. I can." Yeshu cleared his throat. "I have enough reason to believe the general will be onboard. He will work to convince the allies, and the president's men."

"Why should he?" asked Janna.

"He has seen too much death for one person," replied Yeshu. "He has lost too many of his soldiers already. I also believe he does not see an end to the war. Like the rest of our people, the rest of the country, he too, is having reservations about the current direction."

"Has he told you so?"

"Not in words."

"Then you have no reason to think it."

"He agreed to meet. He was the one who offered three meetings. It is an opportunity. For him. He took it."

"There is something to that," Mase said. "Still, I will not commit myself just yet. But I will commit a higher representation at a second meeting, if it is arranged...and after the president's allies agree."

"How will we know whether Yeshu succeeds in having their allies on board and guaranteeing our security?"

"Ha," began Mase. "With pigeons," he smiled. "We have a few trained ones, and we can use elapsed time as part of the message. Two white pigeons, exactly four hours apart if yes, one gray if no."

Asant, Ismael, and Yeshu were blindfolded and lead by armed individuals from Mase's group on the trek back. Asant felt hyper alert and anxious about his surroundings, listening to the sounds of those near him and the receding sounds of vehicle horns. Just outside the urban limits, he could hear additional footsteps approaching them with haste, creating commotion ahead and behind. Then, his group came to a halt.

"Drop your guns." It was a rough, low voice, in a slow tone.

"Drop yours," came a response from a somewhat familiar voice in front of him and Yeshu.

"I will not negotiate. Drop your guns or all of you will be killed," the first voice declared.

The man from Mase's group, just a few feet in front, did not move or make any sounds, and did not attempt to re-negotiate. Asant felt his heart quicken its pace, and guessed that his group's leader was considering their options. Then, the man moved and turned a few steps. Asant felt his gaze.

From a distance, on top of two separate buildings, were three snipers. One had binoculars attached to his face and was watching the incident unfold. The other two were at the ready, their index fingers by the triggers of long-range refitted guns. Behind one of the two holding rifles laid Mase along with two men by his side. All listened to the binoculared sniper, as the other turned what he was seeing into words. The decision was with Mase, of whether to act and fire.

Seconds passed. On the ground, Asant could now hear the boots of the man in front of him shuffle over the soil, moving pine cones, turning to face his counterpart.

"These men come in peace. They are working with your government to end the war. Let them be," the man said with his back now directly in front of Asant.

"The war will end when you lay down your weapons," responded the rough voice.

"Take us. Let them be."

"Your weapons, or your life and the life of everyone behind you."

"Your word you will not kill anyone here."

"You have my word, my word alone that I will not kill anyone here."

The man by Asant waited another moment, then raised his right arm and lowered it as a signal to his armed men.

Machine guns hit the soft ground. The government's men closed in on the circle; the sounds of their boots indicated their deliberate movement toward the center, toward Asant, Ismael, Yeshu, and the rebels around them. One soldier took Yeshu by the arm and led him away, two others followed with Asant and Ismael. A few others collected the weapons from the ground, and led the others from the group in a separate direction.

The soldiers handcuffed Asant, Ismael, and Yeshu and led them out of the woods, and eventually onto a road and into a van. They sat the three deep inside the van's darkened interior, obvious even with the blindfolds as all light vanished. Each was placed in something of a cell; outfitted and separated by metal sheets. The van's engine roared as they sped on.

"Asant?" asked Yeshu, his voice just loud enough to cross the metal sheets and over the noise from the van.

Asant did not reply.

"Asant, Ismael, are you here?"

"Yes," replied Ismael, from the opposite side.

"Asant?" Yeshu called again.

"I think he's next to me," said Ismael.

"Why isn't he responding?"

"Asant?" Ismael called, then knocked his head on the metal to his left. "Asant."

"Yes."

"Why didn't you respond before? Are you okay?"

Asant did not reply.

"Asant?" Ismael called again.

"Asant, did they do something to you?" Yeshu asked.

Few seconds passed, allowing Asant's silence to exacerbate Yeshu's and Ismael agitation and concern.

"Asant," said Ismael.

"Yes," Asant replied. "I feel exhausted, nauseous. I keep dozing off."

"No. Don't," said Yeshu from the other side.

"Why? What happened?" asked Ismael.

"Don't allow yourself to sleep. You have to concentrate, Asant. Think about what is going on. Think about why you came to this land! About your purpose. Pray, Asant, say a prayer, repeat it again and again." Yeshu thought back to his experience, how he decided to begin praying only two days after being inside, and how those prayers rescued him from the shadows of overwhelming despair.

Few more seconds passed. Asant's eyes were becoming increasingly heavy. Unable to open them, he drifted between limited awareness and sleep.

"I can't," he said, then stopped. Another three to five seconds passed. "I feel like I'm drowning, like I'm separating from my mind. I want to sleep."

"I understand. I know. I went through something similar. You can't allow it to overcome you. Keep your mind busy. Pray. Think about people, your teacher, Asant."

"What is happening, Yeshu?" asked Ismael. "Did they drug him?"

"No, I doubt it," Yeshu replied. "Maybe he needs food or something to drink. Or he's just sensing what's coming for us. It's going to be hard times, Ismael, especially for him."

"I don't understand. Are we going to die?" Ismael asked with a raised tone and urgency.

"We need to keep him awake, Ismael." Yeshu said. "Asant?" He called and waited. "Asant, teach me a prayer, something you use frequently."

Yeshu waited, then, after not hearing anything, "Asant, teach me a prayer." He wanted to motivate Asant, thinking a request might engage him.

"Can't remember. I can't think of any," Asant replied with whisper. His voice was barely audible and hard to hear over the van's noise.

"That's no problem. You know, I was wondering, have you been in love?" asked Yeshu.

Unseen by Yeshu and Ismael, a faint smile displayed itself on Asant's face while his head desperately rested on the cell's metal partition. "Yes. I have."

"Really?" Ismael asked with a raised inflection, surprised that Asant never spoke of it.

"What's her name?" asked Yeshu.

"Ahh." Asant seemed to be trying to muster some of his energy. "Bedan!" Asant's smile grew.

"Do you still think about her, Asant?"

"I do. A lot."

"What? But you never mentioned her." Ismael was now even louder, chuckling, incredulous that neither of them asked or discussed it before. *How could we not have talked about this?* he wondered to himself.

Yeshu laughed. "Of course he didn't."

"I tried to forget," said Asant.

"I know, Asant, I know. But not today, not now. I want you to think about her, talk to her. Say to her everything you always wanted to say. Pray with her."

The van made a turn, and then another. It came to halt, and sounds of screeching metal-on-metal announced the opening of gates. The van rolled over the gate's metal frame and inched forward for less than a minute.

"Have we arrived?" asked Ismael, hearing a gate screeching its swing. "What will they do to us, Yeshu? Is there a chance they will kill us?"

"Probably not. They will beat us, attempt to torture us. It's likely they will keep us for months but probably not years. We're too hapless to be much of a threat. These are their methods. It is universal in the prison and intelligence culture. Across the world, the universal tactic is to effect submission through fear and pain but usually not death."

"I want to think that's all comforting," Ismael said with a tremor in his voice, a nervous chuckle.

The van stopped again. Its back doors flung open and let in the day's light noticeable even through the blindfolds.

Five men, each with a machine guns and in civilian clothes surrounded the back of the van. One called out for everyone to step out with their cuffed hands above their heads. Yeshu moved first, bent down and raised his arms toward the van's roof. As he reached the edge, one of the men by the door moved toward the edge and grabbed hold of Yeshu's shirt by the waist.

"Jump down," the armed man said.

A passenger came out from the van's front. He held a gun in one hand, pointed down. He kept it by his hip, walked to the back, and handed a set of keys to the man holding Yeshu. The man holding Yeshu reached up to bring Yeshu's arms down, took the blindfolds off him and un-cuffed him.

"Go stand in line in front of that table. Wait for the officer behind it to take your information," the man holding Yeshu said.

Yeshu walked passed the van and away from it. The space in front of him was mostly open space, with random men walking with a bit of haste, focused and as if with purpose. The sun was high and bright, by then around noon.

To his right stood a small two-story square building. It seemed to occupy the majority of the space, with the entirety enclosed by a high concrete wall. It was the only building, for about a hundred yards on each side. They were inside a compound surrounded by a wall with intermittent towers. Yeshu looked up at one of those towers for some two to three seconds, then quickly moved his head down, aiming to avoid being conspicuous and noticed. He ascertained that the tower was occupied by two soldiers, both camouflaged, each with a machine gun pointed and ready to be used, and each pacing around an edge.

The table was under an open tent hiding it from the sun. Yeshu reached the space, moved into the shadow and stood behind a line of five other men, all facing the table. There were four men behind the table – one sitting and writing. About a minute later Asant reached him and stood behind him.

"Are you okay?" Yeshu whispered.

"Yes. The light is helpful. You were helpful." Asant looked around him and at the building in the center, at its windowless gray concrete, unforgiving and austere. "What is this place?"

"A jail for political prisoners. Intelligence."

"What is your name?" the man sitting behind the table asked someone, then started writing.

Ismael walked over. His forehead was tense and squeezed, showing its ridges. He looked with puzzled eyes at Yeshu but did not say anything as he stood behind Asant.

One after another, the men gave their information and were led away.

Yeshu was next in line. The man sitting was moving his body and dancing to a tune from his phone. He looked up and chuckled as Yeshu approached. "Yeshu. The same Yeshu from the Sanif prison. I did not think I would see you again," he said with a grin on his face.

Yeshu did not say anything.

"And I see you brought visitors with you."

Asant and Ismael watched as Yeshu was led away through the open space. He disappeared down a set of stairs by the side of the lone building.

A few minutes later Asant went down those same steps, led by a man with almost yellow hair, about Asant's height. The man wore slippers and sweats, and seemed to have a nonchalant attitude. Asant did not resist as the man, just second before, had stood behind him, pulled both of Asant's arms back and cuffed his wrists.

At the bottom of the steps, now under ground-level, they stood in front of a metal door, black paint interrupted only by a closed rectangular slit.

The man knocked hard with the side of his right fisted hand. The door swung open about half a minute later. The yellow-haired man led Asant into a hallway with little light, turned him right into another hallway, then left into yet another. They stood before another black metal door, except this one had an opened slit. The man handled a set of keys, ten to twenty of them united by a ring. Asant looked with despair to his left, to his right, behind him. It was a long and narrow hallway, about fifty to sixty yards, two yards wide, lined by black doors, lit by two faint yellow bulbs.

Asant's breath shortened as his heart began to beat faster, becoming louder to his ears than the sounds of slight movement he could hear. Black doors lined the hallway. A pair of eyes stared out of the one directly behind him.

"Do not look around," the yellow-haired man said. The man chose a key, entered it into the door in front of him, and swung the door out. He then looked at Asant and motioned with his yellow head in the direction of the opened door.

Asant took one short step in that direction, then looked back at the man now behind him. The man waited barely two seconds for Asant to step farther in; then, with his left arm and without himself moving shoved Asant deeper into the cell and slammed the door. He turned the key to the sounds of multiple clicks.

"Do not talk with anyone. Be clean. Cleanliness is everything here," he said looking through the slit before disappearing. The sound of his slippers sliding on the floor filled the hallway.

Asant turned one hundred and eighty degrees, away from the door. It was a cell, with a high unreachable ceiling. A window, barred and glassed, somewhere above, allowed some light in. The space seemed to be split in half. Almost the width of two stretched arms. One half, just in front of where he stood, had a hole in the ground, and a lone dark yellow rusted faucet. The other half had something of a bench, or rather a concrete slab from end to end, about the length and width of an average man. Two disheveled dark brown blankets rested on it.

Asant turned right and faced the concrete slab. He stared at it as if attempting to accept it as part of his reality. He then turned again to have his back to it, and sat. He looked around the space, at the walls, at the window, his breathing still shallow and fast. He tried to think, to talk to himself. No words came. His mind shocked, paralyzed as he gazed at the walls – dark, scratched, lined, marked. His mind struggled to see, to discern, but saw nothing – not the lines, not the marks, not even the darkness.

There were too many conflicting thoughts and emotions. He felt humiliated, embarrassed, and self-conscious, even though no one was there to see him. Moreover, with the loss of choice from being confined, he felt life being sucked out of him, mounting his anxiety. And, he felt confused about how he came to be in this space, confused in spite of the warnings he had received and the concessions he had made.

The confusion, the pressure of being inside these walls and behind a locked door, forced his tears, forced his mind to look away and hide in his hands. He cried for minutes, then spread the two blankets, laid on the slab, and slept, going deeper into hiding.

Teacher, do you see where I am?

Pray, Asant, as you have learned with me. Every moment you feel fear, pray, and think of the One. Answers and strength will come to your mind.

He awoke hours later, hearing noise coming from the other side of his door, his now living space. A few moments after, a man extended a hand through the slit, holding a bowl. Asant looked at it, surprised, unsure what to do. Then it hit him. This was his meal. It was mealtime. Brown beans and yellow potatoes. His mind battled with accepting the bowl and the food in it since it would mean accepting the walls and the black door as his new reality.

He took the bowl, but could not eat its contents. After a few minutes half an orange came his way. It was a cross-section – one of the brightest oranges he had seen in his life. It was sparkling. Its juice reflected and magnified what little light there was. It felt like it had come from paradise – a connection to life, to hope.

It was all done within minutes, and he was back looking at the walls, which were now even darker, with less light coming through the window, except now the lines and the scratches were becoming visible to him. Numbers. Names. Different languages. He made out a word, then another. The names of the months. There was counting. Lines counting days.

This is not good, he thought. *Being trapped, by other humans, a punishment, unwarranted punishment, stealing freedom, stealing one's life, one's choice. It is cruel and inhumane.*

The night's darkness came. He slept. His body, shivering, woke him. It had turned much colder within an hour or two. He moved underneath one of the two blankets and left the other one between him and the concrete. Another hour passed before he was forced to move underneath the second blanket.

He stirred with the incoming light and cried. He looked at the faucet, knelt closer, turned it and watched drops of water fall into his hands then down the hole in the ground.

He washed his face. Sat back on the concrete. Someone knocked on his door, handed him bread and jam.

Days passed. Seven identical days. Then, on yet another one of those days, he heard keys clank against the metal door. It was morning, the first meal had not yet been delivered. This was different. A few clicks, and his door was opened.

Come, motioned a man on the other side.

Asant became elated. That was it. He paid the price, and now he was being forgiven and moving on. He smiled, breathed, moved toward the door, looking at the man as if they were equal.

The man reached over Asant's head with an elastic and a blindfold, and covered Asant's eyes. The world turned dark again, and with it the life in his lungs turned against and imploded. Then his hands, in front of him, were tied together.

The man, whose left hand held Asant's right elbow, led him through corridors. He took a step down, possibly through a door's frame, up some steps, outside through crisp air, up another set of steps, and then more walking, likely in a hallway.

"Don't move. Wait here," the man said in the common language as he pushed Asant's shoulders against a wall.

Asant stood, silent, his breathing racing again. He waited and waited. At least ten minutes passed. Each minute brought a new thought on what was happening, and what was about to happen. He saw those thoughts behind the blindfold as he envisioned freedom. He would then be interrupted by thoughts of pain, horror, and torture. He struggled not to imagine what he once perceived as unimaginable.

He heard footsteps and tried to listen to the gait, but there was too much noise in his head. It was the same man who took him out of the cell. The man took the blindfolds off, knocked on the door immediately in front of them before opening it.

A man in a black leather jacket sat behind yet another metal desk. It was wide, larger than the average person's reach. He wore a brown sweater that covered his neck. The jacket's leather was synthetic leather. The man's black hair was combed to the back, reflecting light. Two couches lined the walls on the sides. The man seemed focused and busy writing. He looked up at the guard next to Asant but did not make any gestures. The guard stepped away and walked out of the office. It seemed automatic. The man returned to writing.

Asant looked at him, puzzled and wanting to understand what was happening. His eyes darted around the desk and the papers below the man's hand. Afraid to look around the office another time, he looked down instead, saw his hands in front of him, united by a chain of shiny metal. The floor had plastic-looking white tiles or what must have been white colored tiles at some point...now dirty and discolored.

"Why are you here?" asked the man behind the desk.

"Sorry, what?" asked Asant, jerking his head upward.

The man looked at Asant and did not ask again. He waited.

"Here? Where?" asked Asant, then added. "Sir."

"I want you to start on the right foot. And, so you know, I already made Yeshu tell me."

Asant frowned, unsure what to think, unsure what the man wanted him to say.

"Come," the man said as he motioned for Asant to approach the side of the desk. "Lean down here." He swiveled on a black chair, looked down at Asant and opened his right palm, as if ready to strike a slap. "Do you know how to read?"

Asant, nervous and confused, did not hear the question; nonetheless, reflexively he wanted to show respect and simply nodded. A part of him thought the man asked whether Asant understood the consequence of not cooperating. "Yes," he said.

"Go back to your spot," the man said as he motioned to the center of the office.

Asant walked back and waited.

"What do you see?" the man asked.

"Sorry, what do you mean, sir?"

"Don't play with me."

"Sir, I don't understand, honest."

"You said you know how to read. Are you now changing your statement?"

"Read?" asked Asant, his eyes moving, attempting to revisit the moment that just passed, attempting to understand. "You mean palm reading. No. No."

"You will have to be truthful with me if you want this to work."

"Sir, I misunderstood. I truthfully misunderstood what you were asking me."

The man's face was blank, virtually a portrait without emotion, without expression. Asant, could not help but stare back. He was desperate to understand, to speak the right words. He then looked down at the not-quite-white floor.

"Very well," the man said. "I will see you again."

Asant heard the door behind him open. The same guard from earlier stepped in. He covered Asant's eyes with a blindfold and led him away.

Back in the same cell, Asant sat on the concrete slab, over the blankets. Without intending to, he stared at the markings and the scratches on the wall in front of him. Thoughts that he could handle his circumstances crossed his mind. His mind traversed and skipped from one memory to another. He recalled that he was taught everything had a reason, then he recalled some of the conversations with Yeshu about Yeshu's experience. He also thought of Ismael most likely being in the same predicament, maybe even across from him. He stood up, moved to the door and looked through the slot, tried to scan the hallway. He then looked to the door almost directly opposite him. A pair of eyes appeared in the middle of that door's slit. They stared back at Asant, but they were neither Ismael's nor Yeshu's.

"What is your name?" It was a question asked in a language unknown to Asant. Asant shook his head. The person's eyes seemed to recognize the issue. They moved a bit, then the person asked the question in the common language. "What is your name?"

Asant cleared his throat, relieved at the slightest possibility of communicating. "Asant," he said, then paused. His mind otherwise blank, he wanted to ask a question but did not seem to have any.

"I'm Jey."

"Jey!" Asant repeated and tried to smile.

Jey smiled. "Don't worry, you will get used to this. It's not so bad, unless they beat you. I suppose. But don't worry, really. It will be okay. Other jails are much worse than this one. It will be okay, Asant." Jey smiled again. "Why are you here?"

"Umm..." Asant tried to answer. He turned his face away from the door's slot, looked away from Jey's and began to breathe faster.

"It's okay, Asant, really, don't think about it my friend. We are now neighbors," he smiled. "You can tell me later. We will keep each other company. Me, this is not my first. All the times have been because I carry a book, a book of laws through which I espouse peace." Jey's eyes smiled again.

"You're here because of a book?"

"Effectively, yes. I'm a political prisoner." He looked at Asant, perhaps waiting for a reaction.

"Meaning you speak against the government?"

"No. I speak for peace. I gather my countrymen and promote the rule of law which unfortunately the government finds threatening."

The two heard clanks and multiple slow footsteps from around the nearest corner.

"Talk to you later, Asant," Jey said. He then stepped away from the door of his cell, his eyes disappearing into darkness.

Asant tried to look at that corner, the corner that hid the source of and the reason for the noise. *Probably food.* He thought. *The first meal.*

Another few identical days passed. Asant counted each one, learned from the markings on the walls to keep track, for no reason other than to keep count and maintain some connection to the world.

"Hey, Asant," Jey whispered from the other side.

Asant stood up and moved to the door.

"How are you, neighbor?" Jey asked, with a smile.

Asant looked at his neighbor's eyes but did not answer.

"Oh c'mon friend. Be objective. First off, you're alive. Second, I'm sure that interrogator will see you again. Remember, they want to scare you into thinking they will keep you for a long time; that's why that interrogator hasn't seen you a second time yet. Trust me, they have too many prisoners to keep people like you here."

"Why would they want to scare me?"

"They think you will talk and tell them what you know if you're scared and worried. It's their game." Jey's eyes smiled and moved as he nodded. "This is how it works."

"But I don't have anything to tell."

"Doesn't matter. They will push your buttons until they're satisfied they have everything from you. Just be consistent. Don't change your story, otherwise you give them more to question."

"What about my friends? Do you think they're here?"

"How many?"

"Two."

"Did they bring you in together?"

"Yes."

"Then they're here. Probably somewhere in this corridor, in a cell like yours, or maybe like mine and without a window – if they want to give them a harder time."

A man in civilian clothes, a guard assumed Asant, came to the door the following afternoon. He led Asant the same way, through corridors and stairs, all while blindfolded. Then, he told Asant to stand and stay still.

Asant obeyed. He did not dare move and periodically took in only short breaths - the back of his shoulders touching a wall with each hesitant inhale. After a few minutes, he allowed himself to lean on the wall.

"What are you going to tell me today?" It was a man's voice, three to four yards away in front, but Asant couldn't tell if it was the same interrogator.

"About what, sir?" asked Asant.

Asant heard abrupt movement, a chair scratching the floor, then hands hitting metal. "Are you playing with me?" the man screamed. Startled, Asant's body jerked and bounced forward off the wall.

"No, no, sir, of course not."

"Who sent you here?"

"Where, sir?"

"Are you stupid?" the man's voice was lower.

"No sir, I don't understand your question."

Asant heard quick footsteps and then a hand hit his face. He felt his cheek burn and sting. His mind went blank. "I don't have time for games. Either you talk or I keep here for ten years, twenty if I decide I don't like you."

Still in shock, Asant did not hear the words.

"TALK."

"Yes sir. Please. I will cooperate."

"Good." The man seemed to step back to where he was. "Who sent you to Siljap?"

"No one, sir, honest."

"Why did you come?"

"To help the country, sir. To help stop the war."

"What?"

"To help stop the war," Asant replied, in a matter-of-fact manner.

"Stop the war?" the man snorted once and laughed. "You are stupid."

Asant heard a chair move against the floor somewhere to his right. The first man did not say anything. Someone grabbed Asant's right elbow and led him away, through two sets of stairs, then the corridors. He took the blindfold and the handcuffs off Asant, and pushed him into a cell, a different one, one without a window.

Asant stood in the cell facing the inside wall with the door behind him. He looked at the end of the cell and then to his left. It was as if everything was the same. The same concrete slab under two disheveled brown blankets, the same hole in the ground, the same faucet except this one was trickling drops and had remains of a pink soap bar below it. He turned, looked at the door, then through the slit. He was on the opposite end of the corridor. A pair of eyes looked at him, waiting.

"What's your name?" the eyes asked.

"It doesn't matter." He moved in the cell, looked at the same blankets, moved and folded the top one, as if working to prepare the cell as his new accommodation. Underneath the second blanket, on one end he found a rubble of small rocks and broken concrete. He let the blanket cover it and moved to the opposite end closer to the door. With that part of the concrete still exposed, he saw white powder with trickles of blue that smelled like fresh spring.

"Hello. Neighbor?" Asant whispered through the door.

"Yes?"

"There is some washing detergent here."

"That's good. So, you have extra powder for washing your clothes, and it keeps away roaches, other insects, even mice." The eyes smiled. "Never thought of that, huh?"

"No. I suppose not."

The eyes smiled, then disappeared.

He sat on a blanket over the concrete slab and stared at the wall. There were, again, etched numbers, and the same names of days and months in various languages, some he recognized, some surmised. He even made out a few names of angels. There were some prayers he knew. It led him to think about praying, then about the teachings he'd received – about life, about the purpose of life. He closed his eyes and tried to separate himself from his physical body and its desperation and fears.

But, a loud knock at his door, metal on metal, echoed and interrupted his attempt. An unfamiliar pair of eyes looked through the slot in his door. They came across as rather neutral, not angry or mean. "Stand up, move to the back," the eyes said, while the man behind remained quiet.

Asant did as he was told. "More interrogation?" he asked.

The door opened. A man in civilian clothes, rather plain and unremarkable, stood next to it. He motioned for Asant to step up and turn. He put on him a blindfold, then pulled him to turn around and cuffed his hands.

Asant waited, anxious about what they wanted from him, anxious to appease and be released. He wondered if it would be the same interrogator, if perhaps he could explain that he only wanted to help Siljap.

"Who sent you here?" the interrogator with same voice asked moments later.

"I told you, no one. I came to help." Asant waited, then asked, "Sir, may I please take off the blindfold?"

"Why?" the interrogator asked without pause.

"So you can see my eyes, so you can see I'm telling the truth."

"I don't need your eyes to know when you're telling the truth."

"Yes, sir, of course not. But it would help, so I can talk to you."

The interrogator did not respond. From behind Asant, dry fingers touched his cheeks and pulled the blindfold off. Asant looked in front of him and saw the same interrogator from the first round looking back at him.

"Who sent you here?" he asked.

"Sir, honest, no one, I came..."

"Take off your slippers and get down on the floor," the interrogator stood up and motioned. "Down on your stomach. Flat."

Asant looked at the floor, then back at the interrogator, not understanding what was being asked. The man behind him pushed him down, ordered him to lie down.

"Feet up," the interrogator commanded.

Asant lied on the floor, bent his knees backwards, and before he could think, he heard the air move. The stick from the man's hands sliced through the space and met the soles of his feet with a burn. He held his breath, did not want to scream, but could not help it. At some point, the man started to count, "One, two, two, one, two, three..." until he arrived at ten.

The man then commanded him to stand up. Asant pushed himself off the floor, but as he tried to straighten up, the pain from his feet led him to careen back toward the floor. The man with the stick held his arm to stop him falling.

"Stay on your feet, or I will make it twenty."

He did not take Asant back to his cell. Instead, he led Asant to a foyer. It seemed to be in the middle of the building, with no ceiling. The floor was tiled. Night had arrived, bringing with it a brisk cool air.

"Take off your slippers and walk barefoot. Back and forth, thirty times. It will help with the swelling. And count out loud," the man said, then disappeared.

In the cell, he found he could not stay on his feet. He kept his socks off, bent his knees, and held his feet to the cold concrete, eventually falling flat and going to sleep.

"Pray and meditate, pray and meditate, pray and meditate," he whispered to himself the following dawn, awaking hours before the first meal. His chin hit his chest, hands clasped on his lap. "Pray. Pray. Teach me to cope. Help me see. Help me understand. Help me understand. Help me understand what I must do. There is a reason. There is always a reason."

The interrogator called for him again three days later. Another beating of his feet and his back followed an undesirable and wrong response from Asant. Then, in the cell's darkness, he went under a blanket, lied down, covered his head trying to hide and willed himself to sleep.

He woke to pain in his body, his back, arms, and feet. He felt throbbing in his toes and in the soles of his feet and was not able to stand. His mind took him back to the first beating and then walking on cold tiles after in the sky-lit foyer. He recalled how the coldness of the tiles helped abate some of the pain. The thought reminded him that the concrete in his cell underneath the blankets was cold too and could be as helpful. It did not disappoint.

A day passed in the same fashion, then another. With some of the swelling subsiding, he decided he needed to prepare for another similar session with the interrogator. He realized that his statements were unlikely to change the interrogator's mind and tactics.

He thought that it was up to him to learn – perhaps even to learn to somehow withstand pain – to somehow harden his feet. He thought of the rubble, the rocks and broken concrete at one end of the slap. He wobbled and paced around the cell in short steps. Then, using his knees, he pulled himself up onto the slab, leaned on the wall, and moved to its end, on those rocks, at first with only one foot on the flat unbroken part of the concrete, left shoulder and arm leaning while trying to hold onto the wall. He willed his body to stand straight, and he tried to step and walk on the rocks, wanting to let the sharp points poke and break his skin and the remaining swollen spots. It caused him more pain...to wince with each touch, with each point. For once he was glad he was by himself between the cell's walls and darkness, allowing him to hide his face from the rest of the world.

By then, nighttime provided further cover, as only minimal artificial light from corridor lamps entered the cell through the door's slot and hinges. It was usually quiet by then, with no one being transported to interrogation and no food haulers in the corridors, allowing the softest of sounds to be heard. It came from behind him, from the wall. He ignored it, thinking it was a hallucination, or that perhaps it was the rocks under and around his feet. He continued his endeavor, walked faster, lifting his knees higher, attempting to hit the sharper points with that much more force, keeping count of each step with his fingers.

"At least one hundred steps," Asant whispered to himself. "Must learn to withstand pain."

His mind tricked him into skipping numbers.

This helps, he thought. *I will do this a few times every day.*

He bent down with care, feeling his back was not ready for a quick move, and managed to sit sideways on the slab, knees bent almost to his chest, feet still on the rocks, left ear now touching the wall, resting his head.

There was the sound again. It was easier to dismiss it earlier as nothing, but now it was so close to his ear...what sounded like a knock. Knuckles on concrete.

He moved his chest and head sideways and pressed his ear to the wall. There was a person trying to say something, trying to communicate.

"Hey. Hey," Asant heard.

At first, he did not want to acknowledge the sound, or the person, fearing it was against rules and the possible consequences of breaking those rules. But curiosity, and excitement, hid that fear.

"Yes?" Asant whispered.

"Tomorrow. At this time," the voice declared.

"What?" It did not make sense.

"At this time tomorrow, we will get out."

"What? No. I don't want trouble," he replied.

"It will happen."

"You're crazy. You will cause me to be beaten again, maybe killed. Please stop."

"Be ready. Be awake in case we need you."

"No. I don't know you."

"You don't need to know me. We need to get out. We need to change this country. That's all."

Asant thought for a moment, about the jail he was in, its interrogatory purpose, and the condition of the country. "What's your name?"

"Doesn't matter."

"Yes, it does." Asant paused and thought for another moment. "Why are you here?"

"Come on. Same reason most of us are here," the voice said. "Tomorrow. This time. Be awake."

"What do you mean this time? How can I know what the time is?"

"Five hours after the last meal," the voice responded. "Count. I will knock when we're close. Stay awake."

Asant waited for more words, but there were none. He looked at the space around him, at the walls, asking them for an explanation, for guidance.

The night seemed to move on without him. His mind would not let him sleep, instead forcing him to gaze into the darkness above him, the ceiling somewhere beyond it. He tried to turn under the two blankets to one side, then to the other.

What would I do? He thought. *What could I do? It's not in my hands.*

That's not true, that's never true. I have a choice. I can choose with whom to work.

But how can I work with people I don't know.

I am here to help effect peace. I must choose peace.

It's between two sides. Two sides. Doubtful either side will put peace above all.

Yeshu. I wonder where he is. He must be here, unless they took him somewhere else. But if he is here, and if my neighbor is right, then he would probably be freed tomorrow, maybe then I can work with him again.

It is a risk.

Of course.

Peace. I must remember no matter what, peace is my aim. I came all the way here, to a foreign country, a foreign people. It is the path I chose. I chose it. I must see it to fruition.

His eyes closed, allowing his consciousness to travel elsewhere. He saw Yeshu in the distance, by a large body of water, perhaps a lake or sea. It was nighttime, dark but not completely. He went to Yeshu and stood by his side on the lake's edge, both entranced by the opposite end, beyond the water, beyond the horizon.

Bulbs of lights stretched over the water, hanging down from a cable, a string of yellow stars connecting the two ends. The lights increased, seemed to move back and forth with the water's waves.

"I must leave to that end, Asant," Yeshu said, looking at Asant.

"Why?"

"The land is devastated. I can no longer change it from here, from this side."

"What should I do?"

"That is your choice, as always."

A heavy and loud knock on the metal door startled him. Asant opened his eyes. It was the first meal. He moved his head, looked around the space, trying to understand where he was, willing his mind to recall where he was. There was another knock. This time louder, heavier.

Sounds from the men in the corridors receded. Asant decided that they started to move away from the door, on to the next cell.

He got up quickly as he did not want to be without food. "Wait," he said.

A man dug into a large barrel in the hallway, grabbed a boiled potato, put it in a plastic white bowl, added a spoonful of orange-colored jam and a piece of white bread. He took a step back toward Asant's cell. Asant took the bowl, looked at the food and put it on the blanket.

Yeshu is leaving, he thought, putting a piece of bread with little jam into his mouth.

To where?

Who knows...doesn't matter. He's leaving. Is he leaving Siljap?

What do I do?

I will have to talk to him.

There won't be time if this all transpires tonight.

I will have to decide.

Time – the seconds, the minutes – seemed erratic, sometime passing in chunks, sometimes seeming to not to move at all. The second shift came, also with a startle, catching Asant frozen in perpetual analysis. Guards walked through the corridor and looked through doors. Two men passed bread. It all seemed unimportant and secondary.

What if they interrogate me today? The question crossed his mind. *Doesn't matter. They're too occupied with the revolution and the war. An escape won't cross their minds.*

But what if they know?

Can't do anything about it from in here.

I should be prepared.

He took to stationary walking, over the rubble, then over the concrete, counting the seconds with his fingers. He found himself between the blankets, flat on the slab, almost seeing the ceiling. His eyes closed, sleep crept up on him.

Once, again, he found himself startled, jumping off the slab.

Interrogation, lieutenant, the words screamed in his mind. But it was the evening meal.

I can't sleep again.

He left the white bowl on the blankets and did not eat. He could not think of eating, and instead Asant took to stationary walking and began counting again, the seconds with one hand, minutes in the other.

An hour passed, then a second, and a third...as promised, the knock came.

"Are you awake?" the voice asked.

"Yes," responded Asant. "Who are you?"

The voice did not respond.

"Tell me your name," Asant requested, to no avail.

The final hour passed with his head in his hands and his eyes in line with the floor tiles.

A knock on the metal door led him to look up. On the other side was a pair of eyes, trying to see into the cell. A set of keys clanked. The eyes seemed to be looking down, at the keys, searching, trying one after the other, until one fit and turned. The door swung open and a man motioned for Asant to step out.

Asant followed the instruction, hobbled out of the cell and waited at the door's frame, looking at the man's hands, wondering if he would be handcuffed and blindfolded. Neither happened; instead, the man motioned for Asant to follow.

With Asant limping, they passed the cell directly adjacent, its door also open. They went through the corridor, turned right, and stopped at an open door. Another black door with a slot.

The man walked through the frame and disappeared. Asant looked in. It was a deep room with about thirty or so men all sitting on the floor on blankets, in three separate circles. Two light bulbs hung down from a high ceiling and lit the room. Clothes, underwear and shirts, all hung on ropes on the wall throughout most of the room. A couple of lines extended across, from one wall to another, the clothes on them hiding parts of the room from view.

Asant remained still, looking at the first circle of men directly in front of him, trying to guess what was happening. The men exchanged turns speaking. They were intense, focused, asking questions, making short statements and appearing to be making suggestions.

Some soft noise came from the corridor behind him. Asant was still near the door's frame, wanting the ability to exit the room if necessary. With his shoulders stooped in a defensive posture, he turned to look. Two men walked in. After a few seconds, there was a fourth man, with Ismael directly behind him.

Asant's eyes and mouth opened wide from disbelief. He did not immediately recognize Ismael.

He made his way to Ismael and surrounded his arms around him, embracing him, resting his ear on Ismael's head.

"I'm sorry, so sorry," Asant said.

Ismael smiled, his arms around Asant's back. "Don't be. I chose to come, remember?"

"It's incredible seeing you." Asant said while still holding Ismael. He moved his head back, looked into Ismael's eyes with the light reflecting off a bulb in the room. "More than you can imagine."

"You too!" Ismael replied. "I have much to tell you, Asant."

"I can imagine. Me too." Asant smiled, now looking more at his face. "I'm not sure we have that chance just yet...do you know what is happening?"

"No."

"I'm almost positive the man who opened my door is not a guard, I haven't seen him before." Asant thankful to see a trusted friend. "Are you alright? Did they hurt you?"

"I'm alright. We should find out what's going on though. Can we walk in here?"

"I don't know," responded Asant. "Nobody is stopping us, though."

"What about Yeshu?" asked Ismael.

"I haven't seen him since they brought us to this place." Asant thought for a moment. "Maybe we can ask someone here."

"He is here," Ismael declared, right arm extended, pointing to the right of one of the crossing clothes lines. "Look deep into the room, at the other end by the right corner."

Yeshu, like all the other men, was also on the floor sitting on blankets, outside the circle nearest him, his back against the wall. Another man was next to him, appearing to be slightly elevated by sitting on rolled up clothes. Both seemed to be silent, lips still, eyes on the group near them.

"Should we walk over to him?" Ismael asked.

"Of course," replied Asant while maintaining his gaze at Yeshu. "We're here, inside the same room, behind the same open door, just like these men. We need to find out what is happening...don't you agree?"

"I do. I doubt we have much to lose anyway." Ismael stopped and turned to look at Asant. "Asant, before we go, can I ask you where you stand?"

"On what?"

"On Siljap."

"You mean in regards to my original goal, my reason for coming here in the first place?"

"Yes."

Asant turned and observed Yeshu for a while. He thought for a long moment. "I am committed, Ismael. Committed to helping the country. I don't think I can abandon it now, in spite of what happened to us...how about you Ismael? What do you think is right for you?"

Ismael drew in a breath then heaved out a prolonged sigh. "With honesty, Asant, it has been a strange journey for me. With that said, it has also been rewarding more than anything else. In comparison to my life prior, I feel I have a purpose. And I feel it is an honorable purpose. I cannot say the same of the work I did prior to meeting you....and Yeshu, do you still feel you need to work with him?"

"With Yeshu? Yes. Absolutely. I trust my teacher at home. He pointed me to Yeshu, even though he did not give me a name."

"Things can change!"

Asant thought for a moment. "True. Still, I'm convinced Yeshu has to do this work, at the minimum he has a large role in it. In fact, to that point, I had a dream last night, that Yeshu was leaving. It wasn't clear though to what end. I think we need to find out what he's thinking. And, even before that, find out what is happening right now."

"Agreed."

"Very well." Asant began to limp in Yeshu's direction, traversing the first circle of men, who continued their focused discussion. Ismael followed behind.

Yeshu noticed the two men moving between clothing items, bending below the lines, approaching the corner he was at.

He stood up and walked over, smiled, and embraced each of them. "Come, come. Let's sit here," Yeshu said, pointing back to the corner. "This is Jey. Jey, this is Ismael. And Asant I believe you already met."

"Jey my neighbor?" Asant asked, surprised.

"Jey your neighbor," Jey replied, standing, moved to embrace Asant, then Ismael.

"There are so many questions, Yeshu."

"It's a revolt," replied Yeshu.

"Can you tell us what is going on? Do you know what is happening?" Ismael asked.

"A revolt? They're planning an escape?" Asked Asant.

"Yes, except it's more than an escape."

"More than an escape?" echoed Asant in surprise.

Ismael turned and surveyed each group. "They're rebels, government opposition," he said.

"Yes."

"All of them?" asked Asant.

"All of them. The ones in here, in this room."

"And the guards?"

"Tied up behind locked doors in solitary cells." Yeshu stopped, then continued after seeing Asant being puzzled and lowering his eyebrows. "This room is considered less of a risk, so they use two men from here to sweep the corridors after the final meal. And, after weeks of cleaning, the men here learned the guards' schedules and conspired with one of them to overtake the others."

Asant thought for a moment about the prospect.

Ismael nodded. "It must have taken some coordination with others from outside...I imagine, if anything, they will have to complete this tonight," Ismael said. "Before the break of dawn, before the next shift."

"Exactly. That is what they're planning. They want to do it within a couple of hours, before two o'clock."

"But the towers, the snipers...is there a way out through some tunnel, underground?" asked Asant.

"Not that I know of. They will have to handle the snipers. They will need people from the outside because they won't be able to access the towers from inside. There aren't any weapons inside the building itself, at this level at least. The guards inside this level never carry firearms. It's a well-designed prison – for people like them – for militia and political prisoners, to control revolts."

"Is there a good chance?" asked Ismael.

"Of what?" asked Yeshu, "of succeeding? Small, I suppose, but I'm not sure that matters. To these men it is worth it. They planned for it, and there are just enough of them imprisoned together to have created the opportunity."

"They must've delivered a message to their group," Ismael commented.

"Yes," Yeshu grinned. "Somehow they did. Perhaps someone was released."

"How about you, Yeshu? Where do you stand?" asked Asant.

"Ah...I'm against it all, Asant. I want to negotiate, not take a side like this," Yeshu replied.

"But negotiating has not worked," commented Ismael.

"We don't know that. I've been able to bring up some issues with interrogation officers."

Jey leaned forward. "Yeshu, my friend," he chimed, "you know that has an even smaller chance of succeeding than this revolt. Interrogation officers were playing with you, going along just to get names."

"Maybe. Playing now. But with time I would get to them, get the message across to higher officials. No matter what, either they would have released me or sent me to higher officials for more questioning."

"They could have kept you here, Yeshu, for as long as they wished, even if all they wanted was to teach you a lesson," Jey said.

"Who knows, it's all plausible," Yeshu said. "But I know I will not carry a firearm. I know I do not want to take part in any fighting. Revolting means I would have to. Armed fighting is not the answer to this conflict."

"I am with you on that, on not carrying arms," Jey said.

"So," began Asant, turning from Yeshu to Jey, and then back to Yeshu, unsure if he wanted to ask the question. "What are you planning? Will you leave the compound?"

"If the doors open, I will leave, yes. But not with the others."

"Leave to where?" asked Asant.

"I don't know."

"Yeshu, are you willing to share your thoughts? I'm sure you've thought about it," said Ismael.

Yeshu looked up at Ismael, considered the man's face for a few seconds, then thoughts from the days prior revisited him. "In truth, I don't know."

"Are you willing to share what you think your options are?" Ismael asked.

"Good question, Ismael," Yeshu replied, then took a long breath. "I suppose one option is walk around the country, without aim." He stopped, looked at the blankets under him. "Perhaps Corseeca would be a place, a new home."

"Leaving? You're considering leaving?" asked Ismael with reproach and surprise, his voice and tone raised by reflex.

Asant looked at Ismael then turned back to Yeshu, sharing Ismael's surprise and dismay.

"You cannot leave, Yeshu. Leaving would be giving up, quitting. And, arguably, that is as bad as you claim the war to be. It is not a solution," Ismael retorted.

"It's a lost cause."

"Saving a people cannot be a lost cause."

"This is our country, Yeshu," Jey jumped in. "He is right.'

"Yeshu, if I may," began Asant. "I agree with Ismael, and Jey. But also, another point – if you believe you had a hand in what has become of Siljap – then you cannot escape your responsibility to change the course of this tide."

He did not reply. Yeshu maintained a neutral face and stared at Asant.

"This is unbelievable," Ismael huffed.

"Wait. I think we can make it work, but, like you, yourself said, Yeshu, only if we make the effort," Asant said while maintaining eye contact with Yeshu.

Yeshu maintained his expressionless face and gaze at Asant.

Asant decided to take advantage of the opportunity. "I think," he continued, "together we can work on it..." Asant's voice began to shake, he stopped and moved his eyes, interrupting his eye contact with Yeshu. "We must do it, Yeshu. And I think you know how."

No one said anything. After a long moment passed, Jey interrupted the silence among them. "What are you talking about?"

"Yeshu knows," Asant replied.

"He might, I don't. Please explain," Jey said quickly, exasperated, his words trailing each other.

"Look, Jey, without doubt you've heard the story about Yeshu, about his role in this conflict," answered Asant.

"Sure, most of us have. It emboldened many, but it is a story. A legend. He has become a legend."

"Well, it is true," Ismael said as a matter-of-fact.

"What do you mean it's true?" asked Jey.

"It means Yeshu at the very minimum contributed to sparking the conflict," Ismael replied.

"What are you talking about?"

Ismael turned to Yeshu and watched him, as if waiting for a response.

Yeshu turned to Jey. "I am disheartened, but I am not ready to abandon the effort. I want to travel to the other realm, work from the other side. Jey, sometime ago you mentioned to me you had contacts in the religious circle, remember?" he asked.

"Yes..." Jey began to reply, unsure of the point. "In the capital."

"No. The ones just outside the capital, in your neighborhood," Yeshu said.

"In Raad? You mean the Drakes?" asked Jey, squeezing his eyes and forehead, unable to hide his dislike of the word.

"Yes," answered Yeshu.

"Yeshu, I know of them, where they are...but you know I am practical, and I don't believe in their work."

"I know, but I also know you are an objective and open-minded person." Yeshu said. "If we get out, would you be willing to connect me with them?"

"To what end? What would I tell them?"

"You would tell them my name and that I would like to work with them."

Jey looked at Yeshu, his eyes moved sideways, left to right, attempting to discern what he was hearing. "I don't understand, Yeshu. I am pragmatic and a realist. Their work is ethereal. I don't believe in it. It would not help anyone here. Why would you want to meet with them?"

"Because this conflict is deeper than what the eye can see and what the mind can discern. I believe we need their help. Please do this favor for me."

They heard a pop, a bullet, muffled by the walls and their underground position, but clear enough to leave no doubt. A round of bullets followed, then another round in response. Then more of it but from the opposite end of the compound.

Asant's eyes moved from Ismael, to Yeshu, then Jey, hoping for reassurance. Yeshu and Jey seemed to be taking turns looking at the door and the ceiling, as if expecting information to come from either, perhaps a sudden appearance at the door revealing the outcome of the gunfight or footsteps above indicating a breach.

Instead, after those few rounds, silence befell the space such that one could hear an insect buzzing in the room. Everyone in the room was quiet and still, staring at something – at the door's frame, or the floor – in attempt to concentrate and hear what was otherwise inaudible.

Seconds passed, then minutes. A man, from the middle circle, stood up and moved around the room and began pacing. After more quiet minutes went by, he walked to the door, stepped through the frame and into the corridor. With his back to the room's entrance, he turned his head from side to side, looking in both directions for some sign, then turned right and disappeared.

The others, still in the room, looked at one another. There was banging on one of the doors. First, it was the sounds of hands on metal, then some hard object.

The man who had gotten up and out of the room came back into it. "They're here!" he yelled, then shut the room's door.

Bang! An explosion echoed through the underground, sending debris through the corridor and smoke into the door's slit.

"Let's go, let's go," the same man was yelling through the smoke, opening the door and motioning for others to move.

"This is it," Jey said. "Let's go, Yeshu."

They heard several pairs of loud footsteps and voices in the corridor. There seemed to be running and rushing all around the compound.

Yeshu turned to Jey, "I will wait until everyone is out. You go ahead, Jey."

"What?" Jey retorted.

With the smoke abating and settling, they could make out three figures, but the faces and heads were covered with black cloths. The three figures rushed into the room.

"I will not join forces with any side," Yeshu said. "You go ahead, Jey, please. You are one of the leaders. You must regroup. It is different for me."

The men in the room seemed to scramble, picking up items. One by one, they ran out of the room.

"You will not be joining any side, Yeshu. It's a matter of surviving. They will bring this place to rubble. The country is at war."

"I will walk out after everyone else in this room exits and escapes the compound, and before they bomb it. Don't worry about me."

Jey turned to Asant and Ismael, looking for help. Both looked back with puzzled eyes; both speechless.

"Fine," Jey turned back to Yeshu. "We will walk out together, the four of us."

"No, Jey..." Yeshu began to reply.

"I will wait with you. You will need me to introduce you to the Drakes, remember?"

After a few minutes, an unmasked and unarmed figure walked into the room between the other three. "Jey," he yelled. "We must leave. And we must meet with our group."

"I, we...we will wait another two minutes," replied Jey. "Taylar," his voice became stern and commanding. "Meet me at my meeting spot in Raad this morning, at eleven. Please invite Murthi to meet with us in two days, at his favored location."

The figure, Taylar, watched and surveyed the men with Jey and measured each one. "Murthi the Drake?"

"Murthi the Drake."

Taylar remained still for a split second, then nodded. "Be careful. We will wait another five minutes. You must leave before then."

Part IX – Another Attempt

THEY MADE IT TO Raad - to Jey's spot. It was inside a one-story plain and unfinished structure; its walls, inside and outside, were exposed concrete. It appeared deserted.

"Siljap is an incredible land," Jey started, a sparkle in his eyes. "This place, the building across from us, is over three thousand years old, Yeshu." He pointed through what would have been a window, toward a distinctive structure about ten yards on the other side of the dividing alley. Yeshu stood, waited behind him, along with Asant, Ismael, and Taylar.

"What is it?" Asked Ismael.

Jey turned to look at Ismael. "A place of prayer," he said, smiling. "You will see, in no time."

"What about Murthi?" Yeshu asked.

"Murthi?" Jey squeezed his eyebrows together. "Murthi, Murthi the Drake." He looked at Taylar. "He is inside."

The five of them, standing below the concrete ceiling, looked out through the gray unpainted wall and through that square hole that once may have been a window. Jey took the first step and walked between the two columns holding up a side of the structure and out to the alley. The others stepped forward one at a time, flanked by Taylar.

They stepped through what would have been a door's frame onto yellow ground, onto the unpaved alley. Light-colored walls on each of its sides rose to the height of perhaps three average men. The space appeared devoid of green, with only one or two trees behind the walls, some branches just reaching over the tops of the walls.

They walked towards one of those walls and stood opposite two metal doors locked together, inscriptions adorning each from top to bottom in a language Asant had not seen before. Jey, face expressionless, knocked on the dark brown metal. Then, with his eyes transfixed on the doors, he waited.

"Yes?" a man's voice from the other side.

"This is Jey. Here to see Murthi," Jey replied.

"Murthi? There is no Murthi here."

"Taylar arranged for us to meet with him. He is here." Jey said.

"This is Taylar. I spoke with Murthi two days ago. We agreed to meet here with his group at this time."

There was no response from the other side. There was nothing. No sound, no steps, no voices. They could not hear anything. Then, they heard sounds of a chain being moved against the door's metal. A key was being inserted into a lock. Asant and Ismael turned to look at each other, reading one another's thoughts and apprehension, both thinking it strange that they heard nothing except for the sounds coming directly from the other side of the door and against the metal.

A bar around the middle squeaked against the door, then another near the top, and yet another at the bottom.

One of the doors swung open. A man shorter and much thinner than any of them stood about two feet on the other side. There was a lot more greenery in the foyer than Asant anticipated. The soil between the white tiles allowed several plants to sprout into the air. The man held the open door with his left hand, a shiny silver wrist-watch contrasted with the door's dark brown.

Asant took in the man's stern face and thin frame. Straight gray hair accented with white covered his head. His forehead was arched, eyebrows thick and pronounced and separated by a thin nose with a pointed end. All together the features created a longish face. He wore a short-sleeved button-down shirt that was yellow and striped with crisscrossing gray lines. A brown withered belt held up a pair of gray pants. His appearance told of a civilian life-style and attitude.

"Where are you coming from?" the man asked.

Yeshu leaned sideways to show his face. "I would like to work with Murthi and his group."

"Who are you? What is your name?" The man asked.

"I'm Yeshu. This is... "

"Yeshu?" the man interrupted.

"Yes."

"You are Yeshu?"

"Yes."

"Can I speak with you, Taylar?" the man motioned for Taylar to cross the frame. "Wait here for a moment," he added, to the others.

The man led Taylar about five steps to the middle of the foyer, asked questions while pointing at the door, then at something else in the foyer they could not see from where they stood. Taylar appeared to respond in an almost identical fashion, pointing at the door, then behind and around him. The man nodded with each motion, then the two of them motioned at the four of them standing outside.

"Let's go," said Taylar.

Jey moved sideways and allowed Ismael to step over the threshold. Asant stepped in next, then Yeshu. Jey followed behind them.

"I'm Fodall, come." He guided the group farther into the foyer, toward yet another door, one that was much wider and taller. It rose above the height of at least two men. It had a half-circle at the top, all of it covered with art and more inscriptions. Fodall struggled to pull it toward him. When he did, the opened door revealed a space barely lit, with numerous dim light fixtures spread throughout on the walls and hanging down from a high ceiling. The men stepped in, then waited for their eyes to adjust. The room was at least fifty steps deep, with writings, drawings and frames covering all four walls. There were benches by and parallel to the walls, followed by columns, chairs, and some structures near the middle of the room.

"Murthi and his group are downstairs," Fodall said to Taylar, while Asant, Yeshu, and Ismael glanced at the nearest wall with focus and interest. Fodall noticed and said to them, "You can look around if you'd like, before we go down."

Asant moved closer to the wall to his right. The sitting space was something of a bench and extended almost the entire length of the wall. It was covered with a long red rug. On top of the rug was a wool runner. The wall's paint was barely visible. It was busy with hangings, fabric with drawings and writings foreign to Asant, sculptured bronze and silver, wood carvings, and more red textile. It was a busy room.

The same drawings appeared in many of the hangings, outlines of hands, writings on the palms, an opened book, candle sticks, and more writings leaving virtually no empty space.

Walking to the adjacent wall, Asant found a similar pattern, and again on the next wall. He stepped to the middle section, and noticed a green see-through fence about a foot shorter than him. It was an enclosure, protecting a large white marble. Looking over the fence, at the marble, he discerned three distinct paragraphs, each in a distinctly different language.

Fodall saw Asant standing by and staring into the enclosure. He walked closer to Asant. "It's his grave," he said.

"Forgive me. I am not familiar with any of these languages. Whose grave is it?" asked Asant.

"Our prophet. The city's first prophet."

"First prophet. From when?"

"From his reincarnation into our city, somewhere between five thousand and three thousand years ago."

"Reincarnation? So, he has been here more than once?" asked Asant.

"Yes, of course. But in this city, only once, as far as we know."

Asant observed the marble, then turned to Fodall, questions and disbelief in his eyes.

"Let me show you the lower level, where the prophet slept and studied." Fodall motioned for Asant to follow. Ismael and Yeshu followed.

"This is now a prayer site in his honor. It was where he lived and worshiped," Fodall said while walking.

They walked along the right wall, on rug after rug, each with a different shade of red, each with unique blue and white shapes and figures. A few yards ahead, Asant saw two columns, white, likely marble. A light fixture was on top of each. There was a step up between the two columns and an arched entry way without a door.

As they reached the entry way, Fodall stopped, bowed, and moved his right hand in some odd but specific pattern.

"Come," he said, smiling.

One at a time, each stepped into the space. It was a square room about ten feet on each side. Its walls not as decorated but appeared royal with alternating black and white granite with tall golden light fixtures in the corners with an engraved golden frame on one of the walls.

Fodall stepped to the right, walked through another archway and motioned for them to follow. They stepped down a round set of stairs and then reached a fork. Fodall walked into a chamber to his right.

"This was his chamber," he said, his voice shaking a bit.

In contrast to every other inch they had noticed, the chamber was plain and simple. The walls were covered with white plaster and nothing else. On two of the walls there were indentations of sorts, where windows may have been had the space been above ground level. One indentation had a piece of wood on its base, and a bronze cup in the exact middle with an ominous and still flame in it, the wick not visible. Another bronze cup with a handle was near the edge on the same wooden ledge.

The walls merged at the corners with arches beginning low, extending and gradually protruding away from the walls to a ceiling that lay low enough to be within reach for any of them.

Fodall appeared to be in a trance. A few minutes passed before he moved and stepped out. "I will be with Murthi in the other room," he said.

Yeshu, Asant, and Ismael observed the space for a while longer. Their minds were clear; all three entranced by it in spite of the lack of ornamentation.

"Shall we join the others?" Asked Ismael.

Yeshu turned, smiled. "Yes, probably a good idea to start our work," he said.

The three stepped over the threshold, out of the simple space, and now facing another entrance with the steps they had come down to their left. A drape hung from the ceiling directly ahead, acting as a door. Yeshu led the way, moved the drape and crossed the frame, into another room that was distinct yet again.

It was a circular room. About ten to twelve men were sitting by the room's wall and on a cushioned floor. Jey, Taylar, and Fodall were among them. One of the men stuck out because of his size, his head towering above the others. He looked too familiar.

Asant recognized him. *The guard. The guard who told us about Yeshu's uncle.*

In the middle lay a collection of a few pieces of textiles and small cushions that were neatly organized into a circular pile two short steps wide. It was unclear whether something else was in between and under. A golden plate lay on top of a golden column in the center, a lit lone white candle on it.

The men for the most part sat close to each other with their arms and shoulders touching, but with empty space for three or so to Taylar's left. A bearded man sat to his right. Taylar motioned for them to enter and sit next to him. The three moved across, passed the pile and sat down.

It was quiet. Asant and Ismael looked around, wondering what was happening and whether this was to be a meeting. Yeshu was focused on the pile in the middle.

One of the men picked up a piece of shining wood that was sitting in front of him. It appeared to be a musical instrument, strings extending from end to end. The man began to play a tune, a simple but absorbing melody. A few moments passed, then another man stood up, and moved in a circle around the pile with the tune's rhythm, moving his head and midsection, up, down, up, down, in a bowing motion.

Ismael looked around the space and noticed a discomfort in Jey's face. Feeling uncomfortable himself, he turned to Asant and Yeshu and instead saw open eyes and engrossed looks from both. He looked at Jey again.

Jey changed his expression, shook his head and pursed his lips. He did not accept the environment and now seemed determined or resolved. He turned to his left and said a few words to the bearded man, then stood up, moved to the entryway, made a slight bow, and exited.

Ismael followed with his eyes, looked around at the others, at Yeshu and Asant, then himself decided he was too uncomfortable and wanting to leave. He stood up and followed Jey, avoiding the man near the pile and doing his best not to disturb. Back by the drape, at the room's entrance, he looked back at Asant and Yeshu. Asant smiled, then went back to looking at the man with the instrument and the man moving in the middle.

The man in the middle continued to move, bow and dance, in a circle, in the middle of the room. Another man stood up and began to move in the same pattern, except that this second person added a chant. He said a word foreign to Asant, bowed, then the word again.

The two men moved one behind the other. They bowed and stepped forward together as if on que, in rhythm along with the second man's voice.

Asant's eyes were fixed on them. As he watched the two move, he noticed something move between them, a long cloud, a wave. He focused on the same space exactly between the two moving men, watching the wave oscillate.

"What is that?" Asant wondered.

"Keep watching, Asant. Give it more time." It was Yeshu's voice.

A third man stood up, moved to the middle, and followed behind the other two. Asant's eyes widened. The cloud, the wave, seemed to grow and extend to the third man; its oscillations seemed to have the same rhythm as that of the men, their bodies, the chant, and the sounds from the chords.

The men spread out a bit. They allowed more distance between them. Asant continued to focus on the wave. It grew in length and thickness as it extended behind the first man to the second and third man. Its whiteness contrasted with the rest of the space, with the men, with the textiles and the pillows.

The chants grew louder. The chords strung higher notes. The men's movements became more pronounced. The wave – little by little – grew even more in length and thickness. It came to touch the walls and the ceiling, all the while maintaining its form as a wave, maintaining the same rhythm. Asant, not having any expectation of this gathering, closed his eyes, then lost track of time. He continued to hear the chanting and gradually felt the wave itself oscillating with the same rhythm as the chant. Distinct from the wave and the chant, he felt someone move and sit to his left, where Ismael first sat. Yeshu leaned closer and whispered.

"Asant, look in the exact center, through the wave, at the candle's flame."

Asant opened his eyes and saw something dark hovering above the flame, a sphere circling around itself. Numerous sparks of black, in the thousands, shot from it and towards it, and yet did not affect its spherical appearance.

"That is strange," Asant said, his voice coming through a slow tone. *"It looks like a black ball, but at the same time looks empty."*

"It is empty," Yeshu replied.

"How can that be? What is it?" Asant asked.

"It has something to do with the problems in this land," Yeshu replied.

"In this land? Is it connected to what you did?"

"Of course not." Yeshu focused on the center. *"It has been there...here...for many generations, for most of man's existence. It was created here. But, as for my part, without knowing, I gave it a large enough opening to overwhelm our space."*

"I don't understand, Yeshu. I see an empty and blank space. And a cloud surrounding it. It's a cloud. Smoke. From the men dancing. That's all I see. How can smoke be the cause of fighting and killing?"

"Not the cloud. The cloud is protecting us from it, right now. Think about it. Smoke disperses, correct? But watch the cloud being a wave. It's doing the opposite. It can maintain its form."

"And the thing in the middle?"

"The thing in the middle is different. It is a void. It can destroy us all, everything, if we allow it. If we act without intent. When we react to our vices."

"It's not doing anything to us."

"True. That's because for us here we have a layer of protection. We are looking at it through a shield."

"The men?"

"The Word. Combined with our intention to withstand it. Out intentions manifested in the chant, in the sounds."

"I don't understand. I don't understand the connection, to anything. I don't understand why we're here."

"That's okay. You will. The understanding will come to you. Be open to it. We will need you. We will need every person in this space. We will need your strength. Your intention."

"To do what?"

"To resolve it. To resolve the darkness. What you see is the opposite of energy. It is devoid of energy, devoid of life. A void, and all a void can do is take, persistently and eternally."

"From us?"

"From everything alive and near it, from anything that has energy, until it is resolved. We – man, men – we take when we lose life from us. We begin to fight when this grows to overwhelm us. When we react to anger, for example, we take."

Asant's expressed no thought, his face was blank as he stared.

"You see Asant, we began it. Man began it and allowed it to continue. Today we feed it. We – men, humans – feed it every moment, every instant we succumb to it. The sparks you see around it are exactly that. It pulls on us humans, takes from us, until we give in and look to replace what it took by taking from others, from other humans. That is conflict. Our immediate response, without contemplation, is violent. That creates conflict. When it's thousands of us, it is war."

"So, we must resist?"

"We must resist, yes, but that is not enough. It's all very strange and simple. It's strange because ultimately it will always defeat us; it will always succeed. We may resist at first, but it will get to us sooner or later. Because we owe it, because we created it. Long ago, we created it, caused it, here in this region. Thus, it is men who must address it, here, in Siljap. At the same

time, it is simple, we just need to resolve it. We need to resolve its beginning."

"Is it that we must understand what happened?"

"Yes and no. We have an idea what happened. It was a murder. Theft of life. Theft creates a void because it breaks a cycle before the cycle is complete. The void is the incomplete process. That we know. But we don't know what to complete, we do not have the mental capacity to know. So, we need to discover and learn that part."

"One murder?"

"One murder."

"How can one murder do this much harm?"

"Think, Asant, about the long past. A hundred years ago, there were fewer people. A thousand years ago, even fewer. Five thousand, even fewer. And so on, to the point when there were only a few conscious humans. Murder has a magnificent effect at a time like that. An effect that has persisted and perpetuated with every human birth since then."

"If it's so long ago, has anyone tried to address before us?"

"Many."

"And, they failed?"

"We failed. Men. Us, in our past lives."

"So, can we, us, in this life as you imply, manage it?"

"You can imagine, it would take tremendous work on our part. It can be done, but, with honesty, I'm not yet convinced we can."

"That doesn't make sense. Why are we here then?"

"There is work for us. There is something we can and must do. We can start the process. We can do our part. Maybe before, the timing was not right. Maybe that is why we failed in the *past. Regardless, today we must try again. At the minimum, we must stop the problem in Siljap. It is feeding this void."*

The two, along with everyone in the room through the cloud, watched the center persist in its motions.

"What will it take?" Asant asked.

"I'm not sure. Hundreds of thousands of people. Or, perhaps, the right souls, those focused and connected enough, those of us less hampered by vices. For now, we do our part. And we will learn what it is that must happen over the next few days."

"We're going to be here for a few days?"

"Yes."

"Without food?"

"Without food. Without water. Just us, the chords, the wave, and... it, the void."

"Will our bodies survive?"

Yeshu chuckled. *"Our bodies will receive what is needed."*

"Have you done this before?"

"Not exactly. But you have, at least in some part, probably with your teacher's assistance."

"How can you know that?"

"You would not still be here if your mind was not trained."

"But how about you? If you haven't done it..."

"I attempted it in a past life. My mind has enough from the past to sustain itself.

"Let's move closer, into the wave."

Murthi the Drake, Asant thought. *How can I know that?* He wondered to himself.

Murthi the Drake joined the chant from his spot. The others, one by one, joined in as well.

"You can do it Asant," Yeshu said. *"Repeat what you've been hearing."*

Asant opened his mouth, took a deep breath in, and tried to make the same sound he had been hearing. He felt his body shake, and wanted to open his eyes, to see if he had some control. He wanted to stand, and to leave.

"Stay, Asant. Do it again, this time gentler, slower, with the rhythm," Yeshu instructed.

Asant caressed his mind with accepting thoughts, willed his body to breathe, and returned to silence. He stepped closer to the wave, then felt his body reject the notion. It reverberated and repelled away from the center. He allowed it a moment's rest, then willed it to inhale another slow breath. His confidence and comfort grew as he felt it regain its composure, and he attempted the step toward the center again.

He felt each eye fill with tears, then looked to his right and saw Yeshu wearing a faint smile on his face. Somewhere nearby was Murthi the Drake whose face shone brighter than the rest; even his beard appeared brighter and more white than Asant remembered. The rest of the men completed the circle. They moved and hovered as they closed circle. All of their faces were focused on the center with a smile transfixed on each. They were in unison, moving with short steps, one after the other, in the same rhythm, closer to the center, into the wave.

Asant's body shook another time. It was a rather violent convulsion that brought him images of his physical reality, and of desperation to open his eyes and look around him.

One thought remained and spread in his mind like liquid spreads on a surface.

"Do not worry, Asant." It was Murthi the Drake. *"We will protect each other. Together, we have a much better chance."*

I cannot. This one thought was now the only one in Asant's mind, taking it in and absorbing it like a sponge. *I will collapse. I already feel nauseous.*

"Focus, Asant. Focus on the center. That is all," Yeshu said.

"But I can't. I just can't," Asant replied.

"These are unhelpful thoughts. They are the sphere's, the void's, not yours. Look beyond them."

Asant saw the center sphere expand. The sparks around it grew in size and reached beyond the wave.

"Yeshu. They are outside the wave. They will destroy me."

"No, Asant. Those are our fears and doubts; it reflects and magnifies them in our minds. Remember, we are here together. We will not allow any harm touch any of us. We will do only what is for us to do. Only what is in our power."

"But there is no guarantee. The others can fall and be hurt. The wave can breakdown. We will lose our bodies. We will die."

"Do not allow it to plant doubt. This is its own doubt and fear, not ours," Murthi the Drake said. He seemed to be speaking to everyone. *"This is the only way it can continue to exist."*

"It is its doubt. We will not allow it to infect us." It was the guard.

"His name is Jame. Jame," repeated Asant, smiling in his mind as he realized that he did not know that before.

"Take my hand," Yeshu said to Asant.

Jame moved closer to Asant's left and reached for Asant's free hand.

Their strength grew with their unity. They became one group within its own closed circle, encompassing and containing the void. Murthi the Drake stepped forward, pulling the two men next to him, holding their hands. Others followed suit.

Asant did as well, then he turned his head, looked behind him, saw his body sitting, legs crossed, chest upright, face still and eyes closed. He could see anxiety in his own face. His eyes were squeezed shut and eyebrows were closer together than normal. His eyelids were wrinkled and his cheeks were raised.

Relax. Asant thought as he smiled to himself. *I want to be here, with these men. I want to do this. My teacher knew I could.*

He turned back to look in front of him, at the center, at the void. The wave still between the circle of men and it.

The men, led by Murthi the Drake, took another step, then another, and reached the edge of the wave. The wave was not disturbed. The chanting continued with the same rhythm. The three first men who started the wave were still physically moving. They continued with their motions, perpetuating the rhythm.

Then, the men entered into the wave with a fourth step. They stood inches from the first three men, and were virtually in the middle of the wave, in its heart.

"Our work here is to contain it," said Murthi the Drake.

"Shouldn't we resolve it?" Asant asked, with a rush of energy and excitement. Wondering, asking the question,

reflected how he was feeling in that instant, the instant after crossing the edge of the wave.

"That is not our work." It was Murthi the Drake again. *"It is for others, those yet to come for that purpose."*

"But we can. We should. We are here. We should." Asant replied.

"We would fail, Asant. We were not made for that. It is not our purpose. Our work is to prepare for the next stage."

"But..."

"We are to make the effort to contain it and its seeds of fear. The darkness in Siljap is rooted in it. The same fear and agitation you felt earlier. We will be able to address the violence only once we contain it."

Murthi the Drake took another but shorter step, deeper into the wave, becoming one with the three men. The others followed. Asant felt a resistance that pushed him in the opposite direction, but now his confidence and connection were stronger. He stepped forward with the others, and the feeling of resistance was quick to abate.

Asant focused on the space in front of him, beyond the wave, trying to understand the black sphere and how it sourced difficulties, how it planted fear in him. But he saw nothing. Renewed unease crossed his mind. Bewildered and worried, he looked in both directions at the other men, wondering if they felt the same thing.

"Am I the only one feeling it?" He asked.

"No," Yeshu said.

Each of the men felt resistance as the void pushed at them. Asant felt it grow stronger, pushing him from the center. At the same time, it seemed to reach his eyes, his mind, displaying to him images of pain. He wanted to cry, seeing violence, explosions, killing.

"It is the conflict, Asant. It is what is happening in Siljap." Yeshu said.

"But it's too much."

"Yes. It is the accumulation of hundreds of years, hundreds of cycles and generations."

"Why? Why so much of it?" he asked.

"We have become overwhelmed, blinded, fighting over our languages, our religions, even over the shade of our skin and the shape of our eyes."

Murthi the Drake took a step sideways to his right. One by one, the men followed. Together they took another step, and another, in concert circling counterclockwise around the center.

"We are consciousness in this plane. Our intention is our tool." Murthi the Drake chanted. *"Our intention is our tool."*

"Asant, we need to be in focus. The conflicts and the fighting are with us, today. Here, now, we are working to unbind men from its grasp. We are working to stop the violence."

"Can we?" Asant asked.

"If we maintain our focus...if we, as men stop reacting to unfounded fears and instead choose to make our destiny."

"Yeshu, Murthi, the violence is overwhelming..." Asant commented.

"Remember," Murthi the Drake began, *"all of these are tools. Language for communicating, religion for enlightenment. Our skin, our eyes, our noses, help us with the elements. See beyond this illusion, Asant. In this circle, we need to be one. We are almost there."*

The men continued to move counterclockwise, in rhythm with their chanting. Except for Yeshu and Asant, the men moved together, as if in slow motion. They bowed, moved their left legs back and sideways, then the right, raising their arms, bowing again, humming, breathing, and humming.

They repeated the same movements in unison, acting more as one with the ending of each sequence. Yeshu recognized the pattern. He managed to join and follow and ultimately move himself without thought. It took Asant longer, he managed nonetheless, as the wave, the rhythm itself had pulled him into itself, helped him join the others.

By mid-evening, hours after they had first knocked on the metal door, the men were one form. There was one circle – one encompassing cloud – around the darkened sphere. It calmed the darkness, reduced the sparks and the flares that surrounded it when they started.

On the upper level, Jey and Ismael walked on the rugs, alongside each wall. They admired the contents hanging on the walls and the intricate symbols and drawings.

"These are ancient walls, Ismael," Jey exclaimed.

"How ancient?"

"We do not know exactly. They are at least three thousand years old," Jey replied while maintaining eye contact with one of the frames and its writing, unwilling to let go of it. "I worry, you know. I worry we will lose these."

Ismael turned to look at him, managing to capture the enormity in Jey's thought. "You haven't lost them yet."

"This structure – the doors, the walls, the frames, the writings – all point to the significance of this space, they implore us to protect it, to protect this spot, to show our appreciation and honor the higher power. In truth, it is us who need its protection and assistance. It is a gift to us. You see, long ago, when The One and Only, created this planet as a home for man, certain spots – locations of great energy – were also created. But this energy can be used for good, or for harm. The One and Only gives to man to do as man wills." Jey interrupted his focus. He shook his head sideways, then made short slow steps away from the wall and to the center, moving closer to the green fence.

Ismael remained silent. He wanted to grasp the import in Jey's thoughts, and moved only his eyes to follow Jey.

"We must end this war," Jey said. "Or it will consume us. It will consume the country, its people, its children, its future, perhaps even pulling the region into the conflict like a whirlpool pulls down anything daring to touch even from its fringes."

"How? How can it end?" Ismael's question was abrupt. His voice led Jey to look up.

"We must recognize our common foundation and common interests. We must put aside weapons and..."

"Don't you think that is hypocrisy," Ismael interrupted, "considering that your men carry weapons?"

"The men and women who work with me are my family. They are my comrades and partners, my brothers and sisters. They are their own individuals and lead their own lives. They are not mine, as you say. Moreover, we do not carry weapons. No one in our group resorts to violence."

"What about the men who broke into the jail? The men who rescued you, and Yeshu, and me..."

"Not members of our faction; although I must admit I have been working with them, but it is to reduce the violence, to use weapons less, to convince them of the futility brought on by firearms."

"Jey, they set you free!"

"They did not. While they do know me, I doubt they would have come for me. They came for members of their faction who happened to be in the same compound. The walls came down, and I chose to walk out. It would have been ludicrous, foolish, to reject such an opportunity."

"Why were you jailed?"

"We do not resort to violence. We use truth. The truth. Along the way, we sometimes anger the controlling faction."

"I think I understand. One other point, I hope you will forgive me. The truth can be subjective, wouldn't you say?"

"Never. There is one truth. The rest we choose to believe as truth, or we choose to subvert or deceive to achieve personal desires."

"It all sounds too idealistic, Jey."

"Perhaps. But we can raise our standard only when we have ideals and aspire to them."

"And practically, how will these ideals – of no weapons, of no violence – help you? How is it that you believe these ideals will save Siljap and its people?"

"Simple. Once again, we must recognize our common foundation and history. You see, Ismael, the people in Siljap have a common lineage. We all come from one family. It is nothing more than brother fighting brother. It has been so for ages." Jey stopped and watched the green fence. He became distant, as if his mind was in another world. "Ah, we seem to forget our history and what violence and conflict cause. A vicious lesson we do not learn."

"I understand the conflict has been on-going for generations. But had it become a war before?"

"Oh yes, many times. I have witnessed a few wars in my lifetime, but those were with less destructive weaponry. Each time – each war – it gets worse. There were several uprisings as well. There was one uprising about four years ago. It was quashed quickly within a few months. The last war happened about twenty years ago, but that one was concentrated in one specific region of Siljap. It did not affect other sects, did not spill over into other parts of the country. It was, somehow, contained. Still, it lasted almost ten years. Ten years of destruction."

"Can there really be that much hatred, as you say, between brothers?"

"It is difficult to grasp. But it is so. Caused by blindness. Blindness that occurs behind thick clouds. Clouds mounting from killing after killing, war after war. Now it is so difficult for us to see through these clouds, to see reason. It is too difficult for us to recall that we come from one – that we were once family, brothers and sisters."

"I suppose my country is not all that different. My people have seen many wars as well. Perhaps the difference is that some of these wars were by those foreign to the land, by invaders and conquerors," Ismael said, recalling discussions and arguments he had had about his country's history.

"There is some of that in Siljap as well. Our internal issues attract regional interference. Or maybe it is us, the different factions, who seek help from other countries. It all becomes convoluted and complicated. That's part of the problem. We must solve our issues ourselves. We must come together, Ismael. We need to come together, all the different factions, and the ruling faction. We must unite. There is no other way."

"That's what Yeshu said."

"He knows. I don't know how, but without doubt he knows."

"I don't understand. Do you mean he knows the country's history?"

"Well, he may know the history. But what I mean is...he is an old soul. He is aware of the root of our issues. It is as if he remembers events from past lives."

"How would that help? How could knowing past events help resolve current issues?"

"I do not know. What I know is I want his help."

"What kind of help?"

"That I do not know either." Jey chuckled. "For me, he is helping if he chooses to do so. And now, he is choosing to help. Whatever it is that they are doing in that room, it is effort. Effort from people like them is help, perhaps even necessary."

"Perhaps. I do not know of such matters, so I suppose I cannot say one way or the other. But even if, well, their work, even if their work is helpful, there must still be work by people, by normal people, and by those versed in politics and leadership."

"True," said Jey, turning around the room and admiring the walls. "All true," he continued. "We must come together because we want to. We must do so ourselves. Prayer, magic, whatever it is, will not do it alone. And if it does, I don't think it would last."

"Why would it not last?"

"I believe, in our age, we need structures and guidance, to sustain us through time. In past centuries, it may have been the word of a king or a queen. Today, law is our structure."

"Ha," Ismael chuckled. "It is law that Asant wanted to escape. And yet you're suggesting that he take part in this venture, along with Yeshu, of creating a structure based on laws."

"I don't know Asant well enough to know what he is escaping. Regardless, every person has to face his or her due one way or another."

Ismael gazed in the direction of the archway and the steps. "It's already been a few hours. Do you think they're almost done?"

"I doubt it. I expect they will need the entire night. I've heard that's when the hard work begins. They might even need more than one."

"More than one night?"

"Maybe." Jey wrapped his right arm around Ismael. "Come. You and I should find a spot to sleep. If we're lucky, there might just be a room with a couple of sofas. If not, then it will be the rugs on the floor that we sleep on."

"We can leave, right? We will need food."

"No. We must wait here. As long as they are below, we must not open the gates to the outside world."

In the lower level, the circle, the sphere and the cloud, had become one. Each person retained some connection – albeit minute and thin – to his earthly consciousness and self. There was still a distinct voice from each, Asant, Yeshu, Murthi the Drake, and each other person who had remained in the space – a thought, a faint awareness, from a distant background. At the forefront, however, the immediate thought that is, was one. One thought. Consistent and unchanging, just as a string of light appears infinite and all-encompassing.

But it was not absolute harmony. Something of a struggle was also happening. A struggle to separate. The void, attempting to return to its free form – of wanting, desiring, of pulling from out into itself. It struggled against the one thought. It struggled against unity and harmony, and desired to return to the taking form. The two powers in eternity, from being one to being distinct existences. The void succeeded at separating; the unity succeeded at effecting harmony. They could not co-exist, however.

The void expanded, exploded and broke the circle.

Asant heard voices. Many. First a few, then tens, hundreds, and then thousands upon thousands, chattering, growing in volume, causing him pain. He tried to open his eyes and see around him, but he could not move, could not feel a body.

The voices grew louder and angrier, screeching and hissing. Then, there was an abrupt stop. They disappeared, and were replaced by voices of men, voices he recognized from some past.

"*Yeshu*," he thought. However, only his mind was responding to him; he could not feel or use his body. The voices from the men were coming closer and becoming clearer. They increased in number. There seemed to be several. He then felt a touch on his body. A person's touch. A hand on his left shoulder that revived more of his senses.

"Asant. Asant," Yeshu whispered. He was so near, but his voice seemed to be coming from the opposite side of the room.

"*My body. I can feel my body,*" Asant thought. His entire body remained still; even his eyes and lips were unreachable.

Yeshu squeezed Asant's shoulder. "Asant. Wake up."

Asant ached to see Yeshu. He thought about his eyes, about moving and opening his eyelids. But still thoughts were all he could muster. He felt other movements and heard other voices, but could not place any them to individuals he knew or their whereabouts exactly, except for Yeshu's.

"Asant, wake up; we need to re-group." It was Yeshu again, his hand on Asant's shoulder.

"Is he alive?" Another voice asked.

"He is...his body...he is breathing," Yeshu replied while watching Asant. "Maybe incense or smoke, something to shock his body, perhaps that will help."

"Let's move him, move his back to the wall to sit him up," the other voice suggested.

Yeshu nodded. He supported Asant's head with his left hand. The two, with a gentle and slow pull, held Asant's body upright and propped him.

"Asant. Asant!" Yeshu called again, as both his hands now held Asant's cheeks.

The other person returned with a golden metal saucer, smaller than his palm, with coal and smoking myrrh. He kneeled, then moved the saucer in front of Asant's face and allowed smoke to hover over Asant's nose and eyes.

With an abrupt movement, Asant's body convulsed. He coughed and swayed his arms, coming back, attempting to rescue himself, hitting both Yeshu and the other man along with the saucer and its contents. He continued to cough for another minute, before he managed to open his eyes and focus on his surroundings.

He turned to take in his surroundings, noticed Murthi the Drake with his eyes closed and sitting cross-legged. It was just as Asant remembered him from when the whole event began. A few others were in the same state, same posture. "Why...why aren't we..." Asant mumbled.

"We were knocked out. It was strong." Yeshu observed Asant, considered what to add. "We will have to wait for Murthi."

"Can't we rejoin them?"

"I think it's better if we don't take the risk."

"What?" asked Asant, blinking rapidly and confusion in his voice. He shook his head in attempt to regain a stronger grasp on the sequence of steps he had experienced. He coughed again, moved his body and reached for Yeshu's arm. "We cannot just sit here. We must help."

"There are five of us. We will think of something. But first, we should drink this blessed water and reorient. Then we will plan how to help them." Yeshu handed Asant a cylindrical glass bottle, an inch wide and a few inches long. It was smaller than the size of his palm. On it was an insignia – a star, perhaps a letter, and two figures, one of an animal and one of a human.

"We just need a couple of drops each," Yeshu said.

Asant looked at Yeshu with questioning and confused eyes. He shook his head in disagreement.

"Go ahead," Yeshu said as he extended his arm. "It is water. Nothing to lose my friend. If anything, it will only help."

"I don't understand how taking a drop of water can help. I want to return to work with Murthi the Drake."

Yeshu nodded.

"Take it, so we can get going. We can talk about water another time." One of the other men commented from behind Yeshu.

"Wait." Yeshu looked behind him. "We need conviction, from each of us." He turned back to Asant. "Water is a primary element, Asant, I have no doubt you know that."

"I do, but..."

"Think about it. Water, light, air, earth. The four primary elements, the goodness that life needs. Plants need only them. We, you and I, are more water than anything else. Water is purifying. For sure, people in your country treasure and know of water's role in life."

"I understand." Asant reached for the bottle in Yeshu's hand.

"Believing me is not enough. It's not enough to do it because I asked that you do. We," Yeshu motioned around the room, "we need all of us to be as clear and clean of *sidiki* as possible. Each of us needs to know of the dangers in us and how water helps. Each of us needs to know how the tools given to us work. Believing in them will not suffice because believing is willing the mind to disregard doubt. We must overcome and remove doubt. And doing our work without conviction is even less effective."

"What's *sidiki*?"

"It is what causes us to doubt and hold back. It is how the void works. It lurks around our souls, separating our true nature from our minds and planting seeds of doubt. It leads us to fear life, to fear one another, to fight one another. It is the blinding nature of voids. Do you understand, Asant?'

Asant nodded.

"Water clears off the sidiki, ridding us of our doubts and giving us a better chance in our struggles, if only temporarily. Does this make sense to you?"

Asant continued to nod. "You are right. My elders, my guide and teacher, all have taught me these principles. I understand."

"Good. Give yourself a few drops."

Asant took the tiny bottle and raised it over his head. A few drops trickled into his mouth. He passed it back to Yeshu. In turn, Yeshu put a few drops on each of his hands, rubbed them, added a drop on his right index finger and touched Asant's forehead. "Now, do the same for each of us."

The five sat near each other on the floor. They made a circle of their own, connected their hands, and closed their eyes.

"Trust one another," Yeshu began. "Trust in our work. In life. In the mercy we've been granted. In our purpose here."

With that, silence befell the room. Their breaths slowed. A few minutes passed.

"Feel your body breathe. See it breathing. See the air moving into you, within you.

"Look from outside. Look at the center point of our circle, at the small sphere idling there. It is becoming even tinier with every passing second, with each of our steps. Smaller than the head of a pin.

"Continue walking to the center. It's just us and this point, until we are one."

Their thoughts slowed. More time passed, then disappeared from each of their minds, leaving only the image of the small sphere. In it, in the distance, they saw one discernible matter inside another. They focused on it and moved closer. It was a darkness darker than an unlit room. A hazy and cloudy film surrounded it. The film was malleable with different colors, like a few wide ribbons, each moving in circles, together containing the dark sphere.

"It's Murthi the Drake. And the others."

"We can't wait much longer, Jey, we will have to go out!" Ismael exclaimed.

"Why? I don't see a reason," replied Jey.

"Food. We will run out at some point."

"Maybe. But we will figure something out. There is always a way."

"I don't see it as so. I think being prepared is necessary."

"Ah. My friend, you worry without need. True, preparation is helpful; but really, it is knowing that you will receive what you need when necessary. With that knowledge, you will manage any situation. It will feed your mind with strength and insight, and your body will receive the nourishment it requires."

Ismael looked on without commenting or reacting, unsure he agreed.

Jey smiled. "I see in your eyes, Ismael. The disagreement, doubt and hesitation," Jey continued, "the thought in your mind saying, '*I'm not sure I agree*'. You see, if you *know*, then it would be just as you would know some physical fact. In the same way you might see a piece of food and know that you can eat it, you would know about the universe, you would be connected to our source, and you would receive all you need, because this knowledge draws it to you."

Ismael continued to gaze at Jey. A part of him wanted to look away and to change the subject; another part wanted to look deeper into Jey's eyes and understand his intended meaning. "Can I ask you, Jey, about your involvement?"

"You want to talk about something else?" Jey smiled again. "Do you mean my involvement in the war?"

"Yes."

"What about it?"

"To start, how did you become involved?"

Jey turned his eyes to the bowl between him and Ismael. Soup with dark beans. He allowed it to take him to a different time. "It wasn't as it is today. It wasn't a war. For me, it was about the people in this country, my people. I wanted to help change the government's attitude and its need for oppression. I believed, and still do, that their approach was unsustainable, that sooner or later it was going to lead to violence."

"And it did."

"It did. Yes."

"You don't consider yourself part of the rebellion?" asked Ismael.

"No. Not exactly. My goal is still the same. Bring the people together. Unite them. Unite us. Without violence. This horrendous violence is perpetuating itself. It is giving rise to our internal conflicts and allowing powers from outside our country to become involved. It is exploding the conflict into an uncontrollable cancer, infecting our neighbors."

"But your group is one of the sects; one of the sects the government seeks to destroy."

"We oppose the government, therefore we are by default a threat. We do not, however, carry weapons. We do not kill. We do not kill our brothers, our neighbors." Jey stopped and watched Ismael for a few quiet seconds. "Ismael, killing begets killing. As it is, this violence is going to haunt us for a long time,"

"Yeshu tried, you know, to bring the sects and the government together. You know that."

"Yes. I know. He did not succeed."

"What makes you think you would? What makes you think an alternative method would work?"

"Well, for one, the fighting – the violence – is one of the methods not working. More importantly, not succeeding must not lead to quitting. Not succeeding does not equal absolute failure; rather, it is a nudge to attempt a different approach."

"What would you try differently?"

"Three of the four sects are within reach. They are on board if I get the government to stop..."

"You still haven't described why you think you can manage that," Ismael interrupted.

"True..."

"Oh..." Ismael abruptly turned to sounds coming from the arched frame that leads to the stairs of the lower level.

Jey turned and followed Ismael's gaze. His eyes opened wide as he saw Murthi the Drake step over the threshold and through the frame. The others appeared behind him one after the other.

Jey immediately stood up and moved around the room to collect a few cushions. He brought a few and set them around where he and Ismael were sitting.

Murthi the Drake approached, Yeshu and two others now along with him, Asant trailed a few steps behind.

Jey walked over to Murthi the Drake and Yeshu. "How did it go?"

"Let us sit, Jey," replied Yeshu as he rested his arm on Jey's shoulders.

"Of course. Please." Jey pointed to where he and Ismael were. "I'm going to get some bread and soup for all of you. I will be back."

"No, Jey. Some oranges or water will do. Our bodies need to adjust, having been without food for so long. We must be slow in our taking."

"What happened? How did it go?" Ismael asked, anxious, aching to know.

"It has been a while since I've wanted to work on this...but until now I never managed to attract willing souls." Murthi the Drake said.

Ismael persisted to watch him, desiring more of a definitive and descriptive answer. The others now occupied with sipping water from the available cups, each coming to sense their bodies' thirst.

"We contained it. I believe circumstances will be somewhat better – if only for a period – perhaps a generation or so." Murthi the Drake continued.

"Only somewhat?" asked Ismael, his hands turned with palms up in midair.

"Yes. It goes back too far in our existence. It is not for us to resolve."

"This raises many questions."

"Ismael, please," Asant interjected.

"The questions you have we will address," Murthi the Drake said. "First, however, I would like to make a proposition."

Ismael and Jey, in particular, stared at Murthi the Drake, waiting in anticipation. Everyone else remained as he was, without any change in their expressions, without surprise, knowing what was coming.

"It is contained, not resolved," Murthi the Drake began, then looked up at Jey and continued. "Thus, it is necessary to build a structure, a foundation on which this people can co-exist. This will require a leader who can unite the people. And we have agreed that it must be you." Murthi the Drake cut the air between him and Jey, pointing to his open palm and locking his eyes with Jey's. "You have shown that you can erase divisive lines, and we believe you can create a new fold. We believe you are the best fit to bring the current ruling family into a new structure."

Murthi the Drake stopped, and reached for a cup of water.

Everyone was looking at Murthi the Drake and waiting for more.

"We," Murthi the Drake swung his arm slowly, moving one by one to each of the men who were with him on the lower level, encompassing everyone in the circle aside from Ismael and Jey. "We surveyed the possibilities and now believe that you will need help, from us. We will open the doors for you in hopes of creating opportunities. We want to help you determine the best time to make a given move, such as the best time to approach the ruling family. Once an agreement is reached, we will continue to help you with deciding when to implement each phase of the new foundation and of what this new foundation will constitute."

"Murthi the Drake, Yeshu, you both know I only want to effect stability. That is all. You know I do not want the responsibility to which you allude," Jey said.

"We know," replied Yeshu. "And it is for you to decide what role you want to occupy in your life."

"Moreover, what guarantee do we have that we will resolve the conflict and achieve peace?" Jey asked.

"None, of course," replied Yeshu, his words were quick and close together, expressing surprise. "But you already know that, Jey. You know there are no guarantees, ever. Anything can happen. Somethings we might anticipate, other things will undoubtedly surprise us." He stopped and observed Jey, wanting to give him the space to process his thoughts. "I think a guarantee is besides the point. I think the reluctance in your mind is only a fear, perhaps that you will not succeed. But you must know that we in this, that we are doing this together, each of us, including Asant, and," Yeshu turned to Ismael and smiled, "I hope Ismael too. Each of us is already playing, and will, play his role. Each of us with the same ultimate goal in mind. This land must see peace among its people. It must. Else it will be reduced to ashes and smoke for a generation, and the chaos will spread outside its lines." Yeshu stopped, his eyes still and focused on Jey.

"Jey, my dear friend," Murthi the Drake began. He moved closer to Jey and clasped Jey's right hand. "Yeshu is right. Each of us will play a role. We will be with you, will support you, and will help with making decisions. We will make recommendations to you on when to speak to a given person, such as a leader, and most importantly on when to approach Siljap's president. But yes, we will not see everything, and at other times what we see might be unclear.

Also, as a leader yourself, ultimately your decisions are yours. Our role will be only to give you what we see, and accordingly some recommendations." Murthi the Drake examined Jey's expression and considered how his words along with the implications were reaching him. "What is clear, to me, is that we must make this effort. We must be steadfast, persistent, and focused. We have one goal – to unite Siljap by effecting peace and building a foundation." He continued to examine Jey, and allowed him a moment. "You understand that we are recommending you. We are in effect asking you to be Siljap's leader, starting at this moment."

The meeting between the factions and the ruling family was scheduled; however, the factions' distrust of Siljap's officials and army persisted. Two days before meeting, the factions, except for that of Jey's, again decided against sending their top leaders and opted to send only lieutenants.

Jey saw it differently. Along with his advisers, Murthi the Drake and Yeshu, he decided to be present himself and to have with him most of his able advisers. And, he proposed to his counterparts that he meet personally and alone with the country's sitting president, Daas.

They protested, disagreed, laughed and said Jey was risking his life, and in turn whatever existed of their coalition. History had shown that the country's government could not be trusted – certainly not its army, and even less so its intelligence force. The majority of those who had been present and active in all the preceding meetings had somehow vanished, either abducted or killed.

"I must have a one-on-one dialogue with Daas," Jey repeated several times to the different group leaders. His voice was consistent and direct, showing his conviction.

"What makes you think he would agree? For that matter, what makes you think he will be present?" Janna questioned as part of her leadership role.

"His presence is a condition for arranging this meeting in the first place. In fact, you all demanded it and yet you are not willing to reciprocate by being present yourselves."

"The coalition represents us, Jey." Georjus jumped in and reiterating his group's position.

"The so-called coalition does not qualify as a coalition. It is a coalition by name only. I started it and promoted it, and even I don't have faith in its integrity."

"Daas is brutal. A butcher. If the coalition is failing it is so because of Daas' atrocities."

"No. It is so because we have not yet managed a united and coherent voice."

"That is not true." Yet another one of the leaders.

"It is. And of greater concern is that in the event we do defeat the government's forces, this coalition would not stand, and the country would only continue to be in turmoil. We would find a way to fight each other. You all know that." Jey was persistently calm, but he felt he needed to be even more candid and needing to articulate better what no other leader wanted to face.

The scheduled conference consisted of three days in Vant. The conference was organized by Vant and two other neighboring countries who were beginning to see the risks Siljap's conflict was posing to them. The agreement for this first conference required Siljap's top leader – Daas himself and his top advisers – the factions' coalition and its leadership and at the minimum representatives from each faction.

The factions' top leaders agreed to appoint Jey as the coalition's head, but continued to refuse to attend the meeting themselves. They feared being identified and abducted, citing the intelligence forces' past actions.

The most important meeting, Jey decided, was his meeting with Daas. All other meetings promised to be repetitions of past meetings – more demands than commitments and lacking road maps and timetables. That one meeting between Jey and Daas, however, remained unscheduled. Jey did not announce his intentions to those outside the coalition. He decided it would be best to request the meeting casually and from Daas himself, on the second day, perhaps for a dinner. What remained on Jey's mind was how to convince Daas to meet one-on-one.

On the first day, the gathering was going as Jey expected, likely as everyone expected. Frustration was clear on the faces of representatives from the neighboring countries, most visibly those from Vant.

Daas stood up. Three of his bodyguards who stood directly behind him rushed to assist with his chair. He turned away from the massive round table, and appeared to be leaving. His entourage, on cue, followed suit and rose from the table as if they were one.

"Mr. President, please!" It was a Vant representative who was now also on his feet.

"This is a fruitless discussion," one of Daas' advisers spoke, waving his right arm in dismay and his voice raised, almost yelling. "We will no longer negotiate until we receive commitments from each of our neighbors, Vant first of all, must stop arming these murderers, these so-called friends of Siljap." The man pointed toward the opposite end of the table, at Jey and the faction representatives.

"Mr. Daas..." the same Vant representative pleaded.

Daas stopped just before stepping through the conference room door, held open by a guard. "I will no longer be present unless the other presidents are here," Daas announced and walked through two columns of guards.

Jey hurried around the table toward the exit.

"Stop." A guard asserted, standing outside the meeting room. His right arm was raised with an open palm.

"Mr. Daas, may I have a word?" Jey requested from behind several guards.

Daas did not stop.

"President Daas, I have a proposal I believe will please you." Jey tried again, this time with a louder voice.

Daas stopped, turned around, and waited in his spot.

"I suggest we meet before the first meal tomorrow, two hours before the official joint meal," Jey announced.

Daas turned and stared at Jey. It was unclear to Jey whether Daas' nostrils were flaring. Rather, Daas appeared to be surveying Jey, hovering between becoming furious and, possibly, thought Jey, actually considering the suggestion.

"Just the two of us," Jey raised his arm and motioned at the guards, "with your guards, of course, and two of my advisers. It will be simple and quick."

Daas maintained his focus on Jey and remained silent.

"You are no different from anyone else in that room. What is the point?" It was one of Daas' entourage members, perhaps another adviser, thought Jey.

"I am different from all the others." Jey said to the assumed adviser, then re-established eye contact with Daas. "For one, I am willing to understand and work on getting you what you want, Mr. President. I also have the means and the network to help us end the conflict." Jey stopped and focused on analyzing Daas' face, again attempting to decipher his expressions and measure his interest. "Nobody wants this conflict to continue."

Silent and slow few seconds ensued. Jey thought to himself he could hear each second tick through the air.

"We do not change positions," the assumed advisor stated. "We will let you know if we decide to re-communicate our demands." The words hung in the air. It was not an absolute rejection. The advisor's words conveyed that he did not know Daas' exact thoughts and left open a possibility for Daas to communicate with Jey.

Jey did not receive any word or updates from Daas' delegation. Nonetheless, he walked into the dining room the following morning. It was too early for anyone to be in the vicinity aside from Vant guards and peace keepers who were working on preparations for the second day of the conference. Jey had brought with him only Yeshu and Asant. Both, Yeshu and Asant, requested to take part. They considered themselves less likely to become recipients of the regime's ire since they had already attempted similar efforts when they met General Kan.

The three sat in the room and waited with anticipation mixed with anxiety. Each allowed his own thoughts to help pass time. Yeshu closed his eyes and attempted to focus. He worked to separate himself from his body. He focused on his body as if he were outside, yet feeling its its tension, in its muscles, in its face. He focused on his center and worked to separate himself and retain objectivity. Murthi the Drake was some twenty miles away sitting cross-legged on a white cushion and waiting to connect with Yeshu.

Yeshu directed his thoughts to Murthi the Drake. *"We are ready."*

"Clear the room, Yeshu." Murthi the Drake's voice echoed in Yeshu's mind.

"I'm working on it. Then what?"

"Request the presence of The One and Only. Ask for Guidance. Find the balance between the presence of both your mind and your awareness."

Yeshu opened his eyes and saw in the air droplets, translucent and bright, emitting light that seemed to travel and cross into space for about a foot or two before disappearing into the empty and dark areas between the droplets. The entire space, the air in the room, seemed to be either these droplets or the dark space between them. A dichotomy of light and dark.

Yeshu focused on the light-full droplets. He found them pleasant to look, and admired them and felt a desire to be immersed with them. It was as if they noticed him. They moved and drew toward him, coming closer until they surrounded him. A thought crossed his mind – that they were connected to a source, that they themselves were drawing their light from another, from One. He also saw dark spaces, so dark and devoid of anything that he feared them, feared becoming lost in the darkness, forever. The dark spaces seemed to be connected as well, except that they were sending instead of receiving. They seemed to be sending everything they received, to the infinite void.

"Jey, there are two methods, only two," Yeshu said.

Jey opened his eyes and pulled himself out of his own meditation. He refocused his attention on the room and the objects in it. "Only two, Yeshu."

"He will come – Daas."

"I know. I do not doubt."

"We need to help him choose our path."

"Yes."

"I will work to set the foundation."

"Good. For my part, I will speak little and will choose my words with careful intention." Jey turned to his right and smiled at Asant. "Asant will help us both."

"*Bring them together, Yeshu, the forces.*"

"*How?*"

"*They are meant to be one. Everything in our existence, including us. Remember, they were divided only for us to learn and unite. So, it is, that we do our part today. Know that Light is infinite; whereas darkness, taking, is not. Light travels beyond its boundaries through eternity; darkness is limited and expands only when we allow it to and feed it with our intentions. It is your choice, our choice, to decide to what we give.*"

"Yes, I understand."

"One other instruction, Yeshu."

"What is that?"

"We must cleanse and protect the room – and Daas – for this to work."

"How?"

"Build your desire for the Light source to fully occupy the room and to rid it of remnants of the void. This will help Daas be objective. To protect this space, gather some of your forces, your related souls, as you have done in the past. Instruct them and have them guard the room's entrance – and Daas himself – from the advisers."

"I understand."

"Recall thirty of your warrior souls now." The voice stopped for a moment. *"He is on his way, a mere thirty steps away."*

"We will be ready."

"Yeshu, there are two men wearing ties, both of whom act as advisers. Their minds are far too poisoned and must be separated from Daas. Have your relatives lead them out of the room and close the doors."

Yeshu went to work. Thoughts, instructions and commands traversed his mind. He greeted the light-full droplets as living entities, as equal actors in the realm. They grew in size and surrounded him.

There was an intruding bang on the doors. Something, or someone, had hit the doors and swung them into the room, causing Asant to jump off his chair. Two men entered. Both were stalky and wide and wore common and casual civilian clothes. They appeared to be unarmed. Two more men followed directly behind.

The first two seemed inquisitive. They looked around the room, surveyed it, then gazed directly at Jey and his company. They walked into the room. One scanned the walls with a foot-long black plastic stick in his hand. The other did the same with the table, and then Jey, Yehsu, and Asant.

A fifth man stepped slowly through the door's frame and between two standing at its sides. He wore a frown on his face and seemed different, looked different. He wore a suit and a complicated tie colored in gray, black, red, and blue lines that crisscrossed in a predictable pattern. He walked farther into the room, hissed and pointed at Asant. "He cannot stay. He is a foreigner, and must wait outside."

Jey looked at Asant and nodded.

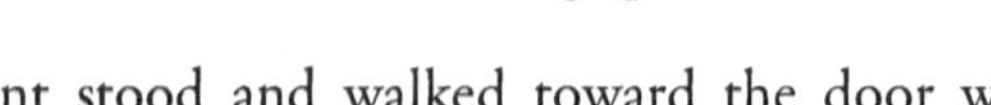

Asant stood and walked toward the door with his head down and wanting to avoid the eyes of the three men at the door. He passed them and stepped out of the room. Two other broad men were standing on the outside; one of them motioned to Asant to move away.

Asant walked a few steps away, then looked behind him and around the space and the lobby. He noticed ten to fifteen men spread out throughout the space, standing at corners and near doors. They added anxiety to the environment. He felt energy drain from him just by looking at them. His back stooped as he turned to his left, opposite the conference room, and saw Daas.

The President was in the middle of a circle of seven to eight men, some in casual civilian clothes, some in suits, with one man next to him inside the circle. They moved in unison and approached the conference room.

One man shoved Asant farther away as the circle came closer and passed by him. Daas walked through the door and vanished inside...as if leaving one world and entering another. Asant saw Jey stand. The doors closed and separated the inside world from that in which Asant stood.

Barely a minute passed when the doors opened again and allowed two men with ties to step out. The two surveyed the lobby with disdain. Both of them had their fists clinched, and their faces spoke volumes. One of them was the one who demanded that Asant exit the room. He said something in the local tongue, to Asant. The doors closed.

"You know I don't speak the local language." Asant said to him.

"Why are you here?"

"In the conference?"

"In my country."

"Oh. Well..." Asant moved his right hand, showing his reluctance and surprise.

"You cannot say."

"I want to help, of course. There is no need for war. There is no need for killing. There is a better way..."

"Better way? *Better way*? You have no clue what this country is going through. It is foreigners exactly like you who have destroyed it. You have destroyed its peace by smuggling weapons, carrying weapons and fighting and killing my kin while all along you claim to care for freedom, for peace."

The man now stood an inch from Asant. He was so close that his spit continued to hit Asant's face even after the man stopped talking.

Asant stepped back. "Sir, I assure you I have never helped smuggle even one firearm into Siljap. I have never even carried a firearm. You must believe, all I want is to help." He recognized his own plea, but he, himself, did not understand it, did not understand why he wanted the man to believe him.

The man's body was as tense as his clenched hands and face. His eyes spewed fire and anger at Asant. He glared, as if trying to affect Asant, to burn him inside and out. Then, he turned to another adviser behind him, also wearing with a tie but still standing close to the outside of the door. The two moved closer to each other. They seemed to say a few words, neither looking at Asant.

Asant, for his part, turned and stepped a few yards away to one side of the lobby. His mind was fully occupied with the circumstances as he looked at nothing in particular. He noticed a few chairs by a nearby wall opposite the conference room's doors, backless chairs like those often found at hotels then walked a few steps toward them, sat, closed his eyes.

His mind slowly quieted as he experienced fewer thoughts and withdrew from the anger near him. It occurred to him to pray. One prayer, thirty seconds. Then a second prayer. Then a third, and a fourth. He watched the minutes pass as he swam in time. It seemed to be an eternity, but in the back of his mind he knew. Logic informed him. Fifteen minutes.

He maneuvered around images of the men around the lobby, those outside, and those armed. He saw pictures of more weapons, tanks and fighter jets across the country's domain. Machines built to destroy. There were worried and anxiety-stricken faces, each fearing the next breath and the next moment life granted them.

Asant's few thoughts traversed him farther in time and space, to his past. He saw his father, smiling. His father's eyes always smiled when they saw Asant.

His teacher came about as well and hovered in the distance, cross legged in the air, elevated. His face was brighter than Asant remembered.

Seeing them was helpful and reassuring. The teacher moved his body and stood upright on the ground. He walked closer to Asant.

Asant, believe. Believe in life. Believe in yourself.

I cannot. He heard himself blurt. *There is so much destruction here. These men have only hate and anger in them. They do not see life any longer.*

That is not true, Asant.

Why aren't you here? Come see for yourself. Please come, if only for one day. I know you can.

I have moved on, my dear son. I am no longer where you are.

You have left too?

Not left. Only working from a different side.

I am alone again.

Focus, Asant. Believe. Do not give up on humanity, that would be giving up on yourself. I know you would not do that.

No.

You are very close, Asant. See it through. You have already become a man. And you have much to give, much to build.

Daas had his eyes locked on Jey. "Do not waste my time," he said.

"Mr. President. Our country is no more a country."

"You are not to insult me. I am saving my country from the destruction that your people created."

"You have saved the country. I agree. We all owe you. Please know, however, that no one with me ever wished to harm the country or any brother or sister. I carry no arms. Never have."

Daas' face was plain, unmoving, without any ridges. His face said nothing. Offered nothing. "Whether you, yourself, carried a weapon is of no matter. Your brothers, as you call them, did the work for you." His tone was monotonous and low, with barely enough pitch to carry his words across the table.

"Yes, some have. Nonetheless, they will disarm if I request it."

"Then request it. Else you are carrying arms by extension, through your brothers. You consider yourselves brothers, correct?"

"I will convince the factions to disarm if I manage to reach an agreement with you."

"No agreement. Disarm, or I will destroy all of you."

"We must come to an agreement, Mr. President. If you destroy me and all the other factions, Siljap will no longer be."

"Siljap must be rid of you."

"What if I promise you the five groups will not be a threat?"

"Your promises are of no consequence."

"I vow to you no faction will threaten Saamad or its province?"

Daas was unmoved. He did not reply. His eyes and face remained as they have been the entire time.

Jey exemplified Daas' tactics and stood his ground. He allowed minutes to pass. "It would be a tremendous benefit to you if you no longer had to concern, yourself, with a threat. It is the same for me." He stopped and considered his position, analyzing whether it would be best to permit time to pass again but decided to continue. "I will administer Raad and the province."

Daas allowed his face to express a mocking smile. He smirked his lips and let out a bit of air. He maintained his silence, and his eyes remained fixed on Jey.

He moved his right arm to the arm rest, as if getting ready to push himself off the chair, to leave the room.

"There is also Vant," Jey said. "It has been your dream to unite Siljap and Vant."

At this, Daas reacted. His eyebrows moved and rose a mere hair's width. It would have been undetectable to an unfocused observer. He moved back into the chair, and rested his right arm back to his lap.

Part X – Seven Months Hence

ASANT, ISMAEL, YESHU, AND STORI crossed the imaginary boundary of the coffeehouse. It was the same coffeehouse where Yeshu brought Asant and Ismael months prior. Each took hold of a chair and sat around a square wooden table.

A man pushed a stainless-steel cart. "Sweet cheese," he announced. "Best sweet cheese in Vant."

Yeshu raised his head. "Music to my ears," he said as stood up and walked in the man's direction. "This is a must. As always," he said after finding his way back to the table.

"You must reconsider your priorities, Yeshu." Stori chuckled.

"Need I remind you, dear Stori, that it was you who convinced me to try this, from the city's carts?"

"Ah, the good days." Stori displayed a faint smile, while looking at Yeshu and recalling in his mind the time when he leisurely walked the streets of the old city with Yeshu. "Tell us, Yeshu, what is happening in Daas' mind?"

"With modesty, I dare say it's more predictable than we make it to be. We all are predictable. I think, Daas, at some point in his life, succumbed to insecurities, resorted to control and hungered for power. Wanting to control Vant played into that narrative."

"At least now he is talking with the groups!" Ismael chimed.

"And that is so because of our work, our collective will. Your work, Asant's and Stori's." Yeshu's eyes showed a sparkle half hidden by his eyelids, showing a combination of a smile and gratitude. "Gratitude to you, Asant, Ismael!" Yeshu reached over the table with his hands to touch theirs. "It was your will. Your travels and efforts. You started this work." He paused. "You reminded me of he Truth." He paused, inhaled. "And, thanks must go to Murthi the Drake and his consistency. I must say, he has been a rock. A rock that I, Jey, and few others relied on."

"Of course. We – Siljap and its people – are indebted to him, and to Asant and Ismael." Stori nodded his head in their direction and smiled. "And, through your objective lens, Yeshu, and practically, is Daas truly seeing the light?"

Yeshu smiled at Stori. "It's always been enjoyable conversing with you, Stori. Your way with words and lightness are helpful."

Stori waited. "Well?"

"Well," Yeshu continued. "In plain words, we are managing to see the benefit of communicating and cooperating. I think it's simple and the most effective structure. It only makes natural sense for Siljap, and Daas, to have Vant and the groups as partners. Partnership would bring all of us more benefit."

"And Daas?" asked Ismael, wanting a concrete answer.

"For sure it is beneficial to Daas. It gives him more recognition, and more influence, as opposed to endless conflict with enemies...or even with subjects. I'm willing to bet warring was not what he wanted, but neither was stepping down. To be honest – Stori will likely disagree with this – I think it was not strategic when the groups demanded that he step down."

"You are correct, Yeshu, on that we disagree," Stori offered.

"But your position now is different. It has to be, correct?" Ismael asked Stori.

"Not quite. If I were leading, Daas stepping down would not be negotiable."

Ismael frowned and scratched his temple, still unsatisfied. He examined Stori, then turned to Yeshu. "Well, Daas is on board, correct?" he asked. His head shook a bit. The question came with uneasiness and reluctance, as he wanted a definitive answer.

"He is on board. A roadmap has been agreed upon."

"That's it," Asant chimed in with an exuberant smile. The news elated him and his voice showed his excitement, contrasting that of Ismael and Stori. "That is the necessary step in my mind. I think it's excellent. Yeshu, good work!" He stood up and hugged Yeshu.

"How long?" asked Stori.

"The roadmap?"

"Yes."

"Over fifteen years." Yeshu pursed his lips. "Five progressive milestones."

"It is good news, I am happy." Asant added, lowering his voice. He looked away toward the west, toward an orange sun mostly hidden behind a building. Only its upper arch was visible. Asant gazed in its direction into the distance.

Stori took a metal fork and dug into the sweet cheese. "I have to be careful with sweets," he said, then added while chewing. "Perhaps starting next week."

"There is still much work to do," Yeshu continued. "This is only the beginning. And as with all beginnings, it is fragile. The work from Murthi the Drake is crucial, so is Jey's." He stopped to observe Asant. "What are you thinking, Asant?"

Asant sighed and followed it with a deep breath. "It has been about two years. I have been away for the better part of two years."

" 'Away' is rather subjective..." Stori said between a spoonful. "We must not forget that Siljap owes you, Asant." He put the spoon down, leaned toward Asant and tapped his shoulder. "You too, Ismael."

"I believe it is time," Asant said.

"Time for what?" Ismael asked.

"For me to return."

"So, you say," Stori said, now voice unclear, mouth closed, busy with the sweet cheese and another chuckle. He brought his hand to his mouth and coughed. His face turned red.

"Stori?" Yeshu looked at him and stood up.

"I am...alright..." he raised his hand, coughed again. "I...deserved..."

"Yes you did." Yeshu punched him in the shoulder.

Stori coughed again. "You are going nowhere, Asant," he said between coughs. "Neither are you Ismael. We need your help."

"With what?" asked Ismael, again hesitant.

"With our future. Would you help us build a school for Siljap's unsupported children and teenagers?"

Asant looked away, again to the distant West, at the yet smaller arch, now pink. He could smell the sweet cheese in front of him, so inviting and readily available. For some reason, its sweet smell took his mind to the bank and the yellow note. For a quick moment, he re-experienced the anxiety he had felt when he was in the bank with a plan to forcefully take money. His heart raced and took his thoughts to the fears and chills he experienced while sitting across from his teacher. The train of thought took him back even farther, to the moment he first met his teacher. He had just lost his mother and was begging and wailing outside his home, in the middle of the street.

The sun flashed behind the white building and brought him back to the coffeehouse, just as it moved one degree further and disappeared.

About the Author

Issa is an attorney working on civil rights issues, writer, researcher, and traveler. His work revolves around law, society, and spirituality, often learning to maneuver cultural intersections with different opinions and views of our world.